A Drowning World

S.R. Ruark

Indies United Publishing House, LLC

Indies United Publishing House, LLC
PO Box 3071
Quincy, Illinois 62305-3071
www.indiesunited.net

Other books by S.R. Ruark

Siren Series
A Drowning World
Siren's Song

Coyote Laughing

Table of Contents

Chapter 1

"Hello, Lauranya." Captain Alen Jameson smiled at her. "Ready for the lift-off?" His smile was in place, but his eyes were looking over the buildings, his hands clenching and unclenching his faux leather belt.

Dr. Lauranya Torvins gave the dark-skinned captain a smile in return. Slower than his, as if smiling used muscles long forgotten. Once the smile started though, she grinned shyly at him, brushing her blond hair away from her face in unconscious reaction to his kind interest and charming smile.

"Ready to stay and do more research…Arianya!" She turned from the captain, catching her daughter about to jump into a well filled rainwater pothole. "Please do not jump into puddles that are over your waistline!" The small blond child of 7, looked up and giggled at her mother. The captain joined in the laughter, which made Lauranya smile, erasing the frown.

Arianya or Arie, as almost everyone called her, was enjoying the relative freedom and the lighter hand of her mother, outside. Water puddles were still a novelty to the child, and she wanted to enjoy every chance to splash that she could. Not to mention the fun of wet stuff falling from the sky into her hair and her skin. It was like taking a shower with momma but warmer and with clothes on!

"Well, doc if you don't mind, I need to round up the scientists and their children for a pre-takeoff cocktail." The captain's slow smile was infectious and his quirking eyebrow a novelty to her. "Meet you in the conference lounge." With that, he nodded and headed back toward the shuttle bay.

Lauranya took a deep breath working to control her obvious interest in the captain, trying to enjoy her last moments outside. The rain had stopped, into a moment of broken clouds and blue skies, but that wouldn't last. She breathed deeply; water and fresh air were what she smelled. She wanted fresh air before her lungs were filled with recycled air and the smell of metal, oil, and people living too closely together. The shuttle would be filled to capacity, always on the edge of almost too small. A few others were enjoying the last few minutes in the open air before being hustled into the shuttle port.

Camdia was sitting on the curb around the shuttle port, her shoes next to her, her feet submerged to the ankles, in flowing runoff rainwater. Camdia's tightly woven hair, had droplets of rain, glinting like diamonds in the dark strands, making her look younger than her 30 years. She grinned up at her boss like a small kid, flashing bright teeth against dark skin, taking a few more years off.

"Just another hour and we'll be strapped down heading back to the world ship." Camdia looked happy at this prospect.

"Eight weeks in close quarters." Lauranya shuddered.

"Again," they said in unison. Laughing as only those sharing the same miserable short-term conditions could.

"Dead Gods, I can't believe we're leaving so soon." Camdia started.

"Well, it has been five years," Lauranya said looking at Arie splashing in the rainwater. Her clothes would dry quickly having the advantage of being made from finely woven synthetics. Lauranya touched her own shirt. Captain Jameson had given her a shirt woven from this world's natural fibers yesterday, as a take-off gifting. She made a face. Her husband was sure to ask about the shirt. Thankfully, their marriage contract finished as soon as she delivered one more child or two more years had passed. Arie might stay with her, when his family sent Lauranya packing, back to her own family but she could not sure. They could be spiteful when given even the slightest provocation. Lauranya was going to have to hide the shirt well. Maybe among Arie's things, which he never bothered looking through.

"I'm going to miss you singing for us in the evenings. And your research has barely begun! " Camdia's voice brought Lauranya back to the present. Lauranya smiled slightly. Camdia was more outraged than she was. Oh, she was disappointed, but the Dead Gods and Lords decided to shut down this world's research during the flooding years, so ship ward bound they were. Lauranya bit her lip to keep from saying what she should not. There were no Overseers, but that did not mean no one was listening. Dissension was not tolerated. Scientists were given a certain latitude, but they were not allowed to actually have an opinion other than what they were told when the final orders were given.

"At least I will not have to fix every computer routing issue or downed screen some idiot savant forgot to turn on, on top of my daily work." That part Lauranya didn't have to fake being happy about. Gods forefend the other scientist could remember how to log into their computers or backup their data. She hated computers, preferring the beauty of water and the creatures in, but computers ran everything, and she had a knack for solving puzzles, biological or electronic. This made her valued, which meant better placements. She said a small prayer to the goddess Yemoja for a water research placement for her next assignment.

"I didn't get any more whip marks this assignment!" Camdia chirped happily. "I hope the next place is as nice." Lauranya didn't have the heart to tell her it had been a close thing once or twice. The girl was brilliant in her narrow field of stress reproduction. Some days though Camdia couldn't focus on other things that didn't pertain to her specialty or hide her true thoughts.

"I hope so too dear." Lauranya feared Camdia would end up strangled by an Overseer for verbally, or Gods forbid physically, stepping over the line. Camdia wasn't a Free Person; she had just spent too much time around scientists who were usually free and very open in their thoughts around their equals and underlings. Camdia would have to have a very good marriage contract to buy out her freedom or any children she produced. She was smart, maybe smart enough for that type of marriage.

Gods, please do not let Camdia be harvested for her genetics, Lauranya prayed silently. The world ships needed more upbeat and lively personalities.

Lauranya had a thought. "Camdia, did you put the animals we were testing down?" Brilliant but not always focused was Camdia.

"Yes." Camdia stopped for a second. "I'm pretty sure I got them all." she amended. "I was sad; they were just so cute." Camdia made a face. "Would rather the ship have room to take them with us. I would have loved to see how the stress levels of the flight affected their hormones for reproduction."

Arianya took that moment to come running up to her mom, blond hair flying in the wind, wrapping her arms around mom's knees. Lauranya scooped up the wet child and blew zerberts on her tummy. Arianya squealed in a high-pitched baby squeal of happiness. Arianya planted a kiss on mommy's cheek before squirming to be let down to splash and get wet.

Lauranya gave a quick nibble to the neck and put her only daughter safely back on her bare feet. No sense in getting her soft leather shoes wet. Lauranya thought of how she might be able to trade the shoes for something of value on the ships. Leather was as rare as fresh water. She reached a hand out to the slight splatter of rain, licking the fresh water from her hand, sweet and free of chemical traces — a rarity on the ship.

She should be able to sell the shoes and the shirt for either food or medicine, possibly even amnesty if things got very bad at the next assigned world or ship. Overseers tended to take bribes and gifts made to the world Lord or the presiding ship's God. Lauranya sighed again at leaving so soon.

Jacks and his two children waved at them through the shuttle port's thick sliding glass doors.

"Looks like it's time to move up," Camdia said, sounding less than thrilled with a definite pout.

"Well, the company will be good for the trip back." Lauranya gave the younger woman a quick hug.

Camdia gave her a sideways grin. "Bet you are glad Tine's left on the second shuttle with the twins. Will give you and the captain a chance for a quickie or two."

"Camdia!" Lauranya said. The girl could not keep her thoughts to herself.

"What? It's no secret ya'll were barely on speaking terms, or that he spoiled the boys."

Lauranya pressed her lips together thinking of the twins, crossing her arms over her not quite ample chest. "Yes, the boys were a bit rambunctious."

The boys had favored their father, and not just in their lovely dark luminous eyes or dark velvet skin. They had become more demanding as if they were little Lords and not children of Free, a dangerous attitude for children on the ships before mental and physical evaluations. Lauranya shook her head; Tine favored the boys too much. Lauranya knew that culled for gladiatorial entertainment or to the tender mercy of the military was a real danger if they did not pass mental evaluations. She could do nothing but pray for them.

"Luckily your contract only has two more years." Camdia continued on blithely as she stood, brushing off the bottom of her pants.

"Or I give him another child." Her voice was tinged with a bitterness she could not quite hide. Lauranya tapped a finger on the opposite arm in annoyance. She took a deep breath trying for a measure of calm.

"He has to actually spend the night with you and not Micah." Camdia said slyly over her shoulder with another quick smile.

"His body slave has no choice. And if I slip the right word into his mother's ear, the conception of another child will be that much faster." Lauranya looked away to hide the distaste for either action.

"Duty but no love." Camdia shuddered, hugging herself. Camdia enjoyed the emotional upward spiral of love. Very few of her lovers left angry or bitter when there was a parting of ways.

"Love costs too much," Lauranya said sadly, her eyes distant for a moment.

Camdia shot her favorite boss a worried look, giving her a quick hug. "I'm sorry I didn't mean to bring up…"

"Camdia, please. Stop." Lauranya sighed gently. "Maison died a long time ago. And his little brother knows he will never measure up to what I felt for him. I can't fault Tine for keeping time with Micah then me, except when I am ovulating."

"But still." Camdia was working on her outrage.

"Stop." Lauranya put up a hand to fend off Camdia's next few words. "We have a shuttle to catch, and I have to arrange my notes for maximum effect. I want a good placement next assignment, preferably without my overreaching husband and his family."

"Yes, ma'am," Camdia said hunching her shoulders, finally catching the hint.

"Thank you." Lauranya smiled to take the sting out of her rebuke. Camdia gathered up her leather sandals, heading inside with a swish to her generous hips. Lauranya had always been envious of the girl's lush hips where her own were not nearly so generous.

"The Gods gift everyone differently," Lauranya said to herself with a smile. Her smile faded as a thick misting drifted over the road, before fading into the scientists' apartments. She frowned slightly. Lauranya couldn't summon ghosts, but she did see the occasional wisp of one. Kori had been the stronger of two of them, able to raise the dead and control ghosts. Lauranya shook her head banishing the thought of her twin. The shuttle would wait for none of them. The ghost could find its own way to Obatala.

She would mention the ghost to Jacks. He might know of someone still left who might be able to lay the ghost to rest, but she didn't think it likely. No other necromancers were on the planet, and she barely qualified being on the threshold of power.

She lingered outside for a moment more. Arianya was soaked and splashing, her laughter infectious. Lauranya knew that the next few weeks would be torturous for the child in the small space of the ship. Lauranya smiled at her daughter, committing this moment to memory for her own pleasure later on.

Her pouch phone rang.

"Yes?"

"Time to come in Lauranya." The captain's voice was warm and rich over the receiver. Lauranya shivered. Damn Camdia for pointing out the obvious.

"We will be there in 60 seconds." Lauranya's voice was throaty, breathless.

"Can't wait." The voice was almost like a physical touch. Warm and lingering. Lauranya looked at the small phone when it went dead.

"He was purring at me. Camdia, damn you." Lauranya smiled at the phone only slightly vexed at her lab assistant. Eight weeks and no privacy. Luckily, exclusivity had not been part of the marriage contract, only genetic combination between her and Tine. Maybe something nice would happen before she had to rejoin her husband. Another good memory to add to her hoarded stash.

"Arie," Lauranya called to her splashing child. The child looked up giggling from a particularly large set of waves in a small puddle, from her stomping. "Time to go in."

"No! Want to play in the water." The child said with an outthrust chin. Lauranya could feel her jaw tightening. She had seen that stubborn look on her husband when he was losing an argument.

"That's nice dear, but we have to go. We're off to see your brothers and father." Lauranya kept her voice calm as she walked towards the child.

Arie seeing her freedom about to be curtailed took off towards their apartments to hide. Ten steps and Lauranya had caught up with the small child, picking her up and putting her on a hip, walking back towards the shuttle pad. Arie went stiff, howling in the unfairness of it all, trying to squirm her way out of her mother's lean arms.

Arie was still howling and crying when the two of them arrived at the Lounge. Everyone else, from adult to small child had either wine or juice in hand with crackers. Lauranya walked in, both wet and slightly embarrassed at her child's behavior.

Jacks tried to give her a glass and Arianya a small juice box. Lauranya smiled gratefully at her fellow research scientist, shifting Arianya to her other hip to accept. This set Arianya into a second screaming fit with flailing legs and arms. The child managed to kick the glass with her mother's fuzzy drink up, into Lauranya's face, and down the front of her cotton blouse.

"Damnit child!" Lauranya through clenched teeth, grasping the child tighter so she didn't fall to the floor like the wine and juice box. "I just started getting us somewhat dry!"

"You're both covered now," Tass observed unhelpfully with a snide grin. He, of course, was looking collected and well-coiffed with studied grace holding a wine cup. The snide look was the usual for the tall, willowy blond man.

"Yes thank you for pointing out the obvious, again, Tass." Lauranya snapped at the other marine biologist. There were a few soft chortles at his expense. He glared around the room turning to see who was laughing at him. Those who were above him didn't hide their contempt, the others kept a straight face, knowing from experience it wouldn't help sooth his petty ego. He sneered at her before turning his back shunning her from his sight. Lauranya rolled her eyes but was grateful for his turned back. She shuddered to think of what his attention would be like.

"You won't be able to change for a few hours once we aboard the shuttle," Camdia said from the side, twisting her hands together tightly. She had had a few run in's with Tass before, only Lauranya's intervention had kept her from being whipped. Aria's howls were not diminishing, which caused Tass to smirk even more. Jacks' youngest child, a tow-haired little boy, took a few absorbent napkins from his dark-skinned sister to hand to Lauranya. She smiled at the children while juggling Arianya and drying herself off.

"Captain says we are leaving as soon as we finish off these four bottles and the snacks." Jacks said. He edged Tass off to the side with two steps and a twisted hip inserted into their little cluster. Jacks gave Lauranya a wink from his honey brown eyes, handing her a few more absorbent towels.

"If only I had your skill at keeping idiots away," Camdia muttered softly.

"Camdia!" Lauranya hissed in shock, looking up from wiping herself off.

Jacks laughed. "It's all in the hips," he said with a suggestive wink and wiggle of the aforementioned part. Camdia blushed hard looking down at the floor. Jacks was a tease, but the exclusivity of his marriage contract with a major penalty for straying kept Jacks suggesting but never following through. Both families were moderately successful. The penalties for breach of contract on either side were job crushing punitive.

"And a few years of battle training," Lauranya said with admonition, handing Jacks the sopping napkins. Lauranya did not mention his very exclusive marriage contract.

"That too." His grin was bright. Tass would never be able to do anything to him or challenge him. He had no fear of reprisal from the blond man who was slinking off glaring in a not so subtle fashion at the smaller but wiry dark man. Jacks just grinned wider.

"Stop teasing the animals, Jack," Lauranya said softly. "Not everyone has your immunity." She nodded to Camdia. Jacks moued in disappointment for not being able to antagonize the other scientist but he did stop making eye contact.

"Damn." Lauranya sighed. Her shirt was still damp and clinging, outlining her upper torso and lack of undergarments. Hardly worth noticing, Lauranya thought dismissively of her own physique more worried about the shirt as the drink had started spreading a pink stain across her chest.

"The shuttle boys haven't loaded the luggage just yet. Think I saw the bags downstairs." Camdia said, bringing more napkins and taking the sodden ones Lauranya handed to her.

"I'll get us changed and see if I can find her stuffed rabbit as well," Lauranya said giving up on trying to dry off the two of them. Arie was settling down to whimpers, laying her head on Lauranya's shoulder.

"Might want a blanket as well for her." Jacks said over his shoulder as his daughter brought him another cookie while she ducked a shy smile to Lauranya.

"Thank you!" Lauranya said with feeling as she moved through the door. In her own rush, she would not have thought of that. Shaking her head at her lack of foresight, Lauranya moved quickly down the side stairs to stay out of the shuttle crew's way. They might need the wider passage hallways for last minute moving of equipment from the labs onto the shuttle.

The inside landing area by the tarmac was still filled with their luggage. Lauranya frowned. There was no way they would be leaving in 15 minutes with all of the bags still unloaded.

Lauranya sighed in annoyance. "The edge of a foot may be how they plan to load our things." Sometimes Overseers were useful, she thought, searching through the bags for her and Arie's. Arianya's bright green bag and her own yellow and maroon were visible among the other brightly colored bags. Seeing the bags made her smile. The vinyl bags had been presents from her family when the announcement came that she would be accompanying Tine on a very plum assignment. She pulled the bags to the side of the curving stairs. Again, she did not want to get in the crew's way if they decided to load in the next five minutes. No one needed more interruptions when the Gods gave a task, especially the menial tasks.

Arianya had stilled to just mostly unhappy whimpers until she saw her bright green bag. Then she was cooperative with helping momma move the bags to the side. "Bunny? May I have bunny now?" She asked, wiping tears from her red blotched cheeks.

Hearing none of the crew coming up or down the stairs, Lauranya stripped off her damp shirt and wiped down with a small cloth in her toiletry bag. "Yes, love we can get your bunny, but we need to get you out of your wet dress as well." She said reaching for the small child's wet hem. "We cannot have bunny getting wet!"

She stripped Arianya from her dress without issue until the child started being wiped down. "Blech! Momma cold!" Arie exclaimed with a pout, wrapping thin arms around her torso.

"Yes, I know!" Lauranya giggled at the imperative statement from her daughter. "We would be warm and dry if you had not had the tantrum."

"But rain is more fun," Arie stated to her mom with the complete conviction of a child pronouncing a truth so obvious even a dense grown up should see what was in front of them. "Don't wanna go!" Arie started to sniff as her eyes filled with tears, tears that welled up and fell more and more quickly down her baby cheeks.

Lauranya pulled the child close. "Oh, baby." Lauranya rocked the crying child close to cuddle warm damp skin to warm skin. Neither do I, my dear. Neither do I." Lauranya held the girl close trying to push back her own tears. She swallowed hard looking over Arie's head to the grey sky that was growing darker by the second, rocking back and forth to soothe both of them. She swallowed again the bitter resentment and anger for their orders to leave. "The Gods will." she murmured the catechism all people of the Dead Gods learned in the cradle.

"They are wrong!" Arie said with a quivering lip looking up into her mother's blue eyes that mirrored her own blue eyes.

"Arianya, we never say that!" Lauranya said with a gasp, pulling her close, looking furtively around to make sure no one heard her child's blasphemy.

"But, they..."

"No. We follow, they lead. That is how it is." Lauranya said firmly. Arie stuck out her chin but she knew from her mother's tone there would be no winning this argument.

"Can I have a cookie?" She wheedled instead.

Lauranya smiled indulgently at the shift in her child's tone. "If you stop kicking wine all over me, yes."

"I can do that!" Arie hugged her bunny close, with a smile and mercurial change of temperament that only small children can do.

Lauranya took a deep breath for calm. "Let's get you dressed, and you can play with Marion and Mia after we get into space." She said, reaching for the child's things.

"Will we be floating?!" Arie asked. The idea seemed

to both excite and scare her.

"Yes. For the next eight weeks, you can hang upside down like a monkey and walk on the ceiling."

"Oh! That will be fun!" Arie clapped delightedly, jumping from her mother's lap to hop up and down excitedly. "Bunny! Don't forget bunny."

Lauranya reached into the bag for the patchwork bunny, with its four eyes and six legs. Arie hugged her favorite stuffed animal close. Wrapping the foot long fluffy faux fur tail around her arm and chewing on the small-cupped leather ears.

"We must get dressed now dear and meet back up with the others, and you have to be on your best behavior, or the captain will ask that you be leashed to your seat.

"I wouldn't like that," Arie said looking up at her mother with a serious expression.

"No, probably not. It would be rather boring."

"Okay, let's get clothing." Arie gave a long-suffering sigh. Lauranya just managed to contain her own giggle, chewing on her lip in amusement. Arie was usually trying to get out of her clothes, not into them.

Aria was swiftly dressed, and Lauranya had a new top and bra in hand when she looked down to her skin, scratching. She was itchy from where the wine had splashed through the shirt, touching skin. Lauranya frowned taking a closer look. This was not a normal reaction for her to wine. Sticky, she could understand but a dermatological reaction was odd. She would take a closer look once they were on the shuttle. Until then she pushed the skin issue to the back of her mind, finishing dressing and rooting for the last minute comfort items either of them might need but would not be available for hours after takeoff.

Lauranya picked Arianya up onto a hip, the child

clutching the bunny tightly, humming softly. The humming made Lauranya smile. "Glad to see someone having a good day now." She murmured into Arie's soft hair.

Arie grinned up at her mother blowing kisses. Lauranya blew kisses back carefully navigating the stairs, with one hand on the stonewalls, back up to the lounge. They came into the main hallway, to the gold and scroll worked door without any further delays.

Lauranya pushed on it inward, the door sticking slightly before cracking open. Lauranya frowned in annoyance. The door had not stuck on their way in or out last time. She pushed harder putting her hip and shoulder into the push. The door swung free from what it was caught on, letting Lauranya into the room.

She stopped stunned at the scene and site before her. Every man, woman, and child were collapsed on the floor or chairs. Jacks was staring at the ceiling with foam at his mouth drying, clutching his youngest. The towhead child was rigid in his arms. His nails dug into his father's biceps. His daughter, with her large lovely eyes, had tried to escape through the door. It was her hand the door had stuck on as she had collapsed a few feet from the passageway with her hand outstretched on the carpet. She had been inches from the door when the poison hit. Camdia was on the floor. Her neck, hands, and chest covered in tattered flesh and blood. It looked like Camdia had tried to claw out her own throat. Each person had died in pain and horror, with sphincters loosening at death's onset.

Lauranya could not move. The horror was overwhelming. Arie's tugging on her sleeve and whimpering brought her out of her stunned daze.

"Mommy, someone's coming." Arie whimpered.

Lauranya tried not to panic. She clutched the child closer, stepping over the bodies of her friends and co-workers. Lauranya moved to one of the couches next to a large multi-paneled floor to ceiling window with a stunning view of the drowning lake. With three feet between the wall and couch, there was just enough room for her and Arie. She dropped down behind it. Luckily, no one had died behind here. The one favor death had done for them.

She put her mouth to Aria's ear. "I need you to be very still and close your eyes till I say open them. Can you do that baby?" she whispered

Arie's eyes were huge, frightened but she nodded stuffing a fist in her mouth to chew on for comfort.

"Shhhh, shhhhh" Lauranya arranged them both on the floor with her back to the couch and Arie spooned against her stomach, an arm draped over the child with her fingers just touching the window in an artful display. Lauranya then shook her hair out over both their faces to cover any telltale facial twitches. The hair blanketed over them as if they had collapsed looking out the window. Arie still clutched her bunny.

"No momma! No hair! It's itchy!"

"Shhhh. Just for a few minutes and we are playing the hiding game. No noise and no movement." Lauranya whispered desperately, trying to convey the urgency to a seven-year-old without scaring her.

"Is everyone else playing the hiding game too?" Arie whispered back, snuggling close to the body warmth and comfort of her mother.

"No dear. They are playing the very still game." Lauranya choked out the lie to her very young child.

"Oh! I can do that." Arie whispered back excitedly. She loved games and loved getting treats after games that she did well at. Arie went very still closing her eyes.

Lauranya combed her hair back over them as voices came from just outside the room. The door opened, with a shush over the carpet. She tensed up then relaxed. Using the same technique for when sex with Tine was especially bad, slowing her thoughts and concentrating on slow, shallow breathing. Footsteps could be heard. Several sets of footsteps into the room. Lauranya opened her eyes to a slit, peeking through her lashes.

"All accounted for captain." A twangy voice said somewhere on the other side of the couch. Lauranya did not know which ship tech it was. They had kept separate from the civilians and scientist.

"I know Jorgie. I know." The captain's voice was at the end of the couch. Lauranya worked very hard not to breathe.

"She's dead. Just like the others." A different voice said from the captain's right. "Easier than most it looks like."

"Doesn't help Tiron." The captain's voice sounded heavy. "I found her to be...a delight."

"Nope, but we can feed our own families now. But..."

"But we have to beat the oncoming storm and deluge." A deep breath sounded. "Right. Let's move out." The captain's tone took on the tone of command. The death of 37 men, women and children brushed under the rug for the survival of his crew.

The door swooshed open again. Lauranya lay still for another five minutes, her mind digesting the captain's words and the horror of the room.

Arie squirmed. "Momma...I gotta potty!" she whispered urgently.

Lauranya nodded into the child's hair. "Ok dear. But we have to be very quiet still."

She rose to her feet and crept to the door, cracking it just a hair. Arie started her potty dance, with a little humming song that accompanied it. Lauranya looked both ways quickly. No one about. She grabbed the child's hand and ran quickly to the bathroom, three doors down and across the hall, their feet barely whispering on the plush fiber carpet.

The bathrooms were huge, multi-tiered, with beige, and gold granite floors and seats, done with painted walls in vivid colors and gems. A bathroom for the Gods and Lords, when visiting. Lauranya felt only a mild twinge of guilt using this necessity instead of the plebeian one downstairs. She took Arie to a bathroom counter with a child-sized opening for her to sit on. Lauranya started to help Arie with her panties when the girl refused.

"I can do it!" Arie said emphatically.

"Ok, sweetie. Please hurry though." Lauranya said in a soft voice. She left Arie sitting, turning back to the door, with an almost tiptoe gait. She cracked the door a hair to listen if anyone was heading towards them.

Two shuttle crew members were roaming down the hallway to the reception room and the bodies. Close enough for her to hear them.

"Thought the boss said 37 bodies?"

"He probably miscounted." one voice said in a deeper baritone dismissively. "Bodies ain't his strong suit."

"Blood ain't his strong suit!" The other voice said derisively.

Both men laughed.

"Remember Thimas hanging from the post and how grey and swollen he was? And Capt going "Oh my Gods!" I thought he was going to puke then and there!" Said baritone voice. The men stopped walking to laugh in braying tones. They were almost to the door, shadows on the carpet.

"I've never seen a more squeamish person in my life. You'd think he'd never seen a game or been around the whipping stocks." The first voice with a derisive sniff.

Lauranya held her breath, whispering "Keep walking, damn it just keep walking by!" Her luck ran out when baritone stopped laughing. "Gotta take a piss. See you on the ship."

"Durn, that's the women's." The other voice said with apprehension.

"And do you see any round here? Other than the dead ones?" Baritone asked with a sneer. Lauranya imagined him curling a lip while saying that.

"Sick man. Just sick and wrong." The other voice just kept walking, passing by the bathroom door, as his earbud started to beep. A slight, younger man, in his mid-20's. "Yes, boss. We're doing the last round of scavenging now." A pause as the man passed out of sight but not hearing. "No sir we'll be right there without dicking around."

Baritone waived his friend off as he grabbed a drink from the water fountain. Lauranya shut the door and stepped behind it with her back to the wall, slipping off a shoe. Two things happened, the man with the baritone voice entered into the bathroom and Arie finished going to the potty.

"All done!" she sang out, wiping off and dropping the soiled toilet napkin down the waste hole. She hopped down to find her mother. The man stopped his forward momentum to stare at the blond child in front of him.

"What are you doing here sweetie?" Baritone asked in a soft, happy voice, his hand had been reaching for the stolen Overseer's asp on his hip but stopped, changing course mid-action starting to reach for the little girl instead. Arie froze looking up at him, like a small animal caught in the gaze of a large predator.

Lauranya stepped forward, soft as a ghost wisp, from behind the door, to stand behind baritone while he was distracted with Arie. She took the shoe, in her right hand, swinging it as hard as she could onto the sweet spot on the back of his head, driven by fear and fury. The man hit the floor stunned, shaking his head while groping ineffectual to his side for the asp. Lauranya skipped to the other side of him, braced by a hand on the floor to kick him on the side of the head, with her shod foot, as hard as she could.

Arie started to scream.

"Arie quiet! Put your hands over your mouth!" Lauranya snarled, fear making her harsh with her daughter, as she brought the shoe down on the stunned man even harder than the first time.

The child did stifle her sobs behind small chubby hands. She watched her mother bludgeon and kick the much bigger man until he stopped moving.

Lauranya came out of her fear and fury filled fugue when her shoe started to sink through crunching facial bones. She backed up sobbing, dropping to her knees. Arie ran to her wild-eyed mother. Lauranya hugged the girl close the view of the destroyed face hidden from the child. Lauranya rocked Arie back and forth on her knees, as much to comfort Arie as herself.

"I'm sorry! I'm sorry!" She repeatedly whispered in Arie's hair to no one in particular.

Arie pulled back for a moment. "Mommy, are you going to do that to anyone else?" She asked in a very quiet voice, her eyes filling with tears as she looked into her mother's wild eyes.

Lauranya ran a hand over her face to scrub off the tears, giving one more sob.

"I hope not baby, but we aren't safe here."

Arie nodded solemnly, taking her mother's hand in her own. Lauranya squeezed the child's hand but let go to approach the body cautiously. She rifled through the pockets, belt, picking up the asp and communicator, and then ran to the sink to rinse off her shoe, and blood splattered hand. There was nothing she could do for her clothing.

"Ok sweetie, stay with mommy. We need to leave here without being seen and quickly." Lauranya walked back to the door, cracking it just a hair to check the hallway. Clear. Lauranya slipped out the door silently.

Arie was wide-eyed and as scared but slipped out the door as quietly as her mother. The hallway was empty. Lauranya could not run with Arie in tow, but they did go at a very quick walk. Lauranya kept looking over her shoulder trying not to run, as she desperately wanted to. Arie struggled to keep up, running on short legs, whimpering at the quick pace but she didn't stop. Arie sensed stopping would be very bad; she tried to keep up still clutching her bunny tightly.

Lauranya stopped at the end of the hallway before the main lobby area. The marble floor and arched gleaming windowed lobby looked pristine belying the bodied 12 doors down. Lauranya heard the radio before the man. Ten seconds between the voice and the man gave her the chance to grab Arie and duck behind one of the many large planters with wilting tropical vegetation. She turned the volume down on the radio she had from the dead man.

His partner was in the hallway they had just vacated.

"No boss. I don't know where he is." Pause. "I saw him heading into the women's lavatory." pause. "How the hells should I know? Maybe he was changing his tampon!" Pause. "Soon as I find him he's all yours!" The crewmember snapped into his radio. He was moving down the hall towards the bathrooms.

Lauranya picked up Arie and ran for the front door. Arie clutched her mother's neck in an almost choking grip.

"Rooms. Have to hide! Rooms are too easy. Lab! Lab was close. Can go there." Lauranya muttered to herself, running and panting through the whooshing opening doors across the water-filled street. Her feet never slipped on the wet pavement even as she was hobbled by a child around her neck and the street was ankle deep in runoff — fear giving her sure-footedness in the rain.

"Mommy, I'm hungry!" Arie whispered into her mother's ear.

"We'll get something in a moment dear," Lauranya said ducking into the science building entryway to fumble with her passkey still attached to her pants belt loop.

"Dr. Jhen had trade bars in his office," Arie said trying to be helpful.

Lauranya grimaced at the thought of the bars, but Jhen had been fond of the overly sweet crumbly things. She juggled the card and child to get the doors to open ignoring her daughter's comments for a brief moment of necessary fumbling.

"Could I have one? Do you think he would mind?" Arie was trying to remember her manners.

Lauranya choked back a sob while swiping her card against the reader. "No baby, I don't think he will mind at all." The door lock showed green, sliding open. The cold interior air whooshed out raising goosebumps on chilled wet skin.

Lauranya ducked into the tidy five-story complex moving to the stairs. Just in case, she did not want a power signature of the lift giving her away. She managed the two short flights without stumbling or loss of breath, trying to breathe through her nose so she could hear if anyone came through the lab's front door instead of drowning out her hearing with loud panting.

Jhen's office was on the third floor overlooking the lower valley. Spacious and sparse, natural light, even on this cloudy day, filled the room enough Lauranya did not need to turn on the lights.

Jhen had packed up most of his books and notes for the trip. His studies always a benefit for his God, so he had been given greater latitude than even most pampered scientists. She had enjoyed the banter and discussions she could have with him, covering a large array of subjects. He had seen her as a person and colleague, never "just Tine's wife" who was a scientist on the side.

Lauranya swallowed, pushing down her grief, to search his office drawers for the bars. The desk bars were cleaned out; however, he had forgotten two boxes worth of bars on a lower side shelf.

Lauranya smiled at the memory when he had 12 boxes there at one time, Jhen had grown up a slave, only to win his freedom with his second scientific discovery. Successful as he was he could not break the habit of having extra food as a "just in case". He would forget he had a box and would stash another there just in case. His need to squirrel away the bars for at least a two month supply, a gentle joke among his friends. Everyone on the ships had his or her little quirks. Jhen's was safe compared to the quirks of a few Lauranya could think of off the top of her head.

Lauranya frowned then searched the other lower compartments. She laughed aloud. "Thank you Jhen and your fear of hunger!" Three more boxes were still there. "I wonder how many boxes he actually had on him when he packed."

"Oh, chocolate!" May I have chocolate please?" Arie squealed in excitement, her hand inches from the bar before she remembered her manners, as she looked at her mother.

"Yes dear." Lauranya gave Arie a bar before she sat down on the sidewall leather couch. She swallowed hard twice. She had promised she would allow herself an indulgent crying session later, but right now, she needed to plan.

She looked out and saw the valley basin had already been swallowed by the center lake, swollen over its normal shore and ring of trees. The trees were drowned with only the very crown branch tips on two or three of the very tallest now showing over the water surface; the remaining trees were just ripples in the newly formed lake. She could see flashes of whiskered cats with glimpses of other animals, on the high grounds melting in and out of the brush. A wave of panic threatened to engulf her.

"Breath! Breath!" she whispered to herself, clutching her knees to her stomach. Burying her head into her knees, taking deep breaths, she tried not to panic. A child hiding under the blankets from the monsters in the room.

Arie was happily munching on her travel bar, going to the cabinet the doc had stocked with interesting things for his children and their friends. She found the Doctor's plastic loc-n-stack set. She pulled them out, after licking her fingers clean, to play with, burbling happily to herself.

Lauranya rocked back and forth muttering quietly. "Cannot go to the hills. Everything will be moving to high ground. A boat? Not certified on the current models. Storms are too severe to chance the inexperienced to... That leaves the building or a platform of some sort." Her mind running in circles when the stat phone on her hip squawked, jolting her out of her circular panicked thinking.

"Dr. Lauranya, I know you can hear me. Respond." The captain's voice came over the phone, urgent yet calm.

Her hands shaking, Lauranya switched on the voice, no video, looking fiercely into the blank screen.

"Why?" her voice shook with fear and rage.

"Why?" The captain repeated, clearly not expecting this singular question.

"Why were….why did you have to kill everyone? We will be missed. You can't think no one will ask questions." Her voice was hoarse from the force being used to speak through unshed tears.

"Orders were to drop the scientist off at whatever port we made and arrangements would be made from there to their next travel destination. The escaped slaves are closing in on this quadrant. Every ship for itself. If there were no drop-offs, there would be no questions and no red tape. You will be missed in a few months or years, maybe, but not until we've had time to clear out.

Lauranya laid her head back on her knees. Truth. They would not be missed for a long time. A thought wove through her brain to her mouth.

"The others? My husband? My sons?"

There was a long pause before the captain's voice came back. "The other captains were dumping all their passengers into space once the thermosphere had been hit." His voice was emotionless. "No one is coming back to this planet till the water levels are stabilized or before those bodies would have fallen back to the earth and burned in the atmosphere."

A sob escaped from her.

The captain heard this small muffled sound, taking

pity. "Doc...Lauranya, I am truly sorry. I...didn't want you to learn this...from me. We..." A heavy sigh. "I thought the poison would be an easier death than implosion."

Lauranya's hand shook on the phone. "Why?" She cleared her throat from the clenching tightness. "Why did you have to kill all of us? What did we ever do to you?!" She whispered glaring at the phone as if he could see her through the blacked out screen.

"Will you come to the ship?" the captain asked, avoiding the question.

"No!"

"There is a critical shortage of food on the outer colonies and sub ships. What we make is sent to the main ship worlds with little left for most of our families. Wives, husbands, children starving to feed the Dead Gods."

Lauranya made the connection. The pilots and their crew needed food and medicines from this failed colony. Everything and everyone else was a liability. Stolen to start fresh away from the Dead Gods, their freedom for everyone else's lives.

"So you stole the food and medicine for yourselves."

"And our families."

"Our families don't count do they?" Her bitterness bled through the fear. "Babaluaye curse you! I hope you like the taste of blood!" Lauranya hissed the old curse at the Captain, switching off the stat phone with a savage twist of the knob. She pulled her knees up to her chin hugging them close sobbing softly at her losses.

"Should we go find her?" the second mate asked. He was worried. Loose ends had a way of biting people in the ass.

"No matter how beautiful and well-made a coffin might look, it will not make anyone wish for death.

Especially not a scientist." The captain chewed his lower lip. "How long till the water reaches the buildings?"

"Three weeks or so." Came the pilot's answer, the handcuffs around smooth dark skinned wrists to the controls, rattled softly as she tried to gesture with chained hands. Her eyes were dark and wide. She hadn't been agreeable to the killing, but they had needed her to get the shuttle off the ground, so she had been chained to the controls till take off.

"Think she'll survive moving to higher ground?" the second mate asked.

"With those damn long-whiskered cats or the sun spiders? Pfft." The pilot didn't hide her scorn for the second mate's comment. She didn't try to duck his blistering backhand that caught her across the cheek and nose. She gave him a sneering glare through the tears while touching the tip of her tongue to the blood dripping from her nose.

"You hit like a pussy." She said softly, with a curl to her lip. The second mate was breathing hard at the physical outburst. He raised his hand for another blow when the captain caught his wrist.

"Stop." His voice was calm, but he turned his hooded eyes to the pilot. "That is what I was thinking." His comment was on the doctor. He shook his head. "No, we'll leave her and let the world do our killing and burying. We have our own families to pick up. This world can hide one or two more bodies. Start the flight check." He released his second in command's wrist with a look the smaller man couldn't meet.

He grabbed the pilot by the back of her neck, digging fingers into her skin, bruisingly. "Do not piss me off anymore. I need a pilot, but we have lots of time to learn how to do this without you before we get to our first destination. Understand?" His voice was cold velvet with controlled violence underneath.

"Yes sir!" The woman swallowed hard.

"Good." He nodded walking out of the cockpit. "Release her once we are in space, Nori. And don't take your bruised ego out on her."

"Yes sir!" came the second's snarled reply.

"Good luck to you doc. May your death be easy." the captain whispered, as he went to check on the rest of his crew, the only blessing he knew to give to the doomed scientist.

Chapter 2

Chapter 2

The beach wasn't quiet. Waves pounded the fine white sand with a steady rhythm like a lover's heartbeat. Five children played in the shallows, searching for shells and clams for the evening's dinner, shouting to each other and low flying blue-green wave skimming birds searching for edible tidbits, each child as precious as oxygen in space bringing smiles to the faces of those on the beach for less joyful reasons.

A young girl, coltish with flying blond hair ran to Brother as he accompanied the village Torch onto a reed walkway over the water. He feigned being unaware of her only to catch Leah just as she tried to pounce on the taller sturdier peace keeper.

"I almost got you!" She squealed as he tossed her into the air as if she weighed nothing instead of the sturdiness of an outdoor child.

"Almost is never your friend." Brother ruffled her hair as he placed her back on the wet sand. "Where are your parents? Surely none of you are here without some sort of supervision?" He looked around with a slight frown.

Leah gave a squeal of outrage brushing the hair from her face into a less messy coif. "Treasher is keeping an eye on us." She motioned to the huge Katherian whose buff fur coat blended into the edges of the forest shadow; well enough that even Brother had to look twice to spot him. Treasher gave a flick of an ear while keeping an eye on the other four rambunctious children he would fondly call godlings within their hearing.

"Mom and dad are at the funeral," Leah asked, digging a toe in the sand, quickly looking down then up at Brother.

Brother's eyes darkened for a moment. "Funerals are sad affairs and this one even sadder than usual."

"Did you have to kill Nathan's mom?" Leah looked into Brother's green-gold eyes with an innocence that made his heart squeeze, and he hoped she would never lose.

"She was poisoning Grenich. When the poison didn't work…"

"Thanks to Mauri."

"Yes, thanks to Mauri. She tried to stab him."

"Why would she do that?" baffled at an adult acting illogically.

"Because Grenich isn't human."

"Why does that matter?" Very confused now.

"Nathan's mom was unable to live with non-humans." Sister snapped.

Brother looked over at his sister with a quelling look as he amended his original response tempered to Leah's age. "On the ships she could stay with humans most of the time. After the shipwreck though, with all of us living in close quarters and no village without at least a few others that weren't pure human, her brain didn't process the differences very well, which made her try to kill Grenich."

Sister snorted, but she added no commentary either.

"That's very sad," Leah said, her lips pulling down.

"Yes it is." Brother gave her a quick hug. "Time for you to join with the others. Sister has to do a Reading."

Leah's eyes got huge and darted to the small, wizened woman waiting patiently next to Brother. "Oh! Bye!" She gave Brother one more quick hug and a bobbing nod to Sister before scampering off to the other children.

"She takes after her mother," Sister said, watching the children with a smile for young antics.

"And we are all happy about that," Brother said with a smile of his own for the next generation of Runners. He turned back to Sister and offered his arm to her with ship formality. Sister inclined her head to her slightly older brother accepting the arm, leaning heavily on her heavy and knobby cane. They walked in silence to the edge of the reed path recently built just for this occasion.

Sister took a deep breath as her foot touched the reed walkway over the ocean water. The skies and the readings waited for no one. With the thought of the skies, she threw a superstitious glance up at the boiling skies. Behind the clouds, the sky was a deep blue. The kind that if you lay on your back and looked up you had a feeling of falling, making you want to clutch the dirt under hand to keep from losing contact with land. Gravity always worked though.

She should have been dead three times over. Wrinkled skin with liver spots covered her face, neck, and hands visible through the loose flowing wrap. She had survived war between the Gods, a world ship crash landing, and years on a world so dangerous the first month saw a mortality rate of over a third of the crash survivors.

Yes, death had kissed her hand a few times but had declined a final dance. Soon she thought, soon Death would want to finish this soiree. She was seeing an extra shadow when someone was close to death these twilight years of hers.

The thought sent a shiver through her. She clutched her bag of Gods' bones a little tighter. She wasn't scared exactly, but she didn't want to leave life just yet. No one ever did, she snorted to herself. Death was a fickle lover, coming and going as it pleased, sometimes at the most inopportune times, either too soon or far too damn late to have been a mercy. Sister shook her head with lips pursed in annoyance. She wasn't dead yet so time to roll the bones.

The clouds were moving in from the east, large, dark and pendulous. The storms were coming soon enough. The water would rise, a vision seen for the last few decades, bringing more than just change to the land and ocean. The other two Torches had gone insane waiting, but Sister had waited with patience akin to the Silvers. Sister was the last of the world's precognitive. A torch to lead the way out from the empty darkness of space, the old saying went. The clouds coming wouldn't reach the island today, maybe not even tomorrow but the rain they shed would be felt and the clouds would be here soon enough.

The water had been shallow for many feet out two weeks ago, now it was deeper than could be measured with heavy knotted rope and wider, wilder than a strong swimmer could dare unless they had fins. The walkway had been bucking and heaving till she stepped foot on the sturdy arm sized bound reeds. The first step onto the walkway caused the water to still for two body lengths in either direction. Water still surged and raged except the area she was walking onto became as smooth and clear as battle plastic canopy on a fighter space jet.

When she had been young, the ocean had been larger but slowly receding. The world's axis had finally tilted throwing the weather patterns from a dry climate worldwide to whipping up clouds and moisture to drown the parched lands. The world was no longer a dry world, but they could still die in the deluge. The shipwrecked survivors on the island and in those living in the waters needed to know the future.

Sister straightened as she continued walking on the now calm water, the bones vibrated at her touch, sensitive were the bones of the Gods, none of which anyone had seen in the last three generations on the islands. The bones had been given to her uncle, of quick wit and fiery red hair in a different pouch, his pouch when the ship still flew through the stars, now hers to read and protect.

The village was down to roughly 150 people. The other villages that were scattered over the area were not faring, population wise, much better. The drying rivers had been low on fishing but the grazing for their animals precarious with the native wildlife finding the goats and pigs as tasty as the shipwrecked survivors did.

The old woman shook her head again. "Getting old and senile." She thought to herself. The years were not weighing lightly, and the path of a Torch usually lead to insanity at a young age or suicide at an older age. Rarely was there another path. She was the last Torch for the shipwrecked, the last seer and guiding light of the Gods. Duty lay heavy across withered shoulders.

Sister was careful never to read too many times in a handful of days. She had been told that her grandmother had the sight in such quantity that bones for focusing were not needed. But the sight had come at any given moment eventually driving her poor grandmother insane. Her uncle had decided swimming during a storm when flathead sharks were mating off the shores, a good idea when the bones became too much for him. Sister still held onto her sanity, but there had been days when she worried. Today was not that day.

She motioned with her chin for her brother to come help her. There was a time when her grace and poise while reading the bones had been perfect. Those years were no longer hers. Unlike her, Brother still looked to be in his early second decade, tall strong and flexible. Things her Power had deemed unnecessary for her to retain. Yet for all his youth, she would not trade their jobs. She told the future and guided the survivors' paths. He had the task of enforcing the peace. Sometimes all that the transgressor needed was a talk reminding them why everyone worked together, other times a grave was added at the foot of the mountain. Those enforcements were the hardest. Every member was valued. Everyone needed.

Brother stepped forward on two legs, not four of his other shape, so silent his footsteps the reeds did not creak once on the walkway over the still water. Sister reached out a hand. Brother supplied an arm to help her down to her knees on the reeds, before backing up off the pathway as silently as he had approached.

She settled on aged sagging haunches with a deep breath, calming her mind. The calm was as important as the medium from which she was reading. With a deep breath out, her hands reached into the squared pouch, with a tying flap, at her side. Flipping back the cover fold, her hands touched the skin with reverence. She gently pulled a folded piece of thin tanned leather from the pouch. The first item she needed was butter soft and smooth, unlike the coarse tanned goatskin laid out for her old knees. The skin was not small, rather thin and compact covering roughly two and a half feet by one and a half feet, the width of most women's backs.

With a flip of her stiff fingers, she laid the skin out in front of her. Next, she pulled bones of various sizes with symbols out in her wrinkled hand, thick jointed with hard work and long years. The pouch held fifteen bones yet only nine or eleven could fit into her hand at a time. Sometimes only five were grasped. The different runed bones pulled, and the number helped her to concentrate her Power to See. The bones, like the skin, came from the body of the Goddess Redeyes in one of her various incarnations after she had died.

This time when she pulled the bones and threw them, she had enough time to gasp once seeing all the bones pulled, then the Sight came. Faster and faster images flooded her mind leaving an impression and images that would never be erased. She let the images flow through her brain until like a cup running over no more could be stored.

Rising to her knees she yelled "Stop! Stop for the love of Gods and my sanity, stop!" She coughed her plea to the air and sky. The images slowed but one last one burned into her brain, a woman and a laughing child, surrounded by the corpses of both the followers of the Dead Gods and Islanders. "They must live," Sister screamed in a whisper before collapsing back onto her knees, tears of pain and the coming deaths pathing down her face.

Sister woke with a pounding head, not an unfamiliar sensation with the sight or with drinking too much. Something she had not indulged in since her late second decade. She looked up into familiar faces. Some concerned and other's hopeful. "Not dead yet, damn vultures!" She snapped irritably, waving a hand weakly above her head. The crowd of five backed up, one or two chuckled at her well known waking temper. She struggled to sit up for a moment to give word of her Seeing.

"We are waiting on your word, Torch." the headman said. His beard and hair so dark there was almost no light reflection. Young, unaged and unknowing, Sister thought with disapproval towards Nathan. Sister glared up at him and his rudeness.

The headman's face was neutral, neither hoping nor hating, though he had more reason than others to hate with both Island and personal losses from her readings or Brother's enforcement.

"The waters will rise, and Dead Gods own are leaving." She turned to look at her brother. He heard the words she didn't speak.

"I will ask if Jolie is available to pull a trireme to the mainland." Was all he said, offering a hand off the woven reed mat she was laying on. She waved off his hand laying back.

"Brother." He stopped as her voice changed to the Torch. "Do not interfere." With that, she closed her eyes and fell into a sleep of recovery. Brother frowned but continued to the beach to find a merman to carry a message.

"Torch." The sitting woman didn't respond to the taller than average Katherian. He tried again with the human's given name. "Atlanta!"

This got a response. The woman looked up with haunted purple eyes and deep bruising underneath from sleepless nights. "Yes?" Her curling red hair, unconfined, seemed to float around her shoulders.

"You ready for this drop?" The Katherian swiveled an ear at her, the tip of his tail twitching. His face was covered with a bone mask concealing the upper brow and cheeks, leaving his orange eyes and short dark furred muzzle visible. The mask could have covered up scaring, but Atlanta knew it covered Redeyes Judgment mark.

The stone steps of Sanctuary were still coalescing in front of the fifteen people, the early morning mist, mixing with the still see-through stone steps and massive metal doorway making the grassy area more surreal than enjoyable. Each of the team members had found a small lightning mark on their hands, a summons for a retraction. Someone or a few beings to be brought into Sanctuary. There was no telling how many or how few Sanctuary was opening up for but Sanctuary answered its own criteria for helping those in need.

The band, for this retraction, was particularly motley; three humans, seven Katherian and five Wolfen. Usually, there was only one token human among the larger races, this time there were three. No Silvers, so the humans would have to do the crawling through tight spots and only one of the team members had not gone through full training. The God with them, their Torch. She didn't carry any variety of swords or disc guns as everyone else had, but she did have a sleek long barreled rifle with top grade sightings, slung over her shoulder. An assassin's gun. The gun and her lack of other extraction missions making the others give her more than the occasional sideways look. The Torch being the unknown element on this mission.

The token leader, the unnamed Katherian was notably concerned with a potential rogue God messing up the retraction.

The Katherian had approached the red-headed woman in the black bodysuit with an aggressive tilt to his head and a growl in his voice. "You can sit this out." He said into her ear, not carrying to the others, though his body language screamed his thoughts.

The implied we don't need novices who are going to hurl or get someone killed. More a command than a suggestion, one that Atlanta, as a God, could ignore. She smiled sickly, waving a hand dismissively at the stated and unstated commentary. The Katherian pulled his lips back over sharp carnivorous teeth in annoyance at this gesture.

"I can handle myself and my gun. Though this time,

they shouldn't be needed" Atlanta said calmly, lying to the Katherian convincingly. She tried to stand but stumbled, the Katherian stuck out a hand to keep her upright, his claws sheathed. Bare skin touched fur covered skin. The Torch flared, and she sucked in her breath as a Seeing occurred by accident.

"Redeyes will forgive you." Her voice a mere whisper, caring no further than his ears, her eyes misting white for a second before clearing to purple again.

The Katherian gave a soundless snarl, baring predatory teeth. "The goddess will skin me, next we meet." His voice no louder than a breathy whisper.

"That was when you stole a ship with some of her best people on it as a gift to the Dead Gods." Atlanta kept her voice low. Roland was a name, that history deemed the worst of the worst. One who had sold every other race on a world ship for his own race's freedom from war. History had not been kind to Roland and his doomed mutiny.

The others coming along on this trip didn't know who the tall Katherian was and neither he nor Atlanta was going to inform them. The others would have shot Roland on principle had his true name been known, no matter how many centuries or for some millennia past his crime had been committed.

He gave a more audible growl this time, drawing looks from those nearby. Two of the band gave the Katherian and the God more than a quick cursory glance, the other individuals looking away to give privacy in close quarters. Ship manners. The Katherian couldn't place the two's uniform, which told him they were from a future millennial than the one he or his regular extraction teammates were from. An unusual team of two post period guardians, a short human male, and a young Wolfen female turned their heads toward them, breaking off a conversation.

The Wolfen stepped towards them, her eyes narrowed at the Katherian, both sets of arms, upper and lower, reaching for sword or guns. Her partner stepping to her side on the left, his left hand resting lightly on his disc gun. A united front, the body language said team, not lovers making Roland reassess their danger level from low to medium.

Atlanta waved them aside. "I'm fine. We are having a professional disagreement."

"If you need help…" The man said with a level gaze, but it was at the Katherian he looked. The Katherian did not need to read the man's mind to know what he was thinking.

With flattened ears, the Katherian glared back. "I don't do humans."

"Not what it looks like to me." The young Wolfen female growled back, her icy blue eyes steady on the Katherian, the ruff down her spine starting to rise. Her lower set of arms resting heavier on the huge disc guns, while she crossed her upper arms within easy reach of either set of swords strapped to her side or back. Roland would bet she had had some training, so the threat of their use wasn't childish posturing.

"I am not forcing myself on the Torch!" The Katherian snapped at the young pup of a guard, his tail fluffing and twitching with his obvious irritation. He was having trouble keeping his hands off his own guns.

"Winisa," Atlanta's voice wasn't loud yet still carried to the Wolfens and Katherians. The Wolfen startled at the Torch's use of her name, her beautiful cupped ears swiveling forwards to catch every word Atlanta had to say. "I am fine. Really. He," She motioned to the Katherian. "Is concerned that I don't have the knowledge or fortitude for this mission. He's just not very good at being told to butt out." Atlanta said with humor at the Katherian's expense, earning her a glare through his bone mask, but the others in the team gave a laugh. The unnamed Katherian was known to be overly controlling for retractions; however, his teams never lost anyone to accident or gunfire. No one asked his name or why he wore the mask. Sanctuary was a safe haven for many reasons.

The Wolfen girl gave an opened mouth smile to the Torch, flashing a mouth of sharp teeth from her long muzzle. The human only raised an eyebrow, but he did touch his partner on the arm settling her down. Her hands came off the guns, and they went back to their quiet discussion, keeping a discreet eye on the other pair to their right. Just in case.

The Katherian turned back to her, a sideways tilt of his head, and a glare.

Atlanta reached up to touch the right sword strapped to his back. The left sword its mate. "Beautiful swords."

"Thank you." His eyes narrowed, not mollified.

"You do very nice work." The Torch Power flared again, this time causing Roland to pull back slightly as a spider web appeared over her left hand. The threads of the future and the past forming a web of possibilities. "Swords that will kill a Dead God in the hand of a Siren."

"Why are you coming on this mission?" Roland said in exasperation. "You're not out of Change or fully a God yet. And Torches are always in short supply." Torches were also rarely stable and this one seemingly less so than the few others he had met in Sanctuary. Those Torches went gratefully into their very own cryo units: no dreams or futures but their own filling their heads.

Atlanta didn't answer for a moment, her eyes on the

changing spider web of infinities. "Because I need to speak to Redeyes' guards." She paused for a second, tearing her eyes from the web to look into the Katherian's fear dilated eyes, her voice dropping to a whisper. "And one of the team isn't going to make it back."

Roland's spine stiffened and his tail snapped twice. "Everyone makes it back in my team." He growled with bunching jaw muscles, turning with liquid grace, walking as far as he could and still be in the group waiting for the steps to solidify and the mission to start.

"Not this time," Atlanta whispered sadly, shaking out her left hand dissipating the spider web of timelines. Sanctuary's light hit the steps, mimicking sunlight at dawn, a new day of safety promised.

Brother shook the rain from his fur futilely, stretching his front paws out and back legs up. His tail curling to the side, the tip of his tail twitching, never still. He yawned. The assignment to watch the colonists had been tedious at best; the rain made it a job to detest.

The colonists had taken longer than expected to realize their settlement was in a low-lying area. This past week had been the most exciting to watch vaguely. Like watching neon-ants scattered when their pebble mounds were kicked open, lots of motion and hand waving, sometimes even fights. The men and women with the whips had taken the first three shuttles out, with many of the others in tow. After that, the loading of passengers and items had gone slower and somewhat smoother. There was no more scent of blood and fear.

Brother, watched, captivated by the dichotomy of the family units. He had seen pale skinned parents with children of much darker pigmentation or the opposite.

Some parenting units were made up of one light and one dark with their children either dark or light. In his one hundred and fifty years, he had seen fair parents produce fair children and darker parents produce darker children. Children with parents of light or darker skin usually had a combination somewhere in between. For the colonists, that did not seem to be the norm. Brother's curiosity was piqued. There had to be a reason for the unusual genetic combinations, unfortunately, it wasn't as if he could approach one of the colonists and ask how this happened. It was as if nature had been denied her normal randomness to follow an unknown but set law of genetics at someone else's' behest.

Brother was looking forward to rifling through any books or notes left behind. Sister and the council wanted to know why the Dead Gods had come here and if they would be coming back. Brother just had his curiosity to settle. He shook his ruff again and settled into a slightly more comfortable position on an uphill brushy covered vantage point.

The last shuttle was leaving today. He saw the last of the men women and children start to bring out their bags, handing them off to the men and a few women of the ship. He flicked an ear as he saw the bags tossed to the side. Every other loading he had seen the bags had been thrown into the ship, but not this one. An odd thing. And odd things should be watched closely. Therefore, he watched and waited.

There was a steady stream of people entering the shuttle port, in twos and threes, some family units with children, other's single adults. He watched the last two people outside, one small child jumping into puddles whose infectious laughter he heard even from where he was camouflaged, her blond hair in wet tangles down her cherub cheeks. She tried to outrun her mother with squeals then howls of outrage at being caught but the slender woman with matching green eyes and long blond hair in the same sun-streaked shade as her daughter. The captured child's howls cut off as they entered into the port.

Brother waited patiently for the ship to take off so he might start to examine the works left behind. Ten minutes passed when the odd happened. The woman with the small child came running out of the port. She stopped for a moment looking around frantically before darting to the non-living facilities. Brother stilled, including the tip of his tail. The ruff on his spine starting to rise at the faint smell of fear and fresh blood he scented on the wind.

Moments later, men and women boiled out of the shuttle port, running to the living quarters. There was hand waving and yelling for a few minutes then those who had stormed the living quarters came back out grim-faced and empty-handed returning to the shuttle port. Within minutes, the shuttle took off.

Brother slipped from the brush, eeling under wet bushes and chin high native plants, careful not to disturb the forest floor detritus, making no sound as he went to step on to the concrete grid worked roads.

He went to the shuttle pad first. Something had happened here. Something unusual. Between one-step and the next, he shifted from a large feline four-footed shape to his human two. Clothing did not shift so he stood naked at the entrance of the shuttle building. The doors opened as swiftly for him as any colonist; however, it was the smell that made him recoil a half step, shaking his head. Even in his human skin, Brother could smell 20 times better than his non-shifting companions of two legs. Here he smelled Death, and it had come neither gentle nor kindly.

He walked through the glass covered vegetation area first. No death, only plants dying slowly. Yet the scent accompanying Death's was not that of decaying vegetation but an almost overwhelming chemical smell of things not natural emanated from the floor's wall-to-wall seamless rug. He walked on this rug, soft on bare feet yet there as a slightly crunchy texture underfoot to the carpet.

He sniffed the air, turning towards a door to the right, pushing it open. A death in this room. A man with pulped facial bones. Not an easy death but the killer was desperate by the looks of the wounds and the man unprepared for the violence that befell him. He sniffed the air — blood, feces and the now almost familiar scent of the woman and child. The blond woman, Brother thought. There was nothing else of interest in the room where human waste was deposited, as softly as he had entered, Brother slipped back out.

The next door to open was on the right and most of the death smells emanated from this room. Brother opened this door cautiously, fearing a trap. The door opened easily if messily. The pulled skin and muscle with much blood, from one small girl's hand, slicking the tan room rug was the first sight that greeted him. The multiple bodies with self-inflicted death wounds or foaming mouths were the first hint of poison.

Brother walked gingerly over the dead to the table filled with empty bottles and the remains of various food items. Not touching anything laid out, he leaned his head over to sniff a small cookie. He wrinkled his nose and sneezed at the amount of poison lacing the treat. A growl broke from his throat. Poison, a coward's tool.

With narrowed eyes, he slipped from this room back to the foyer, only to freeze feet from the door. He dropped to the floor, crawling behind a container of plants raising only his head to observe. The blond woman with the small child was exiting from the building across the way. Her hand held her daughter's as she furtively looked around ready to jump out of her skin at the slightest sounds. Her other hand carried a blanket, oddly bulky. She and the child hustled into the building where most of the others had lived.

Brother watched the door close behind her, thinking. She would know why these people were dead and why she had fled from the ship that would have taken her off the drowning world. However, was it worth her knowing about the islanders or guessing about the sea dwellers? Should he offer her the island for sanctuary?

His sister's voice came unbidden to mind. "Observe...do not interfere." Brother let out a soft growl, shaking dark wavy hair in irritation. If he had been on four feet, his tail would be lashing. He did not like letting the helpless die, but he would not interfere in the Torch's orders. It was important. Even if he knew there was no way the two could survive on their own.

Brother slid to the non-living quarters building, searching for a way in. The doors would not open. He searched his memory of watching the normal day to day activity. Everyone who had entered had used a small rectangular item. He jogged back to the shuttle port and the room of the dead. He searched the bodies finding a couple of small rectangular cards that matched his memory for those entering the other building.

He slipped out of the shuttle port checking for signs of the blond woman and child; the whiskered cats weren't likely to be moving this way, yet. Yet being the keyword. He trotted back to the other building, sliding the card in the sideways motion observed. The doors slide apart with a whoosh and push of cold air.

He glided along well-worn carpet of unnatural fiber, rougher on his bare feet than the shuttle port carpet, though soft enough his footsteps made no sound. He moved around desks and offices looking for paper or odd notes that might help answer questions from the islanders, either belaying fears or preparing for an invasion.

Brother made a face. The islanders had a few of the disc guns left and two of the cannon's left from the ship, but they all knew the outcome if the Dead Gods really wanted them. The only ones who might survive would be the water shifters or himself as he blended in with the native wildlife. Parents would slit throats of their children and their own before allowing capture back to the life of a slave.

He didn't know how to log onto a computer but he had been briefed on what to look for. The small memory sticks that held precious data.

Grenich could probably open the files. The old Silver could work wonders on electronics. He had asked Brother to keep an eye out for the small half circle pull tabs, showing him what they looked like either inserted or laying out on desks and in drawers. Those he found were placed in a small plastic bag, gleaned from another desk. Keyma had the tube to actually hold anything of interest and electronic for the trip back.

Grenich had been very emphatic about keeping the discs dry. Brother winced at the remembered pain of a pointed finger from the Silver's three-fingered hand driving into his chest, leaving small crescent cuts at how the pull tabs were to be kept dry at all cost. Brother had gotten the impression that Grenich's threat to skin him had not been in jest.

Brother had found over a dozen when he stopped

between offices with a disgusted look on his face as a sudden thought made him stop dead in his tracks and he thunked his head into a near wall. The sound carried slightly farther than his voice

"The dead will have these on them as well, just like the cards. I'll need to go back to the shuttle port." His voice was quiet but no less chagrined in the empty hall. He rolled his eyes at his own oversight of the obvious. He continued searching through the offices, leaving the shuttle port for the last place he searched.

"I don't think I'll tell Sister about this." The chagrin in his voice quiet in the empty hall

A quarter of the way through he stopped. He heard a door open, so distant from his current position that even his elevated hearing heard the noise but softly. Brother dropped the rapidly filling pouch onto the floor to shift to his four-footed form. He picked the pouch up in his mouth, silently padding back down the way he had come to observe.

He heard the woman's voice before he saw her. "No damn time! Concentrate…survival first." A deep breath sucked in through her teeth. Brother listened two doors down from the office she was in as she talked to herself. He could smell both fear and sorrow from her, but her voice held determination. He could hear her listing what she needed and could hear what the computer chirped into her ear. The computer's voice was very mechanical in syntax even though it was a good mimic of person, like Grenich's computer on the island.

When the woman left her office to go to the warehouse, Brother followed behind hiding on soft padded feet in the shadows, lurking in the hallways and under desks, making no more noise than fur rubbing against a wall. She never looked back so engrossed on her survival tasks.

He watched her load up her lift the first time, seeing the imbalance, he had wanted to shift and help her load it correctly but stifled that thought. He watched as she broke down as the lift tumbled, then wipe her eyes, stick out her chin in the most stubborn way and clench her jaw unconsciously.

Brother chortled to himself as she picked everything up and reloaded the lift with far more care this time. The woman was a fighter. If there were a chance to survive she would exceed that slim chance and excel.

Brother stopped following her when she left the warehouse, melting back into the shadows to finish his search in the other offices and labs. He had seen the results when Sister's visions and comments had been ignored. The persons usually brought about mayhem by doing what they had been told not to. Brother knew if he helped the woman something would break the threads for her tenuous survival and possibly the islanders as well. As much as it went against his desire to help, he would not break that thread.

Chapter 3

"Mommy, Mommy?" Arie's small voice cut through Lauranya's grief. Lauranya looked up, wiping tears away with a hand. Her daughter was a blurry bundle of blond energy. "Mommy, I brought you a tissue!" Arie held out a tissue only slightly sticky from the trade bar chocolate.

Lauranya swept the child close, hugging her tightly.

"I love you!" she whispered fiercely.

"I love you too, mommy!" Arie squirmed from the tight embrace, tugging on Lauranya's hand. "Mommy come see what I built!"

Lauranya allowed herself to be pulled from behind Jhen's desk to see the child's loc–n–bloc creation. The blocks had been stacked in a tall tower shape, with the blue blocks on the bottom and red blocks on top.

"See? It's the God's tower in the water."

"Water at the bottom. Lauranya whispered. She turned to look out the window to the tower. The scientists had rolled their eyes and wrote unheeded reports on the used materials for a 30-story building just for the guests and Gods visiting when those same resources could have been better used for more research funding.

"Out of the mouths of babes." She smiled. Lauranya ran to the desk for paper and pen. She searched the drawers frantically, her fingers crawling over various paper clips, binders, and small loose.things.

"He's got to have one damn pen that works!" She growled.

"Bad mommy!" Arie said at her mother's bad

language, putting hands over her ears.

"Oops. Sorry, baby. Mommy's a little…" a little what? Sad? Angry? Scared? "A little distraught." The big word wouldn't scare Arie but would convey urgency. "Yes. Mommy should not swear. It does no good and limits my vocabulary." Lauranya took a deep breath and smiled reassuringly.

Arie giggled and turned back to the loc- n- bloc filling in the rest of the city. Lauranya scribbled numbers. She reached to turn on her phone to do calculations then stopped. No telling if the ship could track the phone; however, best not to take chances.

Dr. Jhen had taken his laptop not the main computer with him to the port. Lauranya fired up the desktop computer. She did not remember Jhen's login, so she went in through the back way to boot up the system.

She breathed a thank you for the foresight of her grandparents. "Thank you, G-pa for insisting we learn more than one field." She could hear Nisuo's deep but thready voice. "You will never know exactly what a God or Overseer wants, but the more you know, the better you will be placed. Learn everything!" His whip and sword-scarred face burned fierce in her memory.

She looked up from her math to hear the engines of the last shuttle taking off. She looked out the rain-smeared window, watching the vapor plumes across the sky, raising the shuttle in a bright arc until the clouds swallowed it whole.

Lauranya took a deep, steadying breath. "30 levels, 6 inches a day... slope of the hills... length and width of the valley. Need topical maps," she muttered pulling up the various maps on two screens. Lauranya tugged at a loose strand of hair while numbers resolved into an answer.

She ran a worst case and best case scenario. Neither

set of numbers were comforting, but they were a start. The building would withstand the rising water. The top six floors should be safe from flooding, even in the worst case. Should be. She was betting their lives on her numbers and the information on hand.

"Two weeks for the water to reach the first floor of all the buildings. Eight weeks to flood the living quarters. Weather model says lighter rain and melting snow caps for the next two years." The hair tugging continued as she thought aloud. Worst case, she had two weeks to compile everything she and Arie would need for the rest of their life.

"Looks like we'll finally get to see how the Lords and Gods live on the top floor."

Lauranya threw the remaining trade bars into the loose woven throw blanket and bundled them up to take to their quarters. She then bent to pick up Arie, after a moment of pleading the loc-n-blocks joined the bars.

The green and silver nanny bot lit up when Lauranya and Arie came dripping through the door.

"Good morning, Dr. Lauranya and Miss Arianya!" The nanny bot chirped cheerfully. Lauranya could swear she heard Jacks laughter at the bot's overly cheerful tones. He had programmed the thing after all. A fleeting smile as she remembered the short curly haired scientist and his warm brown eyes, followed by a lump in her throat.

"A prototype." he said with a dismissive wave when she protested the gift. "A hobby, which will probably be destroyed when a real Overseer makes a landing." She had smiled and acquiesced, accepting the gift to help Micah with raising Arie while she and Tine's were at work.

Arie wiggled out of Lauranya's arms to give the familiar nanny bot a hug and a kiss. The nanny bot's long metallic ring-jointed arms gave the child a loose hug back.

"Nanny, I will be out for a few hours. Keep Arie safe and occupied until I return." Lauranya spoke slowly and clearly as if to a slow adult.

The bot swiveled its dome head to Lauranya. The eyes glowed green in understanding. "Yes, Dr. Lauranya. I will keep Arianya safe and occupied." The robot chirped. The head swiveled back towards the toddler who was busy unwrapping the couch throw filled with the loc-n-blocs and bars. "Shall we continue with your lessons in numbers and letters, Miss Arianya?"

"No. Want to play." The child said firmly.

"You may have five minutes of play then we will do our lessons." The nanny bot responded. Arie nodded, used to this answer.

"Nanny Bot, there are trade bars for dinner and there should still be water on tap. Have her fed and in bed at the usual time." Lauranya said, her brain starting to spin with supplies and transportation.

"Trade bars are not the most nutritional…"

"Stop." The bot stopped mid-sentence. "All nutrition is subject to availability from this point on. Only bring up food if what is on hand is poisonous or inedible."

"Acknowledged. Dr. Lauranya." The bot chirped.

Lauranya turned to Arie. The child was frowning at the exchange between her mom and the nanny bot.

"Mommy, why are you mad at nanny?" She asked, tilting her head to the left.

Lauranya opened her mouth then closed it again, thinking. With a deep breath, she tried again. "I'm not, sweetie. I am upset and probably yelling at an object that has no feelings to get hurt."

"That's still not very nice," Arie said with the certainty of a child.

Lauranya knelt, wrapping her arms around the child. "No dear, it is not. Arie returned the hug tightly. "Sweetie, I need to get a few things set up, and I may be gone for a few hours. Nanny will watch you while I am gone. I need you to be good." Before Arie could ask, "Yes you still have to do lessons but after lessons, you may play with the blocs or watch a movie.

Arie squealed at the treat of a movie, giving a tighter hug to her mother. "Okay mommy. Don't' worry. We'll be fine." Arie smiled, kissing her mother on the cheek, then went to see what nanny bot's screen was showing.

Lauranya slipped out of their rooms quietly, just in case Arie had another question that needed answering. Time, they did not have.

"Food, shelter, clothing. Food and shelter first." Lauranya could feel her heart beating faster and the need to run building. She leaned against the hallway's walls, getting herself under control. Where to start, her mind kept circling on the impossible task of surviving in a drowning world like a mouse in a cage.

"Cages! I need to see what is in the labs. Seeds. No animals but generators. Then the tower. Then I start moving things." With a nod, she pushed off the wall. "Right. Lab is first. One step at a time." She stepped quickly. They were running out of time.

The labs were locked. However, Lauranya had her key pass. No one had bothered to mothball the buildings or shut down the electronics. The water would destroy any attempt to preserve, so minimal effort was made. Lauranya's hands shook for a moment. The Gods wouldn't know for years of intellectual property loss. The scientist had been the largest asset to be saved but even that was a lie. The other deaths weighed heavily.

The solar generators could last for a couple of generations in space; however when enough water hit them things would start to short out. The generators were never meant to be waterproof, just water resistant. She chewed her lower lip. What if the generators shorted sooner rather than later? Electronic doors would not open. Should she prop the doors open or leave them closed? She hesitated for a moment, thinking to prop the door open with a chair, but the thought of a whiskered cat wandering in out of the rain was enough to check the locks behind her.

"If something big gets in here while I'm collecting items, I'm dead. So unlocked but take out the electrical locks so they can be manually opened." She headed to her office first. She sat down, flipping on the computer, experiencing a serious sense of déjà vu opening Jhen's computer, causing another moment of hyperventilation. She drove her nails into her thigh to keep from losing it again. "No damn time! Concentrate. Survival first." A deep breath through her teeth and the pain from her leg refocused her on the tasks at hand.

The computer flared to life. She had disabled the voice program months ago. Having a nanny bot speak was grating enough; having her computer imitate her husband's voice made her skin crawl.

"Computer list all solar generators in the compound." She thought for a moment. "Unconnected and connected." Lauranya started to flip through the monitors for the labs. All the large animals had been put down yesterday. No help there. Would not have been able to house the cheo goats anyway, they were too big both in eating consumption and room for movement. Too bad about the chickens or rabbits though.

Lauranya stopped her screen on the incubators. The lights were still on. She gave a puff of laughter. The eggs were still viable then. "Computer list the egg types in incubator 1101, 1102 and 1305".

The screen scrolled through the genetics of eggs listed.

"Chicken, 3 different types listed, over 25 eggs, but only 5 ducks eggs. Cannot fault Tass for wanting to experiment on an actual water-based bird. Competent scientist just as excellent an ass-kisser, just a lousy coworker." Lauranya rolled her eyes, unconsciously muttering about the well-worn dislike of the scientist. "Crap! Do we have enough food for the chicks? I need to find out." She tapped her computer again. "Computer, list all feed for chickens and ducks. Also all edible seeds in storage that can be used for crops. Nutrition density seeds first with care instructions." A tap of her finger on the wooden desk. "Also list soil density needed and soil nutrition needed to maintain with water usage required for maximum growth." A quirk of her lips. "Though water probably will not be a problem."

Her fingers tapped on the keyboard without striking hard enough to type as she thought. Lots of water would be available but then moving the water to the plants or even to the building would be an issue. Clean water for her and Arie would be an issue. They would need clean water on tap for both drinking and cooking. Hygiene would be an issue without water as well. The ground floor generators would be drowned in 4-5 weeks that precluded using the ones in place. Lauranya chewed the inside of her cheek, her head starting to hurt. Another stray thought. Medication! What was left? What had the captain and his crew not taken? How was she going to apply what was left? She was not a physician.

"Computer, list all the skills needed for …" for what? Surviving a drowning world, being lost without technology or at least limited technology …who was going to fix the broken things? "Breathe damn it. Breathe." She reached into her pocket. Drat! Her anxiety meds were in her overnight bag, which was still in the concourse at the shuttle port. She took more deep breaths. One-step at a time.

"Waiting for command." Scrolled across the screen as the computer beeped at her.

She tapped the appropriate keys to keep the beeping at bay. "Computer print all items pertaining to and instructions for growing food plants in a greenhouse type environment…" She stopped mid-sentence a sob breaking free. There were no people, a drowning world, and such a long shot to survive. Would the Gods' accommodations actually be waterproof or just water resistant? Could she find and grow enough food? Medicine? What would they need for the years, hells the months to come?

This time she did start to cry, burying her head in her hands. Was she even doing the right thing for her daughter? Would it have been better if they had drank the champagne? The

thought of her daughter dead, frothing at the mouth, choked her even more, but the image of what had been done to the others filled her with a fury.

"No! The Dead Gods be damned!" She wiped her eyes angrily. Lauranya clenched a fist. "So mote it be. We will survive!" They would make a go of it at least trying to survive. The practical side of her brain kicked in. In a worst-case scenario, there should be something on hand to slide them gently into death's arms.

She took a deep cleansing breath and continued to dictate to her computer.

Lauranya stepped into the labs. The computer had listed the edible seeds stock inventory as ¾ full. The planting from last year had gone amazingly well but this year's planting had not started. The spring rains had never abated.

There were enough of each seed to plant two acres each and still have seeds to eat. Well, those seeds that could be eaten, she amended. The fruit tree seeds were not going to be edible, no matter how long she boiled them.

She looked in the animal lab wistfully. Camdia had done her job though and had euthanized and disposed of the bodies. The protein would have been useful if not for the strong euthanizing drug in their system, so no salvaging of meat was available.

All four incubators showed green lights. Lauranya grinned; walking up to the incubators to visually confirm the power on green lights were working. Bless Camdia and her forgetful genius! That girl could map out genetic codes on reproduction, but she was absent-minded on anything not in her area of specialty.

"Thank you Camdia! May Yemoja, the all mother, hold you close." Lauranya whispered. She flinched and looked around guiltily if someone overheard her prayer. "No one here but you, woman!" Lauranya shook her head, hissing her breath out between clenched teeth. Her back ached from the last time she had prayed to the forgotten Gods and not the undead god of her world and had been sent to the Overseer for correction.

She touched her earbud, connected to the computer's interface. "Computer I will need all growing …raising instructions for chickens and ducks from the incubator." She stopped for a moment looking at the hatching estimate. "One week from hatching to full growth."

This led to the next train of thought. "How do you even cook one of these birds?" She spoke into the empty office.

She flinched when the computer responded. "There are over 200 recipes for chickens and ducks."

"Damn…Never needed to worry about turning off the computer's voice for the earbud." She shook her head but continued without disconnecting the voice. "At least it is not Tine's voice. Computer, add all recipes pertaining to chickens and ducks with grains from the seeds listed at this location." She continued to explore the fowl lab. "Add that to the manual being printed."

"Would you like recipes for the grains, legumes and root vegetables with the spices on hand?"

"Yes." She said absently and then stopped. "Spices on hand?" She queried with a frown.

"The hotel has a rarity of spices on hand. Some of which are in seed or clove from that could be grown for further replenishment of stock.

Lauranya's mind raced. If they left spices, could the ship crew have left other food stock?

"Computer, is there food stocked in the hotel as well?"

"All lower kitchen food stocks including spices were removed…" The computer started.

"Damn you for raising my hopes," Lauranya said through clenched teeth, her hands turning to fists at her side. She felt the prickly sensation around her eyes, as tears started to form. She missed the first few words of the computer's next sentence.

She almost sobbed, whispering instead "Repeat."

The computer droned on, "However, the upper suite

portion of the hotel is fully stocked with spices and food items. Shall I list all the foods and spices on stock?"

Lauranya stopped with her mouth open and then closed with a snap. "No, wait." She thought for a second. "How long will the food last one adult and one child? Are the cooking facilities only in the lower portion of the hotel or in the upper portion?"

The computer gave three soft beeps while computing. "The food stocks will last one child and one adult for three years on three meals a day. There are cooking facilities both in the lower and upper portions of the hotel. The upper kitchen is not dependent on the lower kitchen for operations."

"Computer, can the kitchen cooking facilities be attached to a solar generator for use?"

"With the use of one connecting solar power generator, the entire kitchen facility will be operational."

"What other equipment does the kitchen facility have?"

"Food preparation stations, cooking station, freezer sections and pantry. The pantry and food preparation areas only require lighting for use."

Why did the captains leave the food? Like her did they just assume the kitchen had not been stocked? All the slaves who had filled the pantry and freezer gone with the first transports off so no-one to correct this assumption.

Lauranya sagged with relief, leaning against the wall. Her hands shook for a moment and then steadied. Three years they could survive, while she and Arie learned how to raise plants and birds on a rotating year long basis.

Lauranya passed through the labs, confirming no other surprises until she got to the personal offices next to the children's lab. There she paused for a moment as she heard a high-pitched squeaking, like rusty wheels spinning repeatedly but un-synched. Lauranya hesitated but followed the noise moving as quietly as she could on the tiled floor.

The sound got louder the closer she got to the far side of the labs. Here she found the second bit of good news in the source of the squeaking wheels. The kids would come in with their parents and be given small tasks with personal pet projects. There were eight cages, each cage holding either one rabbit or a rabbit and her litter. There were five singulars and three mothers with litters.

"Yes!" Lauranya gave a small whoop. "Bless you, Camdia, again for not thinking outside your orders." She leaned close to one of the cages for a better look. Fat and sassy, the six-legged mammals seemed not only well fed but happy to see her. The closest one rolled onto its back with all six legs up and loose, as if asking for a stomach rub, with a toothy grin. This reminded Lauranya of her own pet rabbit before it had been contributed to the family dinner one lean year. "We'll get back to you eight as soon as I can," Lauranya promised, with a smile. She checked food and water levels. All seemed to be stocked well enough to last another few days if necessary.

She continued on to the warehouse storage. The warehouse was right behind the labs, with a walkway wide enough to accommodate two lift jacks at one time. The sound of rain beat steadily on the metal roof walkway between the labs and warehouse. Any other time she would have enjoyed the effect of the rain, but now it just drummed out in a staccato pattern that reminded Lauranya she was running out of time.

The concrete had been sealed, leaving the floor shiny and reflective. The overhead lights pierced the gloom, but did not really alleviate the shadowy corners at the ends and at the bottom of the high reaching rows of equipment.

Lauranya swallowed. The shadows could hide so many things, and usually nothing good. Taking a deep breath to clear her mind and steady her nerves, she headed deeper into the bowels of the warehouse.

The warehouse, even after the ships had cherry-picked the contents, was a vast treasure trove of survival items. She went to the area listed for holding the solar generators. There were four. "Damn you, to the hells!" Lauranya whispered. The computer had listed over thirty. It seemed the various transport crews had helped themselves to the generators as well. Lauranya had to crawl to them, as they had been pushed to the back wall of the holding pen. Of the four left, one looked to have been cannibalized for parts, the interior wiring and electronic boards showing through a gaping open panel. The remaining three did not seem to be missing any parts. One was dented slightly on the side, but not serious enough, Lauranya hoped, to be damaging.

Each one weighed 90 lbs. There was no way she was going to get these to the hotel by herself. She stopped for a moment, chewing on her lower lip. "Right. I need moving discs. Now, where the hells are the discs stored?" She muttered to the ghostly silence.

"All frictionless discs are in the first row by the office door, third shelf up. There are also keys to unlock the lifts and tarps varying from 6'x4' to 12'x20'." The computer chirped into her ear, causing Lauranya to jump up startled, smacking her head against the metal shelving row above the generator section.

"You bloody sand wasted piece of..." Lauranya held her head, clenching her jaws, as her breath whistling through her teeth in pain.

She crawled out of the pen to locate the discs she needed for moving. The discs were exactly where the computer had stated. She gathered six-- two for each generator. The discs did what they were fashioned for, making a heavy load easy to slide over any surface with the touch of a finger. These she moved to the warehouse bay door to the left. She found the barrels with the markings for seed grains.

"Why the hells did you not take these, Captain?" She looked for a forklift to move the grain plastic barrels to the hover lift. "There's enough here for years of growing…ahh…growing. You need dirt or hydroponics, and most small ships will not have those. Only the world ships. And I am betting you didn't think you could eat those or have room for a growing medium." She stopped with her hand on the forklift, closing her eyes. "Dirt or hydroponics. How do I grow these now?" She said, realizing the same dilemma that kept the seeds from being stolen in the first place. She shook her head. "Seeds and eggs with power generators. I will find dirt next!"

With her computer's help and judicial application of machine help for moving equipment and supplies, she spent the next few hours sorting useful from not so useful into sections near the warehouse doors. The most useful items went next to the bay doors, while those not immediately necessary further back from the door. The incubators she would leave until she had a space cleared out in the hotel main floor.

On the first trial run of packing the lift, she overloaded the seed side, causing a tilt on turning. The seeds did a slow tumble to the left, followed by the solar generators with only a thump.

"Esu!" Lauranya snapped irritably and then started crying. "No Overseers and I cannot do a single thing right." She angrily wiped the tears away, pressing her lips into a stubborn line. She straightened her shoulders, with a deep breath. "The road to the end requires many steps," she whispered her grandfather Savo's favorite quote. It took her two tries to reload the lift correctly with the heaviest items center, picking up the various items that had spilled.

"Doctor Lauranya, I have a problem to report." The computer chimed into her ear.

"That's a surprise…?" Her voice was dry in response, as she concentrated on each item's placement.

"Excuse me, doctor?"

"Nothing. What is the current issue?" Lauranya swallowed her sarcasm.

"The map of the suites shows all rooms to be filled with furniture or bedding. There is no room for your influx of equipment."

That stopped Lauranya cold. She had not planned on there not being room. "Computer, is there enough space to move the furniture into a room or a set of rooms?"

"Not without much lifting."

"Visual."

The computer projected a hologram in front of her eyes with the upper floors schematics and furniture.

"Lots of furniture. Inefficient use of space." She tapped her upper lip with one long finger. More lifting, it looked like. "Well, I will have a lift with me." Another thought. "Computer, keep track of all the items I am moving. I will want to move the equipment into the main lobby while moving the furniture into the rooms."

"Yes, Dr. Lauranya." The computer intoned.

"Arie and I will take the upper suites, and I will fill the lower suite with furniture. Sheets, towels…those will need to be found as well. Cleansing suds for us and clothing. Add that to the list of items to find, computer."

"All cleaning supplies and fresh linens can be found

on the first floor in the laundry rooms. To a lesser extent, there are also cleaning supplies and fresh linens in the laundry room on the upper floor."

"Oh! Yes that is perfect." She stood for a moment, gathering her thoughts and rearranging the order of items needing to be collected. "Computer add to the list all medical remaining and take notations. I will need to move the supplies to the upper floor, second room from end right. That can be our medical."

"Acknowledged, Dr. Lauranya." The computer flashed a holo to her right with the list already compiled and a line drawn through the warehouse items on the lift.

"Second floor can hold equipment, cables, computer and generators here." She said pointing to one suite of rooms. Another thought. "Computer, are there discs on the furniture or do they have to be lifted?"

"Final inspection has not been completed by the majordomo, so all furniture items are on frictionless discs."

She breathed out. "Something going right for the moment. Ok, we will start with the leftover moving items, and I will start arranging furniture over there. Have a list ready with each moved item and their location so I can put them on the moving lift easily and quickly in order of need. Priority to food, generators, medical, and animals. Each move needs to contain a portion of each.

"Acknowledged, Dr. Lauranya."

With a shake of her hair, she returned to the task. The lift was loaded without wobbles. She used three tarps to cover the generators and other items from the downpour.

She pulled the lift with her to the bay doors, opening them only a fraction so she could look outside, no whiskered cats in sight. She opened the door, pulling the lift behind her. Once cleared of the door, she reclosed it.

She was soaked to the skin within seconds. She came to realize her office flats would not work after a few feet on the water slick road. She was stumbling, catching herself against the lift, as one foot or the other would slip out from under her on the running water covered concrete. She did not swear at the slips just grateful the water was still running downhill and not pooling around her ankles or higher.

It was a short walk to the hotel, but Lauranya kept stopping every few feet to check the lift, not trusting her packing for this first, most important load. What should have been a quick four-minute walk was a good 15 minutes.

Lauranya tried not to think about how much more dangerous and time-consuming trips would be when the water was pooling at her feet and rising fast. She concentrated on her footing and breathing pushing her anxiety aside.

The service door was wide enough to hold three lifts at a time and twenty bodies. The door was a palm reader, which had Lauranya worried for about 30 seconds. "Computer have biometrics been set for the Lords building?"

"Not yet, Dr. Lauranya."

"Ok, let's give this a try before I have to gladiator stomp this thing." She placed her hand on the door. The idea of her trying to kick in the metal door makes her smile for a moment. The door plate beeped thrice then opened to let her in.

"Generic hands will open it." Lauranya was both grateful and appalled at the lack of security. She pulled the lift into the dry service elevator over the rough stone tiles on wet squelching shoes. Cold air blew on her from the ceiling air vent, causing shivers.

"Please no key." She whispered, reaching with shaking hands to hit the uppermost floor button. A heartbeat in time that felt like an eternity, later, the button lit up. The locks had not been set. She leaned her forehead against the smooth steel walls. The service elevator started to move up and the music started to play — soothing classical. Lauranya rolled her eyes at the sporadic touches for the building. The music reminded her to add another list for compilation. They would need music on file.

"Computer, download all music into the hard drives. Duplicate all information requested not just music, no triplicate into multiple files areas." She shook her head. "Redundancy must have more than one." Another thought. "All entertaining and educational videos as well."

"Yes, Doctor." The computer chirped compliantly.

The ride up gave her the time to chew on her lower lip thinking. Her brain kept turning over the thoughts of what might be missing, like a burrowing rodent tunneling through her brain.

"Shhh…calm…shhhh." She whispered to herself as she would to Arie. Her hands were shaking so she gripped her upper arms to quell the hands. The hands still trembled but not as badly.

The double doors opened onto the bottom floor aerie suites entryway. Even with her anxiety spiking, Lauranya stopped and stared. The entryway was the size of the lab building. The windows stretched from floor to ceiling, showing a grey drenched view with rain-streaked glass. The stone floor was muted sandstone pavers, covered with natural fiber rugs in geometric patterns in floral and mechanical interwoven. The overstuffed couches were in dark brown and red colored leather. Lush and luxurious furniture and materials, and Lauranya had to move it all.

She set the gravity lift to the side and went to explore the rooms to assess the extent of moving that she would need to do in the hours of the day remaining.

Chapter 4

"Momma!" Arie ran to her mother with the energy and enthusiasm of a child, while Lauranya dripped water onto the tile floor of their rooms.

Lauranya scooped up the child in a fierce hug, whispering "I love you," into the squirming child's ear.

"I love you too!" Arie whispered back, giggling, squirming out of her mother's arms, vanishing into her mother's room for a moment.

Lauranya staggered to the unit's couch, sagging into the welcoming cushions, ignoring her dripping hair and clothing puddling on the vinyl.

"Doctor, we have covered the basic numbers and--" The nanny started.

"Stop," Lauranya said tiredly vaguely waving a hand to stop the robot. The nanny stopped mid-sentence. "Any relevant health issues or nutrition concerns?"

"Arianya is healthy. Nutritionally the bars will suffice for a few days before…."

"Stop," Lauranya said in an irritated voice laced with exhaustion, this time not even bothering to raise a hand or her head.

"Momma that's not very nice." Arie scolded, climbing next to her wet and tired mother with a large dry towel. Lauranya hugged the child tightly, the towel wedged between them for a brief moment, sparing Arie from the dribbling rainwater.

"Thank you, love and I know, baby, I know," Lauranya said with a sigh to Arie. "Too tired to remember my manners." She faced the nanny, standing slowly. "Nanny new task." She started pulling off wet articles of clothing while talking, dropping them on the floor with disregard to the growing puddle of water or warping of the linoleum floor tile.

"While we are sleeping, pack all clothes, bedding, medicinal and any food items that do not require refrigeration into bags from all apartment units. Load these bags into the foyer. All refrigerated food items bring to this units refrigerator for holding."

"Doctor, I cannot take things from other occupants." The nanny intoned.

"Drat you, Jacks. Forgot you added this portion in." Lauranya pursed her lips, looking up, trying a new tactic. "Nanny, confirm evacuation notice." Hands on pants that were half off her padded hips. Arie took this moment to run back into her mother's room again for another towel and she wiped up the water puddles on the couch and floor.

"Confirmed, Doctor." The bot intoned.

"Confirm removal of all personnel except Arianya and myself." Lauranya continued to shimmy out of the skin grasping wet pants, kicking a leg at a time to help the wet material slither off her legs.

This took a few moments longer as the nanny internally reviewed port records and manifests. Lauranya took this time to pick up then place her wet clothes on the back of the couch to dry.

"Confirmed, Doctor."

"Confirm all items left are now subject to salvage and scavenge due to lack of ownership or former owner returning," Lauranya said toweling herself off with the original towel Arie had brought.

Internal dialog for the nanny, lights flashing on her

chassis as this too was processed. Arie was fascinated by the unusual light display. Lauranya pulled the child's hands back to their side, instead of letting the curious child fiddle with the robot's internal query lights.

"Lack of ownership confirmed. Salvage allowed. Scavenge allowed." Nanny intoned to Lauranya.

Lauranya nodded with a brief smile but muttered to herself. "Thank you Jacks. I should have kicked you when you gave us this "educational prototype toy." To the nanny, she said. "Good. Now scavenge all bedding, medical, clothing, and food as directed in my earlier instructions." Lauranya looked at Arie a second with another idea. "Also add any toys and games ages 7 and up." Lauranya stopped for a moment thinking. "No duplications. If duplicate toy or game is found, secure the more gently used item with all or more parts intact, please."

"What are you going to do with all that stuff mommy?" Arie asked, her head tilting quizzically.

"We are going to move everything into our new living quarters." She said with a smile to her daughter the vigorous toweling muffling her voice.

"New living quarters?" Arie asked worriedly. "But I like these!" She gestured emphatically to the handprints on the wall that led to the height measurements on the door jamb with hers and the twins' heights, for the last five years. The various pictures drawn by the children or taken by the family taped to the wall adding bright notes of color.

"I know dear, but with the rains, the water table is rising very fast. We will not be able to live here, as these apartments will be underwater." Toweling her hair off, combing the tangles with almost nimble fingers.

"Oh. That would be rather hard to live in. Unless we

had gills." Arie said almost excitedly. She was contemplating life with gills, open and closing her mouth as if she were a small fish, staring at the ceiling while doing so.

Lauranya smiled tiredly. "Yes, if we had gills it would be much easier. We are not far enough along to give ourselves gills, my dear. Maybe one day, though. Until that time though, we have a new place to go to."

Ari was quiet a moment. "Is it as nice as here, mommy?"

"Nicer. You can see for miles through windows taller than you and thick carpets for your toes to sink in." Lauranya slumped a little lower on the couch with a jaw-cracking yawn.

"Oh! That does sound nice." Arie said, climbing up next to Lauranya to snuggle and contemplate the idea of a new home. She absently patted Lauranya's breast to show her approval. Lauranya giggled slightly for a moment, children having no body taboo or shame at young ages. Lauranya stood up, scooping her small child into her arms for a hug. "That's my girl. Now momma needs a shower and a nap before moving more items." Giving Arie a tummy zerberts in the process.

Arie squealed, but let her mother take her into the main bedroom without fussing over bedtime.

Lauranya had set the alarm for an early hour. When the alarm sounded, she turned off the clock with a silent groan not wanting to wake Arie up. Getting dressed in the dark was a series of fumbling through drawers for clothes by touch. Staggering from sleep deprivation and manual labor yesterday into the brightly lit bathroom, it took her a moment to notice her top and pants were very mismatched.

"Not like there is anyone to notice." She muttered. Everything hurt as she continued to stumble into the main living area, dragging a brush through her long blond hair before twisting it into a messy bun to keep out of her eyes and away from her neck when it got wet.

"Good morning, Dr. Lauranya…"

"Stop." The nanny bot stopped mid-sentence. "New instructions."

"Waiting for directions." The nanny intoned. "Pack all clothing, bedding, toiletries…pack up the apartment except the furniture and bring down to the lobby." Lauranya tapped her lower lip with a finger for a second. "Save one…no two days of clothing for both Ari and myself. Keep Ari busy while doing so."

"Yes, Doctor."

Lauranya nodded walking to the kitchen to grab a travel bar on her way out. The first bite was almost enough to make her spit it out, grainy with an almost rough texture and unexpected round squishy parts. Her stomach had other ideas, cramping so hard she almost doubled over in hunger. Lauranya swallowed with difficulty, managing to choke down the remaining bar in four bites. Her stomach seemed content, but her mouth felt gummy yet dry. Lauranya made a face, trying to rub her tongue along the roof of her mouth to get the taste and feel of the bar out while keeping all the caloric value possible. She was mostly successful, but just.

The rest of the morning consisted of moving the bags from the living quarters to the new rooms and throwing them in a pile for later sorting. The first thirty minutes were slow as her muscles warmed from yesterday's moving. Once the bags were moved, she headed to the office and warehouse for more long-term essentials-seeds, computers, incubators, and fluorescent lamps necessary for indoor plants.

"Dirt. Damn it, dirt." Lauranya muttered to herself, looking at the copious amount of seeds. Hydroponics could be done, but only if she had all the supplies and did not have failures in the nutrients. Half hydro and half dirt? Would that work, she thought? Tower farming? "Oko knows I could use any help offered." She let out a breath, contemplating the items in front of her.

An epiphany hit as she found a box of military grade rations packs. The packs were not the epiphany, tasting flat and of chemicals, but killing, her hunger pains. The epiphany came from the memory running from the shuttle crew. There had been planters, very large planters, in the lobby of the shuttle port. Lauranya was betting there were planters in the main lobby of the hotel as well. The Gods and lords liked plants. The green zones on a world ship were better cared for than most of the human chattel. The human chattel was replaceable; the plants were actually life-giving and necessary.

Lauranya took another bite of a military ration. The taste was just as bad as the first bite. Lauranya choked it down. She knew they could survive on these, but she was sure survival would come at the cost of her taste buds. She put the box on the cart of items to go to the hotel. These would be for only the direst of emergency in food. There was no way Lauranya would feed this willingly to Arie or herself if any other choice were available.

Lauranya checked on the incubators. The lights were green. Lauranya turned the eggs manually, scanning for moisture content. The eggs were in fine shape and should be hatching in the next few days. Sooner than Lauranya needed them to, but they would help keep Arie busy as

Lauranya continued to gather items for their survival.

Lauranya packed the remaining seeds, lights and one incubator on the lift along with hoses, wires, various tools and goods thrown into plastic tubs. The trip to the hotel lift was much faster this time around.

Lauranya placed the incubator on the far right wall, closest to the kitchen. She put the solar generators next to the incubator. The seeds went next to the generators. Everything else she moved to the floor and started in on moving the furniture, starting with the large couches first, placing the moving discs underneath the legs so the metal and leather couches moved with a touch of the hand.

She ignored the bags of bedding and clothes piled along the back wall next to the lift, on the way to the bottom far left room. She had moved the furniture in this room to line one corner of the back wall, emptying the remaining rooms and filling with the main lobby area furniture.

The lobby's arrangement of furniture looked like multiple groupings of couches and chairs in various patterns. Some were cozy little four-piece groups with natural woven fabric pillows next to the chairs for personal slaves to sit, set against the windows for a commanding view of the valley and sky. Larger group sections were composed of three couches with occasional chairs. This setting had both fabric and leather woven pillows and mats for the slaves to kneel on while awaiting commands. Small tables, either round or square tops, finished so smoothly that they invited one to touch and pet the silky wood. The fittings were of dark gold or silver to contrast the glowing amber wood.

Piece by piece the lobby area was emptied until only the rugs remained. The one room could not fit another piece of furniture; the door would barely close, almost bursting with most of the lobby furniture jig sawed into place.

She moved to the next room, to the left and against the back wall on the bottom floor, adjacent to the lobby. This was another two-room suite. She moved the suite's furniture to the back wall opening up the room for more items from the lobby and more warehouse supplies.

She had time for one more warehouse run. This run she gathered the remaining seeds and incubators. She checked on the rabbits, filling water bottles and feeders. "Tomorrow, I'll move you guys too." She promised, heading back to the grav lift and her final load for the day.

She moved the final incubators next to the first, checking energy levels and lights. "All green," Lauranya said with a sigh as she bent backward stretching her arms overhead, then slowly raising upright to roll her shoulders back. "Any more exploring can wait. I think I'm good for the day." She tapped her ear bud. "Computer, have a list compiled for any primary survival items I missed and set for prime move tomorrow."

"Yes, Doctor."

It was dark when she had cleared all the furniture and rugs. Another ration pack and she headed back, taking the lift by the labs first. The water was ankle deep and running downhill less slowly. Lauranya noted this change, chewing her bottom lip. She could not see anything past the building lights, but she could imagine what was in the dark. She heard the screams of the whiskered cats and shrill calls of other wildlife, moving through the dark seeking higher ground. Lauranya did not want to think of how bad the displaced animals would be in a week, as she tried to move Arie, while all the animals were also looking for shelter. She dragged the lift behind her back to the apartment building, parking it in the foyer. Tomorrow morning it would be time to move the child to the new living quarters.

The cove was only a few miles from the Dead Gods installation, but the climb up was at a 48% angle. Almost more than the very hardiest or foolhardy wanted to try. With steep vegetation and unexpected rock out thrusts and loose stones, the hills going up or down were leg breakers just waiting to happen. Brother had shifted as soon as he had hit the shoreline, leaving Keyma to wait for him until he returned. The return could be in a day or three weeks, was all he had growled mid-way through his shifting.

Keyma lounged on a smooth tree trunk trireme, in a small natural cove. The first few days Keyma had spent exploring the surrounding waterways around the cove. She was uninterested in shifting to her land legs to explore the shorelines, finding the changing waterline more interesting. The formerly shallow cove would normally have a sandy shoreline with crystal clear water and a shallow depth; however, the runoff from the hills had turned a once clear cove into a rapidly rising mud bath. The water was so silted that no mer could see more than a few inches in the dark rising depths. The water was deep enough that there was a real danger of a flat head shark deciding to try for a snack. Not an issue if one could see, but dangerous under the prevalent conditions.

She lounged, bare stomach on the wet but smooth wood, cleaning her half-moon dagger-like fingernails, flipping her tail in a board fashion against the low side railing. Her tail, leaned over the edge of the trireme dipping into the water, making small tapping plinks against the rain dimpled water surface. Her blonde hair was tied into a rough braid, draping warm and wet over a bare shoulder. Carving intricate designs into the floorboards helped to stave off the boredom when she wasn't hunting the clearer waters outside the cove. With nothing exciting for the last two weeks, the floor had little space for any more designs.

The trireme dipped and swayed for a moment, then stilled. Keyma's eyes narrowed and she put her knife back into the eel skin sheath at her waist. With a quick flip of her tail, she pulled her tail up from hanging over the edge of the trireme rolling to her back. Slowly she sat up, shifting to two legs. Her hand on her spear, she watched the rain dimple the muddy waters around her.

Another slow double ripple rocked the trireme, this time from the right side. An underwater exploratory nudge moved the trireme half an inch.

Keyma scrunched her lips in irritation at the unexpected and unwelcome company. She rocked with the trireme, moving her weight with each ripple, gaining her feet but in a crouch, trying not to give the flat head any more of a silhouette then necessary. One hand flat on the trireme, the other gripping her spear tightly. She tensed as another set of ripples marred the surface. She waited, tensing her shoulders, ready for an attack, counting the seconds under her breath. Three minutes went by slowly. The water remained dimpled only by the rain. Keyma's thighs started to scream at the unaccustomed position.

Keyma took a deep breath, releasing slowly. She rolled her shoulders down, twisting her neck to either side, lowering herself to a sitting position on her knees. "Thank the Gods." She whispered. Six feet. Her rough estimate of the double ripples compared to the tail ripple. A small one but even small ones had enough of a bite to rip off limbs or gut a mer, with one bite pulling entrails, and the mer clinging to their guts, down into the preferred depths for slow consumption.

The trireme lifted with a celerity that made even a regular shark attack heart-stopping. Keyma's nails reflexively bit into the wood, as the trireme lifted to a 60-degree angle, but did not tip over. She held onto the spear with a white-knuckled death grip as she and the trireme fell back down, hitting the water with a resounding thud, knocking the breath from her lungs in a whoosh.

"Sand and coral, I will fucking eat your heart." She gasped in a wheezing almost scream, scrambling to her feet, silhouette be damned. The shark knew she was there and it was hungry.

The shark had backed up, leaving sets of ripples as the double row head ridges went almost to the entrance of the cove. Room to move, building up speed. Keyma had seen this exactly twice before. Her leg scar ached from the last close-up encounter with a flat head.

"Oh fuck you, you overly smart piece of fecal bottom feeder," Keyma growled. The shark was going to ram the trireme, forcing her into the water. Deep enough for it to maneuver and dirty enough she couldn't see. The damn things were too smart by half. The shark paused for only a moment; then with a flick of its powerful tail, the shark pushed forward picking up momentum with every thrust.

"One shot. Don't fuck this up coral diver!" Keyma shifted the grip of the spear in her hand to both hands, readying the change from legs to tail. The effect felt of electricity burning along her spine and down her legs.

"Three, two, one!" With a scream of fear and rage, Keyma leaped from the trireme almost straight up, aiming her spear's razor coral tip for the point slightly forward of the head ridges. She shifted forms on the arc, as spear touched water, adding the extra bulk of her mer weight to the down thrust.

Had this been clear water, the move would never have worked. Yet what kept Keyma from swimming blinded the shark from an overhead attack. Her point landed between the optic capsule and the vertebral column, severing spine from head.

The shark thrashed stirring up the water to an ochre-tinged mud bath. Keyma held on grimly, wrapping the damned thing around her tail to keep from being bitten as the head, even severed from the spine, kept trying to bite. The dust and silt choked Keyma as she tried to gulp water over her newly sprouted gills, holding on for dear life to the spear with both hands and the shark with her tail.

"Die! Die! Die!" She choke chanted, pushing down on the spear, arm muscles bunching with adrenaline as she tried to nail her spear hilt to the ground.

She pushed harder, twisting the spear point and haft, trying to punch through the hard cartilage of the shark's head to end this battle. Death did not have a full grip on the shark yet. The shark's attempts to roll and twist, dragging Keyma against an outcropping of jagged rocks along what would have been, four weeks ago the cove's hillside. Keyma's skin split, sending more blood into the dim waters. She could taste salty copper as blood, water and silt flowed through her mouth and over her gills. Her stomach clenched at the taste, unconscious memories of other water battles and hard won scars flashing along her synapses.

She felt, as much as heard, a roar of challenge above the water line near where the trireme had been abandoned. There was another set of splashing and ripples to her left. Keyma let loose with her left hand to grab her knife, fearing another predator joining the fray. She slashed widely, feeling a slight resistance then a hand clamping on her wrist.

The hand stopped her from slashing, but it was the half shifted face of Brother, vague in the murky waters, that made the coiled fear in her gut release. Brother released her hand, careful not to dent or cut her skin with his almost claw-like nails, as he dug into the shark, rabbit kicking the stomach with powerful hind legs. His feet, tipped with nails ceramic sharp, cut through the half inch shark skin as if it were paper. The water went from muddy brown with tendrils of red to ochre-hued, spreading ripples as the shark was eviscerated.

The shark shuddered, rolling onto its back with Keyma still riding on top when Brother released his hold. Keyma let go of the spear, unwrapping her tail, to emerge spluttering from the spreading red gore in the water.

Keyma started to spit and cough out dirt and small bloody goo, holding up a finger to stall Brother from asking any questions.

"Looks like you've had a relaxing day." Was all he said in amusement, panting from the watery skirmish. Keyma looked up with a glare and changed the finger from the first to a three finger wiggle of "Go screw a snake." Brother just gave her a wide grin before diving back underneath the shark, tilting the body to have full access to the spear haft. The spear was in a better position for punching through the toothy lower jaw than being pulled out.

"Smartass. This happens to be dinner now." She coughed out in a gravelly voice, trying to clear her throat, knowing he would hear her through the shallow water. The spear pushed through as if skewering unshelled clam meat. She grabbed the haft two feet below the tip and pulled. She resisted smacking him with her tail while he was underwater, but just.

He rose from underneath the side with the partially

exposed head, exhaling noisily, "Dinner is going to be...Holy engines." Brother stopping mid retort. "Your shoulder!" Brother's eyes grew large and his expression horrified at the wound on Keyma's shoulder. She hadn't felt the pain due to adrenaline until he spoke, then the line from her shoulder to her ribs burned like fire.

"Gods that hurts." She whispered, flexing her nails along the haft of her spear as the pain throbbed in time with her heart.

"Get on the trireme and I will get that sewn up." Brother looked at her shoulder with concern. "And don't shift! You'll do more damage pulling the skin then by staying in your water form."

"Dinner," Keyma said faintly, motioning at the shark with a slight bob of the spear in her hand. She hissed as her braid bumped against the open wound.

"I'll pull the damn fish up behind us, but your shoulder needs looking at now!"

"Fine." But there was no heat in her word or face as she tried to comply with his directions. Keyma laid the spear on the floor of the trireme and then moved her braid to her non damaged side. She tried to pull herself up on to the trireme but kept failing. Her injured arm wasn't of much use, her tail weighed too much, not giving her any leverage up with one arm pulling. Brother got behind her and gave her a bit of a push, propelling her over the slight lip of the trireme's side. Keyma gave a pained yelp as his lift landed her in an ungainly position putting pressure on her injured shoulder and ribs.

"That'll teach you to be a badass killing tail spinner." He grunted, lifting her heavier water-form tail.

"Remind me to spike your next set of sushi with zebra spine poison." She gasped with more pain than animosity. The toxin, in small doses, made men unable to achieve erections; in larger doses the ingester died, as the poison enlarged pores of the lungs, letting water seep through tissue, drowning them slowly. Jilted wives and girlfriends had been known to add a few drops when their mates went out on midnight swims.

"Now you're just being cruel!" Brother said in mock horror, as he helped her shift her body into a more comfortable position on the trireme.

"And your girlfriends will be sad." She mimed moving her good hand down her face as if the hand was pulling her face into sadness.

He gave a bitter laugh. "Only a mer girl will admit to sex with a shifter." He said to her, putting two hands on the trireme edge, next to her, launching him out of the water and on to the deck. He landed on the balls of his feet with his knees under him, cushioning the landing with his hands, as if this type of gymnastic move were a daily exercise. Brother knee-walked to the back side storage box where a small medical kit had been placed, next to fruit, a pair of pants, and dried jerky.

He pulled out the kit, knee-walking back to the prone Keyma. She had flipped her tail in half so that her tail fin made for a very odd half umbrella over her shoulders and head. She didn't want to worry about something else trying to take a nibble from her today.

Brother took a look at the wound before selecting a hand sized bottle of precious plastic. "This is going to sting." Was all he said. He did not give Keyma any other warning or time to brace as he poured the antibacterial over the wound.

"Nova!" Keyma swore, digging nails into the trireme's deck. She turned her head, not moving her sodden braid, to glare at Brother and show him her slightly elongated eye teeth. "I swear I will dump you in the middle of the ocean." She whispered in a thready pain-filled voice.

"Want me to stop?" He asked mildly, pulling out needle and thread, looking down at her calmly.

"No. Get it fucking done!" She enunciated, clearly through gritted teeth, chewing each word as if it were gravel.

"This will add to the mystique of your couriering service and how you get such fascinating scars." He tried to distract her with humor as he threaded the needle.

"Rather have had good sex than this scar. Shouldn't have happened."

He could hear the embarrassment. "Ready?"

Keyma nodded once, firmly. She closed her eyes. She couldn't see him pull the thread through the flesh but she could see him pull the needle and thread back out as he stitched her close, and that was just too much for her to take.

"Breath out." Was her warning that he was about to stitch her back together. She exhaled, and he pushed the needle through her skin. Her eyes opened at the first insertion, her jaw clenching on the scream, teeth grinding hard enough almost to break enamel. The thread slid through skin, sending chills down her spine at the weird painful tugging sensation. The needle entering the other side of the wound had Keyma biting the trireme to keep from screaming. Small mewls were the quietest she could do.

"Shhhh…I will be done in a moment, promise." Brother's voice was gentle. He had seen and even performed much worse operations in the last 143 years. Keyma would survive, but she would have a hell-of-a scar to boast when it healed over in the next 5 days.

The sutures took the longest twelve minutes of Keyma's life. The anti-bacterial Brother poured over the wound again, made those twelve minutes seem like heaven, leaving her breathing heavy and limp from exhaustion and pain.

Once Brother had put the kit away, he knee-walked back to her side. "I need to start stripping the shark for meat."

Keyma just looked at him blankly for a moment.

"I will need your knife." He said gently.

"Knife. Right." She started to reach with her good arm but stopped when he put a hand to her arm to keep her from completing the motion.

"I'll take it from here, darlin'. You rest." He reached for the knife but it was missing from her belt pouch. "Damn." He sighed.

"Damn? That doesn't sound good." Keyma said, tilting her head to look up at him.

"It fell during the fight. I'll have to find it on the cove floor." Brother looked annoyed. The water was thick enough to chew.

Keyma blanched. That knife had cost her two months' worth of ferrying and couriering in winter storms. Brother saw the color drain from her face.

"Hey, I'll find the knife. Don't worry." He touched her cheek before sliding off the side of the trireme, feet first.

The knife was found half an hour later and one long slice along the bottom of his foot. Keyma gave a weak chuckle at his inventive selection of words. "One way to find it." She said weakly.

"Hush or you'll be eating shark anus tonight," Brother warned in a not too serious tone.

"Deadheader." Keyma huffed at him, laughing.

Brother pulled the corpse of the shark back to the trireme before it could drift past his reach again. The best parts took a few minutes to fillet, the rest he would leave for the smaller fish.

"Leave the flat head in the water right?" Brother asked looking up elbow deep in sliced up shark. Various bits clinging to his face and in his hair, his normally lightly tanned skin streaked in dark red.

Keyma roused from a light doze with the question. "Yes. Flat heads hate the blood scent of another dead flat head." She thought for a moment. "If we had rope or vine I would say tie the damn thing to the trireme to keep them from trying to follow us as we sail back to the islands."

"Wouldn't we have to worry about other things?" Brother asked uneasily. He was a good fighter, even an excellent swimmer, but some creatures could neither be beaten nor out swum by a mere land shifter.

"Flat heads are the major predator. They don't like the upper levels to eat in, preferring to hunt around shoals and shallows then pulling their meals deep."

"The larger sharks in the deep…" He started to ask.

"Filter feeders, with minor predators that will flee if you splash at them." She said dismissively, waving a hand.

Brother took a deep breath, letting it out through his nose. He was not an expert on the water predators, but it was hard to trust someone else. "I can probably get us the rope. But I'll have to leave now to be back by late at night." His concern went unspoken.

"Park the body between the rocks." Was all Keyma said, laying her head back down.

"Okay darlin'." Brother laid the best of the edible pieces within Keyma's reach, the rest he stacked to the side of the trireme, till he could find leaves that would both flavor and protect the meat for the next couple of day's trip.

Grabbing the shark firmly by the spears entry wound

on the top of the head, Brother pulled the shark up the hill, far enough where there were good rocks to wedge it in and far enough out of the water to not float away as the water rose tonight. He grabbed the plastic bag from the hillside where he had dropped it, coming to Keyma's aid.

"Keyma." He had to call her, wading back to the trireme.

"Yes?" Her response was weak and groggy.

"I need to go to the Deadhead's colony to get rope." He hesitated for a moment. "I will be gone most of the night. Will you be okay?" He fished around in the storage box for the watertight plastic container that Grenich had given to him for the tabs' travel storage.

Keyma thought for a moment. "I should be. No flat heads will come into the cove and the whiskered cats are going up into the hills. Go. I'll be fine." She waved her good hand at him to send him off.

"I'll be back in a few hours." He leaned over, kissing her on the cheek. Keyma smiled weakly.

"Your trip sucks. I want a damn good tip when this is over." She murmured.

"Anything I can give you, or even to you." He teased in mocking lasciviousness, wiggling his hips teasingly.

Keyma gave a breathy laugh, making Brother smile. "Go. I'll be fine!" She reiterated. Brother slipped off the trireme and back into the woods, shifting between one step and the next. The rivulets of water etching into the hill making the normal slippery dirt and rocky loam treacherous. Another long run, forage and run back. He pushed his own fatigue to the back, pulling on years of training for the stamina he would need.

Chapter 5

The morning was a repeat of yesterday with the exception of an excited child. Lauranya staggered out of bed when a small child went shrieking by, butt bare followed by the nanny bot. Lauranya blinked, pursed her lips, but continued on her own path to the bathroom. Once her morning brushing of hair and teeth were done, she followed the giggles into the kitchen. Arie was half dressed missing pants but not panties, munching down a ration bar.

"Watcha giggling at oh favorite child?" Lauranya asked with a smile, brushing a stray strand of hair out the child's face.

"Nanny Bot."

Lauranya gave a quizzical look at the pink and silver robot. "Why?"

"She says I need to learn to pray." The child started to giggle again.

Lauranya's humor drained away leaving her stone faced. "Eventually everyone prays, but today packing up our clothing and personal items will take most of the morning moving to our new home." She made a mental note to delete that programming process from nanny bot's cache.

Arie squealed in delight, not quite able to reach the octave for breaking glass but close, while trying to devour her trade bar even faster.

"Easy child, easy." Lauranya laughed at Arie. "You still eat slowly and not like a starved slave." Lauranya moved around the counter to start hot water for tea. They had a little time this morning and she needed to give her tired muscles a chance to warm up.

Arie jumped down from the stool to the counter were a bag of items were waiting to be carried to the hotel. "Here mommy!" She said rummaging in the bag for a second before handing a trade bar to her mother. "So you won't be cranky later."

Lauranya smiled at her child taking the proffered bar, trying not to crinkle her face too much. "Thank you, love." Lauranya took a sip of the tea sweetened with honey. The tea helped the trade bar be palatable, but only barely.

"Eat mommy! Eat." Arie said with childish imperative.

"Go and get dressed dear. I need to savor my tea for the long day ahead." Lauranya said. The bar she would eat in small bites only because she knew she would need the calories.

"Oh! Pants!" Arie dashed off to her bedroom with nanny bot close behind. Lauranya exhaled, savoring the 30 seconds of quiet she would have while the child shimmied into her pants.

"Ready mommy?" Arie dashed into the kitchen. Her pants on, but the seam was crooked from being put on hurriedly.

"Almost," Lauranya said finishing her last bite of the trade bar and taking another sip of tea. "I need another five minutes to savor my tea; then we can start moving to the tower."

"Good! Cause I wanna see the new quarters." Arie was almost vibrating. Her excitement barely contained.

"The word is because and I want or would like," Lauranya said reflexively correcting Arie's speech.

Arie giggled and enunciated the words clearly again, bringing a smile to her worried and distracted mother.

Lauranya took a deep breath and released with a smile. For a moment, the morning felt like every other morning before the evacuation notice, so much so that Lauranya could almost see Tine and the boys coming in to ruin the morning's quiet.

"Nanny, grab all remaining bags and place them on the grav lift in the building foyer."

"Yes, Doctor." The robot intoned, trundling to Arie's room, and then Lauranya's to finish packing bags with bedding and the dirty clothes from yesterday. Lauranya raised her voice, synapses firing after a moment's reflection in her tea, "And make sure the load is balanced!" after the bumbling if dependable metal servant.

Arie ran back into the kitchen all knees and elbows, ready for the day's adventure to commence. "Come on child, let's wrap up our few personal items and head downstairs," Lauranya said brightly, infected by the child's enthusiasm for the new day.

"Yes, mommy!" Arie bounced from the kitchen back to her room, with a bag in hand. Lauranya had only a few items not already packed in their suitcases by the tarmac that she wanted to bring with her. The tarmac reminded her of one other thing she would need to do. "Computer, a reminder to collect bags in the shuttle port for transfer to our new rooms."

"Acknowledged, Doctor."

The trip to the new rooms was short but distressing. Lauranya got a much better look at the rising water while pulling the 'lift through the rain. The water was now midway up the hill where the complex was situated. A quick calculation; and her remaining time went from two weeks to five days, maybe three. Three days. She had three days for sure to move what she needed. Every day after that would be a fife from the dead.

"Mommy! Look!" Arie squealed, in delight, as she spotted one of the whisker cats moving several hundred yards past the outskirts of the complex.

"Stop!" Lauranya hissed at the child, pulling Arie behind her, fear rooting Lauranya to the ground.

"But mommy!" Arie was confused at the hard jerk her mother had used to pull her close. Mommy never jerked her; only her nasty older brothers did that. Arie sniffled, tears forming in her eyes, the large kitty forgot at her mother's unnatural behavior.

"Shhhh…love. Just a moment." Lauranya said very softly, watching the large carnivore. Lauranya's hands searched in vain for the shock stick left in the labs. The cat barely glanced in their direction, being more concerned with finding higher ground and a dry spot to shake the now ever-present falling water from its coat. He…no she was giving out discontent yowls. There were answering growling coughs further ahead.

Lauranya swallowed. The answering calls were not close and not in the buildings. This was Lauranya's only consolation as the large female passed beyond the buildings heading upwards towards the less dense woods on the hills. Lauranya waited for the cat to move further in before hustling Arie into the Gods Tower, Nanny following placidly along, with oddly shaped bundles draped around her oblong body.

"Mommy!" Arie whispered excitedly.

"What dear" Lauranya said distractedly while scanning the underbrush and manicured "forest" area next to the small complex on their way to the tower.

"I thought you said the cats never came to our housing

complex," Arie said with a child's curiosity.

"Normally the would not, however, their homes are being flooded, which means they have to move up and out of the water's path, much like us, displacing all the hunters and their food source." Lauranya moved Arie and nanny into the elevator, pressing the top button.

"Was that a hunter?" Arie asked excitedly.

"A young female. Not quite old enough to form a pride of her own but old enough to try and carve out a territory of her own with a mate."

"Will we see others?" Arie's eyes went wide at the thought of seeing more of the elusive creatures.

"Yes," Lauranya said with a touch of something Arie couldn't identify.

"You don't seem happy 'bout seeing more." Arie looked up wide-eyed at her mother's lack of enthusiasm.

"It is one more complication for gathering supplies," Lauranya said with a downturned mouth.

"Will everything be ok, mommy?" Arie said with worry, clutching Lauranya's hand tighter.

"I am hoping so my dear." Lauranya smiled down at her child with a reassuring smile and a gentle hand squeeze. The smile was one she had perfected years ago under the crèche supervisors to avoid getting lashed.

"Mommy."

"Yes dear?"

"Your smile isn't reaching your eyes."

Lauranya blinked and chuckled slightly. "That is because I am worried about the cats' but do not want you to be worried."

"Should I worry?"

"No dear. That is what Mommies do."

"Oh, I don't want to be annoying!" Arie's bottom chin quivered.

"Unless we meet any Runners on this planet, it is unlikely you will be," Lauranya said gently to her very observant child.

"That's good," Arie said with the conviction of a child. Lauranya only gave a small, sad smile in response having no idea who or what a Runner was at this point.

They reached the elevator without any more wildlife sightings. Arie startled when the elevator moved up, clutching her mother's hand, eyes wide in excitement. Lauranya smiled down at her beloved child. Arie would probably never get another chance to ride in the elevator again in this life. Lauranya dropped to a knee and gave Arie a long hug. Arie returned the hug, grinning from ear to ear, enjoying the moving sensation.

The doors opened into the lobby. Lauranya let Arie go first into the lobby. Arie went from wide-eyed stunned silence to exploring on hyper-drive mode, squealing at each new find or interesting piece of furniture or piece of artwork. The opulence, seen through a child's eyes, was amazing. Lauranya smiled as Arie kept finding something new every few feet to squeal in delight over. While Arie was busy exploring, Lauranya went to check on the incubators and the bug farm.

"Mommy, what are those?" Arie's breathless voice asked within inches of Lauranya's ear.

"Ack!" Lauranya jumped up, trying to spin on her heels but ended up landing on her butt instead. Arie jumped back at her mother's startled exclamation; her face scrunched up to cry.

Lauranya scooped the child to her lap, snuggling her close. "Shhhh...no baby. You are fine. You just startled me a little." She rocked the child back and forth. Arie buried her head in her mother's shoulder for a few moments.

"Mommy, what are those?" Arie asked when the initial shock wore off, pointing to the square metal boxes that had fascinating lights and clear windows on them.

"Those are incubators for baby chickens," Lauranya said gently smiling at the curiosity that Arie was always displaying.

"Like the ones we eat?" Arie reached a hand to touch the clear window displaying the eggs inside.

"Exactly. Just like the ones we eat. Except these are fertilized." Lauranya caught the questing hand before a touch could be realized on the machine, kissing the fingers.

"Fertilized?" Arie's brow scrunched up at the odd word, but she held her mother's hand instead of trying to squirm away.

"That means the mommy chicken and the daddy chicken had sex and a baby chicken will come out of these eggs."

"Will we be eating these as well?"

"Not these eggs; however these will be the babies so we will need to let them grow first. We are only going to eat those that can't produce eggs or are too old to produce eggs. So once these chickens produce eggs, we can eat eggs again."

"I love scrambled eggs!" Arie chirped happily crawling off her mother's lap to look inside the clear plastic lid excitedly.

"I do too honey. Now they will not produce eggs right away. First, they have to hatch and that is what this is for." Lauranya said trying to emphasize patience, something very hard for a young child to grasp.

"But why are no mommy chicks here to hatch them?" Arie said looking to her mother for answers.

"There are no mommy chickens at the moment dear.

So we are assisting mechanically."

"Can I touch one?"

"No." Arie's face crumpled. "Sweetie. These eggs are the only eggs we have to hatch. We need all of them to hatch chickens, and if you reach in to touch one it may damage, not just the egg you touch but all the eggs. And this means we will have nothing to eat if the eggs do not hatch."

"Oh," Arie said dejectedly, looking longingly into the incubator. "We won't have anything to eat?"

"Not much if anything at all," Lauranya said gravely. She relented and gave Arie a quick hug modifying her statement. "When the chickens start to lay their own eggs, you may help me collect them. Is that better?"

"Oh yes, mommy!"

"But you have to wait. So do not touch these." Lauranya's face echoed the stern voice she used for very important things.

"Yes, mommy. No touch until they are older and laying their own eggs." Arie was very solemn in her statement but her eyes never left the incubators.

"Very good sweetie. Thank you for understanding; this is very important."

"Is this a spanking promise?" Arie asked with a serious look on her young face.

"Yes. If these machines are damaged, the eggs will not hatch, and we will starve." Lauranya said calmly, trying to convey the seriousness without scaring the child.

Arie thought about this for a moment, looking into her mother's eyes. "I like food."

Lauranya smiled at her daughter's upturned face. "We both do. So promise me no touching?"

"I promise!" Arie said solemnly.

"Good girl!" Arie stepped out from her mother's arm,

tracing with small footsteps roughly 10 feet from the incubators. "What are you doing child?"

"Marking the no-touch boundaries, in case I slip and fall."

"Smart child," Lauranya said with a slight laugh, and then her face went serious once again. "Arie, I need to get dirt for growing plants inside."

"Where will we put all the dirt?"

"I plan to bring in the large planters."

"The ones from the shuttle bay? Where everyone is… not sleeping?"

"Yes, those too," Lauranya said with a frown at Arie's reference to the dead. She dismissed her concern as time was pressing. Hopefully tonight they would have a moment to talk about the day's adventures together.

"I thought we were eating chickens?"

"We will but we need vegetables and so do the chicks to get big enough to eat."

"Blech!" Arie was not a fan of most vegetables.

Lauranya laughed, with a smile, she turned towards the nanny. "Nanny."

"Yes, Doctor?" The machine seemed to perk up at its name.

"I will be in and out all day. Keep Arie occupied. Review letters and numbers as well as the usual physical coordination work."

"But I want to watch Armoire!" Arie whined, her good behavior over the incubators evaporating.

Lauranya chewed a corner of her lip for a moment. "For every two lessons, you may watch one Armoire."

"One lesson." Arie was trying to bargain hard having watched her brothers wheedling extra time or treats from their father.

"Two." Lauranya held up her fingers to emphasize her

instructions. "And you can pick which upper floor suite room we will use as our rooms." Lauranya countered.

"Oh! Ok!" Arie scampered to the stairs to explore the six penthouse suites on the third floor. Nanny trundled behind her, trying to keep up with a small child who was all energy with no off switch.

Arie's voice could be heard floating downwards from the first of the suites on the far right. "Look, mommy! Look!"

Lauranya looked up to Arie leaning over the banister, waiving down to her. Nanny bot was behind her, steadying the child.

"I see you, dear," Lauranya said with a smile upwards, waving, then stretching her arms and back, trying to ease sore muscles. "I need to go now, sweetie. Have fun exploring and do not forget your lessons!" Arie was already off into the suites again, squealing in delight at the room's visual and tactile luxuries.

Lauranya headed down the service elevator to the first floor. Instead of heading out towards the warehouse, she opened the doors that lead to the front lobby and the large glass window expansion. She stood at the rain-slicked glass doors, looking both ways for several minutes. There were no whiskered cats in evidence, either by the buildings or in the brush nearby.

She walked quickly to the warehouse making a detour to the guard's area first on the far right of the lobby. There were no guns but a couple of different shock sticks and a cache of charges had been left behind. Lauranya curled her lip in dislike. Those things hurt. Neither the short nor the longer ones were singly deadly; however, either could drop a full grown man on a rampage into screaming convulsions. Depending on where the shock stick was applied, a person could be rendered unconscious with one application. The occasional heart failure or brain rupture occurred, but those were to be expected, though an Overseer could be fined for the loss of a good worker or slave if death happened accidentally. Death caused by convulsions from continued shock sticks were more for cowing slaves and workers. Whips, while symbolic of station, were still used but left unsightly scars on the property. Overseers were more likely to try for a non-scarring "touch up" of attitude if necessary, and the sticks always brought a change of attitude.

So she gathered the sticks, not from want but as a just in case need. Her grandfather had a saying. "Prepared keeps luck in hand." He had found this saying useful when training the young and even old gladiators from being stupid. The young didn't know what advantages to keep while the old tried to keep every advantage they could find on the Sands. Lauranya took two shorthand length sticks, one to hang from her belt and the other she slipped into her front pocket for easy access, along with a handful of charges.

She turned to walk out and then stopped the memory of her grandfather's voice saying to the new gladiators in training. "Better to keep an enemy at arm's length then ask for a kiss." The grandparents all laughed at this when he said this at the communal dinner table as if it were the best joke ever. Lauranya had never understood the joke; she did understand keeping people at arm's length.

"People or whiskered cats in this case." She whispered. She grabbed a long one, roughly 18 inches, for a just in case.

She checked the batteries for each, testing the on switch. She dropped the 18-inch stick on the hard concrete when it fired instantly with a crackle. The smaller ones had a smaller crackle more like a "pzzt" then a "ZZPzzT" popping. Her lower ribs ached in memory, yet she picked the larger one up resolutely.

"For our protection." When that did not work, "There is no one here to report me." She whispered to herself trying to quell the fear and anxiety. Her hands still shook so hard that the stick seemed to tremble and shake with a life of its own. "We will survive."

She hoped any returning expedition had supervisors willing to listen to why she needed the shock sticks to survive. The voice ratcheted down only a little, but Lauranya felt better with the justification.

She found the loader with lifting forks to the side of the closed bay doors where she remembered vaguely seeing it in her rush to get other survival items to the tower. The loader was electric green and dented from hard use. The heavy wire roll cage had dents dimpling the top and both doors were gone. At one point, possibly more than once, the loader had rolled and dropped from more than a few feet if the dents were any indication of toughness. The lifting forks had no paint left on them and not a few rust spots. Jumping into the cockpit's plastic seat and taped up shifting handles, she saw that her luck was only partially in this morning. The keys were in the ignition but the engine battery was low. Almost too low for more than 30 minutes of work.

"Nova! It will take a day to charge the damn thing," she swore with a frown pursing her lips and glaring at the hulking machinery. "Wait." She touched her earpiece turning it on. "Computer is there any batteries that will fit the loader?"

"Yes. Two in row 4 section B-2."

Lauranya started the lifter up and headed down the rows to find a new battery. When she got to the battery bin, she almost cried. There were indeed the promised two batteries glowing gold for fully charged and another four solar generators. The old battery she started to pull out of the loader when a bit of metal caught her hand and ripped skin. Swearing softly in words neither her husband nor her daughter had ever known she knew, she found a medical kit to patch up the bleeding rip then a pair of stout metal and plastic gloves.

Once she was armed with protective gloves, she pulled out the low battery to place on a charger while placing one back into the loader and the other full battery next to the solar generators. "I'll be back for you beauties after I get the dirt!" She grinned pleased at the gifts of her Gods.

She placed the longer shock stick next to her within arm's reach and turned the key. The loader roared to life and Lauranya went hunting for large planters.

Lauranya started with the tower bottom lobby first. The planters were glorious pieces of artwork frothing with various plants filling every space in the eight foot by five-foot container. They were made of a thick ceramic with geometric semi-precious stones and gems, meant to highlight the color schematic of the growing plants. The designs gleamed dully in the clouded muffled light, no less beautiful but Lauranya could only imagine how glorious they would be in full sunshine.

She noted the discrete grow lights in the ceiling above the planters. There was no way she would be able to remove the grow lights in the lobby downstairs. She glared at the inset lights. "I will steal the bulbs though!" to herself as she moved to the first planter.

Each planter was 3 feet high with ceramic feet underneath. This made using the loader a sure thing instead of needing to lift each planter and placing braces underneath. Here she lifted and moved the fifteen planters, from the lobby to the emptied top floor lobby area.

Lauranya moved the first six planters to be in front of the windows horizontally. The next nine she moved into vertical lines of five each with two feet between each planter. The first planter took the longest to position, as the loader was unfamiliar and the planter's size did not lend to moving quickly.

"Mommy!" Arie squealed and ran from the unexplored kitchen toward Lauranya who was still on the loader placing the first planter.

"Arie! No!" Lauranya stopped the loader with feet to spare but her heart thudded as adrenaline flooded through her system. Arie skidded to a stop at her mother's imperative. Lauranya jumped down from the loader and grabbed the child up into her arms.

"But mommy, you need to see…" Arie started, still excited in her news barely deterred by the not close encounter of the loader.

"Arianya! Do not come running towards the loader while it is in motion! You could get hurt. Badly! Lauranya raised her voice to cut through the child's single-mindedness and lack of preservation or observation.

Arie started to cry at her mother's raised voice. "Mommy, I just wanted to show you …"

Lauranya hugged her daughter close. "Shhhh. Shhhh. I love you child but I need to get this done before the waters take away any chance of gathering anything useful. Do you understand?"

"Yes, mommy." Arie snuffled into Lauranya's shoulder. Nanny finally trundled into the room to stand by the wayward child. Lauranya glared at the machine but knew that the robot would have never been able to hold the squirming child if Arie had really wanted out of its arms. Nanny was a test model for child learning not a true human child caregiver.

"That's my girl." Lauranya sat back to look at Arie and ignore the robot. "Did you find the rooms you want for us to have?"

"Yes Mommy. They are really huge!" She started to get excited again.

"Ok love. I will come look at them this evening. Have Nanny move our things in there and I will see you tonight." Lauranya had a thought. "I will be coming in and out with the loader all day and part of the evening. When I come in I will look for you either by the kitchen or on the upper balconies and wave. Can you wave back to me?"

"I can do that mommy!"

"Good girl! Now I have to get back to moving things into our new rooms." Lauranya said firmly standing up and setting Arie back on her feet.

Arie scrunched up her face at not being able to finish her initial thought but only said, "Ok mommy."

Lauranya went to the shuttle port next in the rumbling slow moving loader, knowing there were several planters there to retrieve along with the suitcases. And the dead. She would try to give last rites to the dead as best she could. She approached the building with trepidation, wet from the rain, falling through the large mesh top but ignoring the water in favor of trying to hold back her own tears. She was shivering from more than just the rain.

The front doors slid smoothly apart as she approached on the loader. Two more loaders could fit through the open doors, which bode well for moving the planters in the front area without having to break glass and damage the doors trying to get them out. Not that she needed to worry about damaging property; she didn't want to pick glass out of her new garden container.

Once inside she stopped the loader next to the first planter, a beauty of ten feet by six feet, overgrown with lush vegetation dropping slightly from lack of care these last few days. Nothing she could identify as an edible but many had flowers and a few small seed pods. She would have to do some research before removing anything out of planters. She stopped herself from examining the plants closer though she wanted to. She was trying to put off the inevitable, stalling for time with the plants on her way to the dead.

Lauranya turned off the loader swinging down from the seat with stiff muscles. She swallowed back metallic saliva as she headed for the meeting room. She had seen dead people before. One of her grandfathers had died peacefully in his sleep. He had been on display in the family gathering hall for friends and families to pay their respects before being cremated. However, she had seen more violent deaths than peaceful, not including those poisoned on this planet.

There was no way she could bury all of the dead, nor cremate them all. The building itself would not burn unless explosives were used. Giving a proper burial would damage the tower she needed to survive. Not that she had the explosives in the first place. She gave a shake of her head dismissing the useless thought.

With bowed head, she placed a hand on the handle to the door. She opened the door, forming the words for death's safe passage when she stopped dead in her tracks. Her voice freezing on unspoken words as the hairs on her arms rose.

Every corpse was standing.

There was only one other person, besides Lauranya, close enough to have affected the dead this way.

"Oh Arianya. Love, I am so sorry." Lauranya sobbed, her knees gave way sending her to the gore-soaked carpeted floor. Her child's gift of necromancy could not be denied.

Lauranya could do no more than stare at the dead, clutching the door handle, sagging against the frame. The dead ignored her. They stared through concrete walls, facing the tower with only slightly milky eyes and blue/black or grey skin. Decay had not started to set in.

A zombie would rot but slower than a regular corpse. A necromancer with the power over the dead could retard decay. Low-level necromancers could only delay decay for a few hours. Some Gods could delay decay for decades while trapping the souls of the deceased inside the rotting human shells.

These undead showed little decay but they had not been given a command. So here, they would stand until even nature could not be ignored, the flesh would fall from bone, their brains liquefying, rendering them once more into components of earth. Days or years from now the bodies would start to decompose, depending on how strong the new necromancer was.

"Esu, I ask you to hear my prayer for the fallen." She whispered. "May Osoosi bring them justice and Obatala give their spirit wings to fly to safety and freedom. Sleep until Yemoja sees all safely born again." Her voice cracked as the tears fell at the loss of so many friends, almost family and for her child.

She clutched the door for support to stand, her eyes so blurred by tears she did not see the heads of two zombies turn towards her as she slowly shut the door behind her.

Chapter 6

The next few trips went quicker until the final load seemed to fit into its predestined spot easily. She and Arie exchanged waves and the occasionally blown kisses, which made Arie giggle before Lauranya started back to the moving task on hand. She found a plastic pallet in the warehouse, which would fit four of the 3 to 2 square foot planters in the bottom lobby at a time. She ran into her next problem. The round planters three feet across and three feet high, with their large trees would block any light if placed around the windows.

"I will yank the trees out later. Must have the dirt now!" She placed the planters along the left wall since incubators occupied the right wall. The first planter was placed right next to the wall. The tree showed her the error of this as its branches buckled and cracked bending the tree outwards from the wall. Lauranya pursed her lips in irritation and her lack of foresight into the tree's need for branch room. She jumped from the loader to pull the tree planter out until the branches were no longer touching the wall, roughly four feet. The next planter was four feet from the wall and from the next planter.

Lauranya stopped for a moment after the first four planters were placed, tapping a finger to her lips. She looked at the dead space behind them realizing this was not a good utilization of space. "No matter where I put them they will need a bubble of growth. It would take Oko to figure this out. Too bad I can't just grow the trees flat against the wall." She said with a sigh...then froze.

She ran to get her laptop among the things brought over that morning.

She clicked through discussions of the world ships until she found the Cerveteri. The fifty-page description included a portion on both aquatic hatcheries as a cheap source of protein for the population but as fertilization for their stunning topiary plants. Lauranya remembered this article was vaguely about plants but she had been more enraptured by the different floor to ceiling aquariums.

Her younger self had been fascinated by the world ship's ability to keep food fish as well as a few of the more dangerous species known. There had been a video of the toothed and multi-limbed predators being fed recalcitrant slaves with the dual purpose of feeding and entertainment for the Gods.

"There you are!" There was a small blurb on the many trees and their usefulness for pulling CO_2 from the air while helping the ship filters and producing oxygen and rare fruits. The ship's space issues for the trees were handled in different ways, but the one Lauranya could use was to train the fruit trees to less space by removing the back limbs. "I can keep the aisle branches for more fruit but trim the wall facing branches, so they lay flat. Yes!"

She especially liked the image that showed 15 trees growing in V's with their outward arms crisscrossing with their neighbor for a visually stunning picture of the trees flowering in various colors mixed together. "Beautiful but too much of the tree is lost for maximum production." She said to herself sadly. "Wait…That tree looks familiar." She went to one of the trees to examine its leaf, and then went back to her laptop for consideration. She pulled up all fruit trees with long narrow leaves and a sharply pointed tip. She pulled up a bewildering variety. Four of which might match the tree in the pot.

"Fine." She glared at the bending tree. "I will examine all of you when I return tonight. Even if you are useful, you will not be keeping those back limbs." The tree did not disagree with her stern directive.

She closed her laptop, placing it back on the clothes carefully. She returned to the tree pots to place them against the wall with care to not damage the trees much more until she had a chance to examine the types and their usefulness.

"It would be too much luck to ask of Osanyin that all of these are trees that produce edibles." She said with rolled eyes at the fickleness of Gods and gardeners.

Lauranya climbed back into the loader, a wave of grief flowed through her, nearly blinding her with tears. She had to blink rapidly and shake her head to start the machine. She sniffled and used the hem of her shirt to wipe the moisture away, having nothing else available. She gathered the first of the planters, taking three tries to balance the heavy object so it would not tip in route.

In the lift to the upper floor, Lauranya stopped halfway up to let herself cry as she had not since Maison's death. Her first three children would never be able to call the dead but her fourth child, as much a light of her heart as her first, could call the dead and the dead would always call to her. Arianya would never be free of them.

"How am I to train you, child? How can I keep you from going insane? How can I keep the Gods from stealing you?" Lauranya sobbed. Lauranya allowed herself only a couple of moments of crying. "Somewhere there are videos or instructions. Someone has to have written something down. I will not lose my child to her power!" She swore, shaking her head fiercely as if shaking away fear and doubt. She bowed her head thinking of the dead in the shuttle. "They need to be laid to rest. She cannot keep them."

Lauranya remembered her sister. She thought of what could happen if they were on a ship and Arianya was being evaluated. "Arianya is not Kori." She said to the small voice that spoke of power-hungry necromancers. The voice was quiet for a moment, but Lauranya feared she would dream of the dead tonight and Arianya in Kori's place.

She wiped her cold sweaty palms along her pant legs. The God's visit and her sister's sale to him had haunted Lauranya for years. Lauranya thanked Yemoja for her low testing on necromancy every day afterward for years. She had tested so low on necromancy that she was almost a null. Almost. She could see the occasional ghost and speak to them, but they did not find her interesting enough to speak to her usually, nor could she command them, making her useless as a spy or even as an arena necromancer in the Games.

Lauranya remembered the slaves carrying the God, a mix of black and white men with rolling muscles, neither moving nor blinking as they stood under his weight and the weight of the chair. They were smooth skin that was well oiled. It was not until Lauranya looked into their blank eyes that she realized they were all dead. Zombies. For a second, after the first realization, that she saw their ghosts chained to the undead un-rotting bodies, mouths open in soundless screams. The Undead God Menodisces had raised these men from the dead to serve him body and soul. As long as he willed them to serve, their bodies would never rot, and Obatala would be denied the spirits of the dead.

Her sister Kori had had the gift so strong that the day

after her testing the Undead God Menodisces himself had descended upon their families' apartments to take her from them himself. Her family had frozen in silence when the ship's leading God had come to their humble interconnected family apartments. Her grandfather had met the God before but this time grandfather and the family saw the God close up. Kneeling was expected and performed, with practiced ease, from Grandfather to the lowest body slave.

There was no preamble from the God. He did not deign to descend to touch their floor but spoke in a voice smooth as the steel that made their ship walls and as dark as space. The God's white chiton shimmered from luminescent silk, touches of gold for trim at the hems were the only overt luxury on the God. It was not what he wore that made him powerful but what he could command.

"Your daughter has a talent that should not be allowed to linger in the mud any longer. I will raise her as my own and train her myself." He had said from his open-air sedan chair.

Kori was summoned forward. She was taller than Lauranya by almost a hand even though the sisters shared the same birthing day and mother but subtly different in looks from each other. Kori held her mother's guiding hand tightly, as awed by the God in their presences as everyone else.

Lauranya's mother could not hand over Kori; she bent, bowing her head over her daughter, letting long braided dark hair fall over her fair child, veiling them both for a last moment together be it ever so brief. It was her father that had to take Kori from their mother's last embrace to hand her up to Menodisces. Neither parent cried though their mother's eyes were bright with unshed tears behind a blank face. Tears they would share in private.

Menodisces had smiled with a slow spreading of his thin lips and an almost animalistic contentment in his half-lidded blue eyes gaze, as the blonde child was handed up to him. More predatory than paternal.

The Undead God looked at Lauranya's grandfather, acknowledging the old man's own power and training of fighters. He had made Menodisces and Menodisces' now deceased uncle very wealthy men when he was a gladiator.

"Your grandchildren have potential. Not for the undead but either the Arena or in Science. I wish to patron your family. The children shall be allowed into any school on any ship for their areas of specialty. Any child that wishes the sword instead of books, I give you leave to train them and present them in any arena." Menodisces voice carried through the apartments, his word law. The gossip would reach the market later that day before the ink was dry on the God's Commandment.

There were three scribes, all living, walking at the side of the carried sedan chair. They were furiously typing into their pads so that God's decree would be carried out. Should Menodisces fall to a stronger God, the family would be considered a renewable resource in both fighters and high mentality with the chance of producing once in a generation necromancer, safe from purging unlike political allies of Menodisces in a straight up fight for the world ship.

"I would also present you with a gift." His secretary, a tall willowy woman with skin so beautifully dark and eyes so luminous she could have been a goddess herself, stepped forward with a natural fiber woven pouch in a vivid shade of yellow that shimmered with embedded red threads. The pouch matched the woman's peplos, covering only one shoulder, showing more beautiful skin and rounded shoulders. The pouch took both of the woman's long elegant hands to hold up for Menodisces.

He took the pouch from the woman with a flicker in his eyes and a lingering touch on her hand. The Undead God reached down to hand the pouch to Lauranya's grandfather.

"We thank you for your generosity and patronage." Grandfather's voice was steel and subdued; he accepted the payment for his grandchild's sale with a bow of reverence and downcast eyes.

Neither spoke of Kori, who would never be part of their family again.

Menodisces nodded, but his smile was all for Kori who tried to not shrink back from the strange man's touch. It was not until the chair turned to leave that the Lauranya's sister realized she would be going with the God and not put back down to her family.

"Mommy?" The child began with a quaver, twisting in the chair to see her family retreating behind her.

"Shhhh, child. Your family can no longer keep you." The dark woman's touch seemed to soothe the child into an unnatural lethargy. Kori slumped down into Menodisces arms almost relaxed but with vacant eyes. Precious cargo still young enough to be trained and bred appropriately.

The sedan with its undead carriers and the scurrying scribes left without another look back. Lauranya would see her sister only once more and that would be at her uncle's wedding to a Small God. The Small God resembled Menodisces and the dark woman favoring her mother in looks than that of her very dangerous father. Kori did not recognize Lauranya when she came up to hug her. Kori had looked down at her as if she were nothing;

the look deterred any further attempts at family renewal between the sisters.

Lauranya mourned the loss of her sister but her sister seemed uninterested in her birth family. Lauranya never wanted to lose her only daughter to a God or the Games. Taking a deep breath, Lauranya continued with her self-appointed task of gathering planters and dirt. The undead could wait another day or two.

Lauranya pulled every potting container she could find from the shuttle port and then from the labs. She found an extra eight small containers and three large ones from the lab lobby. She lucked into an extraordinary find while getting lights, wiring and the remainder of the solar generators with parts. The horticulturists had left two pallets of compost in the warehouse she snapped up as quickly as possible.

"Computer, are there any schematics on which plants were used in the planters left by the gardeners?"

"No doctor."

"Oko!" she swore then took a deep breath, shaking her head. "I am lucky enough with the dirt, too much luck and Esu will take everything back. I shall be grateful for what I find and just do the research." Jumping back into the loader, she carried the solar generators and light supplies back to the upper floor.

Between the planters loading and unloading, then the last three rounds of generators and dirt, night well advanced when she returned to the upper floor.

Lauranya opened the service elevator to a hushed silence. She dropped the dirt off by the elevator doors to damned tired to do more then turn off the loader and crawl down from the driver's seat with a groan. There would be no setting up or moving anything else tonight.

"Arie?" The lights were still on bright but hours past

Arie's bedtime. She walked to the light switches, turning the main lights to dim. "Arie?" she called louder heading up the stairs. "Nanny would have Arie bathed and in bed by this time." She said with a yawn to herself with a smile. "Thank you for Nanny, Jacks."

Lauranya stopped midway up the stairs thinking for a moment there was a whisper of sound behind her. She frowned listening. Only the sound of rain on the windows, so ubiquitous now as to be white noise, only noticed when gone. The sound did not repeat either her imagination or the rain hit the windows harder at a different angle. She continued upwards with a slight shrug.

She walked into the large living area filled leather and wood furniture with lush rugs that begged to be walked on barefoot. She dimmed these lights as well. Both bedroom double doors, decorated in woods done in intricate patterns, were slightly ajar showing no light, but a deep restful dark.

Lauranya smiled slightly thinking of how nice sleep would be. If they managed to survive, they would be living like the Gods. Spoiled with luxury items but not pampered with body slaves responding to every whim without the fear of whips or shock sticks.

"I can live with that." Lauranya finished her thought aloud in a whisper, her fingers running over the back of the butter soft leather couch on the way to the left hand bedroom. The dim light from the living room showed through the door that Lauranya opened to body width. She found Arie's toys and clothes were here, mostly piled neatly with scattered drifts here and there, but no Arie in bed. Or nanny. Lauranya frowned.

"Arie probably insisted on my bed then." Lauranya turned heading to the other bedroom across the living area that could have fit three of the scientist quarters with room to spare. Arie would slip into her mother's bed when Tine was with Micha.

Lauranya opened the door carefully so as not to wake the child, but there were no soft snores of a child in her bed. Lauranya stopped for a moment at the doorway confused for a second then felt the first threads of panic winding through her brain and stomach.

"Arie!" Panic sounding in her voice. Nanny would not have taken her to the other apartments. Those rooms had been stripped of anything necessary or useful. "Arie!" The floor's open rooms swallowed her cry as she started to search the other upper floor's five suites. None of the third floor rooms held her child. Nor the empty second floor. The rooms with equipment and furniture had not been shifted from their relocated spots. There might have been room for Arie to eel through the gaps but Nanny would have been close by and responding to Lauranya's frantic calling.

"Lights! Must have lights!" She turned on the lights in every room entered and the main living area, flooding the entire upper floor to glare like a beacon in the night.

Lauranya frantically ran to the last dark room unexplored. She turned the lights on full in the kitchen. Neither Arie nor Nanny were in here either. Lauranya turned to start her search again ready to head outside to search every other building. A mist drifted to the right of her eyes, catching her gaze. The mist settled by a large metal freezer door and Arie's rabbit resting on the floor next to it.

Arie!" Lauranya cried rushing to the toy. Arie would not have left that behind without a fuss. Lauranya started to throw open the cabinets and tall pantry doors. Nothing. The mist caught her eyes again. Fading then coalescing semi-solid by the freezer door again. A ghost. Lauranya felt her hairs stand on end.

"Oh no, Arie." She whispered at the door, her mind blanking in numb fear. She walked to the door as if in a nightmare, her feet leaden. Freezer doors were supposed to have an opening latch on the inside in case the door closed behind them. A push latch. Arie was too small to reach but nanny should have been able to push the door open unless something had happened.

Lauranya heaved the door open. "Arie," Lauranya called but did not expect a response more a whispered plea as her breath fogged the freezing air.

"Mommy?" The voice was faint. Lauranya's eyes widen and she rushed to the sound of that faint voice. "Please not a ghost please not a ghost please not a ghost," she whispered crawling over boxes dumped on the ground from toppled shelving to the back of the freezer room.

Lauranya found a small bundle wrapped on the floor the size of a child. "Arie!" Arie was huddled on the floor in a burlap sack around her shoulders and another over her head. Her lips were a pale blue from the cold, but she was definitely alive.

"Oh baby!" Lauranya bent to scoop the child into her arms, struggling to stand.

"Cold mommy." Whimpered Arie, looking at her mother through large red-rimmed green eyes, frosted ever so slightly with icy tears.

"I know love, I know." Lauranya staggered out the freezer door to the kitchen sink, turning on the water tap to lukewarm. The door closed behind her with a soft click.

"Let me undress you dear. The water will warm you up." Lauranya started unwrapping the burlap from around the shivering child. There was a layer of plastic under the top layer of burlap and another layer of burlap next to her skin, under the plastic.

"Smart girl to layer like this," Lauranya said in a soothing calm voice as the child's shivers became even worse. Lauranya's hands were shaking while peeling each layer off the child's cold skin.

"Camdia."

Lauranya stopped pulling the layers off to look at her child. "What was that?" her voice going even softer for a second before tugging off Arie's clothes.

"Camdia told me to layer like that," Arie said in a shivering stutter looking up.

"Okay sweetie. Put your feet into the water then slide in slowly." Lauranya urged throwing the plastic and burlap to the kitchen floor.

"Hot mommy!" Arie whimpered, clinging tighter to her mother

"Not hot, you are very cold. We want to warm you up slowly." Lauranya soothed while easing Arie into the barely room temperature water. Lauranya grabbed a clean metal bowl from the counter and started to pour the warm water around Arie's shoulder then head. Arie hugged herself tightly shivering, looking wet and miserable.

After a few minutes, the shivering began to abate. "Water's cold Mommy."

"Ok hon, we'll warm it up a bit then." Lauranya turned on the tap to a higher temperature until Arie said good.

Lauranya let Arie soak for a few more minutes before speaking. "Arie...you know Camdia is dead, yes?"

"I know mommy. We saw her not sleeping at the shuttle port."

Lauranya thought back to the dead. Had she seen Camdia's body there? She could not remember off hand. "Did Camdia come in ghost form or did she walk up here?"

"She was misty and pale." Arie tilted her head and perked up. "Jacks tried helped as well. He tried to get nanny working again but her brain pan was shot he said."

Lauranya felt her knees start to go weak and gripped the counter tightly. "Did any of the others say anything?"

"No. Should they?"

"Hopefully no." Lauranya swallowed bile. "Sweetie how did nanny stop working?" is all she asked.

"We went into the freezer. I found some good foods and was trying to get to it. Nanny came to help. The food was too high, and I fell." Tears began to trail down Arie's cheek slowly. "The shelf fell. Nanny tried to protect me but then something hit her in the back, hard. She started to splutter then stopped." Arie started to sob harder reaching for her mother. Lauranya wrapped her arms around her terrified child.

"Is that when Camdia and Jacks came?" Lauranya asked carefully as she checked Arie for signs of frostbite.

"I couldn't get out, and I was getting colder." Arie sobbed huddling in the sink of warm water, trembling at the memory.

Lauranya wrapped her wet child in her arms. "Shhhh." Lauranya took a few calming breaths herself and began to hum a lullaby for comfort. Comfort to Arie or herself, she was not sure but the humming helped them both. The lullaby filled the kitchen with warm, rich tones that seemed to cut through the gloom to brighten every surface with the vibrating notes.

Arie could talk after the lullaby, but just barely.

"I pushed on the bar to get out, but it was stuck. I started to cry; it was so cold!"

Arie snuffled into her mother's shoulder.

"It is very cold in there," Lauranya said softly, squeezing Arie a little tighter. Arie was alive, and there was no frostbite that Lauranya could see.

"I got scared. Then Jacks showed up next to nanny and Camdia came to hug me." Her lip started to quiver. "Jacks…Jacks said that nanny wasn't working anymore and I would need to try and get the door open if I could. But I couldn't mommy I couldn't!" She wailed clutching her mother closer.

Lauranya rocked her as best as she could, water splashing over her clothes and onto the floor. "I know you did baby, I know." A soft calming hum to the murmur.

Arie's snuffles slowly subsided. "Camdia…Camdia said I would need to get wrapped up in warm things…so I had to svav...scavenge things from inside the freezer. I made a mess mommy." Arie looked up with huge red eyes and nose, afraid her mother would be angry with the mess.

"I would rather the freezer be a mess then it clean and you frozen." Lauranya said with a smile. "Frozen children just are not as much fun as children who can run jump and play! Don't you think?" Pinching the tip of Arie's nose gently between thumb and forefinger.

Arie giggled, wiping her nose with the back of her hand. "Very much!"

"Are you warmer now, love?" Lauranya asked gently as Arie's spirits seemed to lift.

"Yes, mommy." Arie nodded emphatically, showing wrinkled fingers and waiving wrinkled toes at her mother, bending in the middle as the flexible child that she was.

"Ok. I think you have had your bath tonight; however, I am still in need of one. So off to the showers for me and to bed with you." Lauranya started to let Arie go. "Let me get a towel to dry you off child."

Arie whimpered, "Don't leave mommy!" Clutching Lauranya tighter.

"Arie, I need…." Lauranya started.

Arie just clung to her mother, starting to sob, whispering, "Don't leave!"

Lauranya wrapped her arms back around her daughter. "Shhhh. Mommy is here. I will not leave you love." She lifted Arie from the sink, letting the wet child, drip onto the floor and herself. She carried Arie up the stairs to their room, slowly. The adrenaline was wearing off and Lauranya's body was reminding her how very exhausted she was already.

Lauranya went to Arie's room, freeing an arm to hit the light switch. Lauranya found a set of children's towels next to the bed among a pile of clothing. She sat on the bed, bending with Arie in her lap making the child giggle as she was turned upside down as Lauranya picked up the towel. Arie was clingy but suffered through the gentle toweling as only a child could. She only started to whimper when Lauranya set her to the side to find clothes.

"I am right here love. Just need to find you some clothes and then I need to take a shower." Lauranya's hands were starting to shake again. She picked up a shirt and panties three times before she could keep them in hand. "Arie, we need to get you dressed." Arie scooted into Lauranya's lap. Not the easiest of ways to get a child dressed but they managed. Lauranya rocked Arie for a few moments.

"Arie dear, I need to get a shower," Lauranya whispered into her child's soft hair.

"Don't leave me please mommy." Arie buried her head into her mother's chest.

"You can come with me while I shower if you want or you can lie in bed," Lauranya said firmly even if a bit wearily.

"Can I sleep with you tonight?" Arie looked up

hopefully.

"Of course hon." Lauranya kissed the tip of Arie's head. They would both need the comfort of proximity.

They turned off Arie's room light then walked across the living area to Lauranya's room. Lauranya switched on the light in the bathroom, her jaw dropping. Arie's room had been nice but this room went from opulent to drop dead bejeweled. As she walked in the windows to the left were floor to ceiling, covered in diaphanous curtains and a rich blue heavy brocade curtain pulled to the side. The windows would showcase the glorious forests on either side of the building, tonight there was nothing penetrating the deep black of the night through the pale blue transparent curtains hanging to the floor.

The remaining walls were done in wood murals of forest scenes with gems, precious and semi-precious used for eyes, nails, jewelry, and accents. The ceiling had small light sensitive gems embedded in the blue and pale blue mural. The gems glowed faintly with the light, but Lauranya knew when the lights went out the gems would glow in the ceiling like stars in the night sky. The carpet was thick and plush like the living area and done in the same cream color. The bedspread was swirls of blues and blacks that played off the unusual mural and ceiling. The bed itself could sleep eight with room between each person and then some.

Lauranya reached a hand out to touch the bedspread. Soft to the touch. Natural fibers, she thought enviously. Softer than the pet cat she had as a child. Arie climbed into the bed with a squeal of delight, sinking into the plush top. The bed hugged the child in warmth and comfort.

The Gods lived far above those below them, Lauranya thought. In a child's gesture, she slapped a hand over her mouth even though she had not said the thought out loud. She buried that thought deeply as soon as it floated through her mind. No Gods here, just her and Arie. They would enjoy those items that had been intended for the Gods now. This thought gave her a small shiver of delight and fear.

"Ok, love I am going to get washed up," Lauranya said, recovering her voice from the ostentatious display of the room. Arianya sat up whimpering, reaching for Lauranya's hand.

Lauranya reached across the soft bedding to clasp Arie's hand. "Shhhh. I am right here dear."

"Don't leave me, mommy." Arie's fear was palatable in her wide eyes, as she started to shake in small uncontrollable trembling, shaking her limbs.

"I need to shower baby. Do you want to come with me?" Lauranya asked with an exhausted smile. She did not dare sit on the bed, or she would never get up.

Arie nodded solemnly, climbing out of bed, oblivious to her rucked up shirt and panties. She looked as if she were swimming in thick water, all arms legs and wiggles. Lauranya could only smile and take her child's hand when Arie finally made it off the huge bed.

Lauranya walked into the bathroom, flipping on the light switch and gasped. "You would think I would have gotten used to the Gods over the top décor." She commented more to herself than to Arie. The bathroom was as large as a bedroom. To her left was a vanity with a single sink, large enough to qualify as a shallow tub just for Arie with smoothly fluted carved sides in a native rock marbled in white flecked blue and gold veins winding through the stone in random patterns. The actual tub was sunken and of the same material as the vanity. Beautiful against the wood patterned of Gods in various poses, again accented with gems.

There were no windows facing the surrounding forest, but there was a large window above from which Lauranya could both see and hear the raindrops splashing down from above. There were several floor to ceiling mirrors that reflect both Lauranya and Arie in the bright light. One bedraggled and covered in dirt and muck while the other looked back with huge eyes. Both figures had the same deep green eyes.

Lauranya's reflection mimicking her snort and eye roll. "Well if I didn't already feel grubby the mirrors certainly tell the story better than I."

Arie giggled. "You are a little dirty mommy."

"A little?" Lauranya in mock outrage. "I could plant a field of grain in the dirt on my shirt! It is definitely time to get cleaned up."

With that, Lauranya started to strip out of her clothes. She piled them to the side with a lip curl of distaste for later cleaning but not tonight. Arie turned to the mirror, pulling up her hair while turning her head to observe the effect. Lauranya looked in the mirror and saw a stranger. Her blonde hair was clinging to the back of her neck and cheeks, cheeks sunken and circle under her red-rimmed eyes. Lauranya looked away with a deep breath. "Beauty will only get you so far, child, only to be replaced by a younger prettier face in a few years. Use your brains they will take you much further." Her mother's advice rang in her ears but did not cushion the blow that survival was making her look old and tired.

"Vain woman, you need to survive first then worry about the wrinkles and grey hair!" Lauranya thought aloud.

"You're not old mommy!" Arie said with conviction catching her tired mother's eyes in the mirror.

"You are sweet my dear, but I feel old. And at least ten more grey hair for today." Lauranya smiled at her child. "However I need soap…and lots of it." With a glance down at her dirty clothes.

Lauranya took a long shower. Arie decided she needed to shower as well, joining her bedraggled mother. Lauranya quirked a smile at her clean child who liked this warm water experience. She and Arie sang songs. They were simple learning songs of numbers and letters, learning rounds that made everyone smile, easy enough to forget a harsh reality with a hot shower and silly songs.

Lauranya reached for a towel on the stool next to the shower, rubbing dry Arie first. Arie smiled and giggled at the soft cloth against her baby smooth skin. Lauranya grabbed a second towel for herself. The material was almost heaven against her water heated skin. She smiled at this small bliss, luxuriating in the feel, for just a moment. With a reluctant sigh, she finished toweling off, warm air from the vents like a second caress after the toweling. Lauranya hung the towels up to dry, including Arie's wet clothes. Her own clothes she left where they were in a pile. Tomorrow will come soon enough to handle dirty clothes and cleaning, she thought.

"Ok, darling…let us see about getting some clean clothes and sleep." Lauranya said giving her singing child a weary smile, then picking Arie up to be carried back into the huge bedroom. Lauranya put Arie on the bed and looked across the room to the open door and the path to Arie's room. Lauranya shook her head.

"We can sleep in the nude tonight." She said after calculating how much energy it would be to walk across, find clean clothes and return.

"Nude?! Mommy no swearing!" Arie said in a huffy voice.

"Nude means naked my dear child." Lauranya tried to suppress her laughter but failed. A giggle escaped which started Arie in giggling. They both giggled as Arie got under the covers while Lauranya turned out the lights.

"Mommy?" Arie's voice was tremolos in the dark.

"Shhh…I am here love." Lauranya used Arie's voice to locate where the bed is, barking her shins slightly on a miscalculated step.

"Oww!" Lauranya said reflexively but without heat. The bed was soft, yielding to her knee without any pointed edges.

"You ok, mommy?" Arie's voice was less tremolos but no less worried.

"I'm fine sweetie." Lauranya found the edge with her hand and followed to the edge side by the windows. "Just the bed attacking my defenseless legs." Arie giggled not believing that beds could attack anyone. Smart child.

Lauranya tugged the tightly tucked in sheets, flipping them back so she could crawl in. Arie's small warm hand was searching for her in the dark. Lauranya linked fingers with her daughter. Arie rolled to her side then scooched to snuggle up to her mother for comfort. Within moments the child's breathing was deep and even, her body relaxed and limp.

Sleep was more elusive for Lauranya. Lauranya snuggled her child close, brushing Arie's bangs away from her forehead gently, enjoying the warmth and illusionary safety of the moment. Lauranya closed her eyes, feeling shudders wrack her as she replayed what if of the freezer but a far different ending, the fear of losing Arie still too fresh to let go.

"Safe. We are safe!" she whispered into the night.

Eventually, her body let loose of the day's work and fear to let sleep in.

Chapter 7

Keyma surfaced in the shallows with a push of her tail and sweep of muscular arms. The rain causing rivulets on her slick skin and seaweed tangled honey blond hair. "As far as I go." She said looking over her cut but healing shoulder at Brother in a tired voice with a slight smile. Pulling the trireme had been hard work, but even the sore muscles were worth pulling Brother back to the islands.

Brother jumped from the small trireme into the warm surf, stumbling through the tugging riptide to stand by her side for a moment. "Thank you." He kissed her on the cheek. "For bringing me home safely." His arms wrapping around her firm and curving waist, dripping from the ocean water, for a hug.

She chuckled in a smooth contralto. Brother enjoyed the sensation of her laughter along his skin. He could understand the appeal she had beside her sexual proclivities.

She slid the braided plant harness off with a slow roll of her naked shoulder handing it to him with a wink, leaning close enough to press bare breasts against his skin. "Anytime you need a ride, lover boy." She murmured coyly into his ear as the morning sun turning her skin the color of wet gold. With that, she dove back into the surf with a flip of her tail.

He took the proffered harness with a smile as water from Keyma's hug dribbled down his chest, ignoring how his pants now molded to his thighs showing his interest in her visibly. He took a moment to enjoy watching her backstroke out of the island cove. With a sigh of real regret, he yanked the harness and rope over his shoulder, trudging through thigh-high waves to reach the high tide mark on the sugar sand beach.

The tropical trees and brush gave welcome shade, but the warmth of the sun was already causing a sweat to break out. Brother propped the trireme against a tree before jogging towards his village at a ground eating lope following faint footpaths that were more hints than actual paths through the undergrowth. His bare feet making a bare whisper on the plant detritus and sandy soil.

He heard the wailing at the river before he saw the villagers. He slipped between the trees to observe before stepping into view. Yeara was on her knees, hip deep in the river. Her husband was at the rock dam, picking something up out of the water, his back to Brother but only for a moment. Nori turned, and Brother could see not a what but a who. Yeara's eleven-year-old daughter, fair skin bruised with wet blond hair, her arm hanging limply from her father's arms. Nori staggered on the rocks. Not from the weight of the child's body but from the crippling knowledge his only child was now dead.

Brother ran from the trees to Nori's side. He helped the large burly man stand. Nori looked into Brother's eyes with the pain that no father should ever have — outliving their child.

"She's…" Nori couldn't finish the sentence, taking a deep breath as tears rolled down his face.

"Let me help Nori," Brother said gently, a hand on his shoulder. Nori clutched the body closer, head bent down as a quiet sob shook him, but he nodded once and held out Leah's body.

Brother took the small precious bundle into his arms as Nori struggled to the shore next to his sobbing wife. A small crowd had gathered but part for Brother and the parents. A ragged band of wailing and tears welcomed him back.

Brother would have turned back towards the beach where the village had stood but Grenich gave him a discrete tug to the right for the village's new location. Brother gave a nod of thanks, but his mind was on the child's death not where he was going.

Sister came out hearing the noise. A look of annoyance on her face till she saw the cause. A look of horror and pity crossing her face.

"No damn it no!" She whispered, tears leaking down soft wrinkled cheeks. Children were so rare that even one death was a blow to them all.

Yeara saw the Torch standing among the villagers who had come out to see why so much noise was being made and started to scream at her.

"Why didn't you see this? Why is my little girl dead! Why didn't you help us old woman?" Yeara would have gone after Sister if Nori hadn't wrapped his arms around his distraught wife. Yeara couldn't budge his arms. "Why? Why is my little girl dead." She sobbed turning in his arms to sob on his chest.

"You didn't see this for a reason," Brother said from behind Sister as anger and guilt chased across her face. Sister knew he didn't mean to insult her, yet the village would wonder why she had not seen this death. The sight was not always on time and Sister would always blame herself for this death.

"Shhhh." Was all Nori said. His tears fell into his beard and Yeara's bright blond hair. The same hair Leah had. Had. He bowed his head over Yeara's head holding her close.

Brother looked for Mauri. He lifted his head inhaling,

trying to scent the Wolfen, as the new huts were not in the same pattern as in the old village. Mauri stepped out of her newly finished hut that doubled as medical a heartbeat behind his first sniff.

Mauri tilted her head, her ears going flat. She bowed her head, towering over Brother's tall frame by a couple of feet as he brought her Leah's small broken body.

Mauri took the body in three of her arms. Her fourth arm was atrophied and stick thin. It hadn't worked in over 80 years. She looked down at the body, her upper right hand feeling for a pulse. A faint hope as the head wound over the temple was as ugly as it was deep.

"There is nothing I can do," Mauri said. Her cheeks wet from tears. The village children were cherished by everyone, no matter the race or parentage.

"She will need to be buried." Brother stepped back letting Nori and Yeara in with Mauri.

"What will you do?" Sister asked coming in behind Brother.

"Now it's up to me to find out who did this," Brother growled. He undid the tattered wet khaki pants so he could shift. "We can't have a child killer loose." Brother shifted, bounding out the door to try and find any trace of the killer near the river before rain washed the scents away. Yeara, Nori, and Mauri looked up at the shifting and away just as quickly. A shifter was never comfortable to look at as blood bone and skin changed from one form to another in the most stomach-churning way possible.

Leah had been laid out for observation, giving the grieving parent's extended family and villagers a chance to say goodbye. Tomorrow Nori and the other men would dig a grave at the base of the sleeping volcano where the others were buried, and the whole village would process to Leah's final place of rest.

Yeara had not moved from Leah's side. Mauri had removed her sodden clothing. Mauri worked around Leah's mother, washed away the bits of leaves, bark, and detritus from the river, before clothing her in the gown her mother had just made for her 11th birthday.

Treasher stumped into medical to pay his respects along with the others. His tan fur a dull gold in the light turning to dark bronze at his points. The Katherian's footsteps were neither soft nor even having to use a peg for his lower leg lost in the final ship battle that had stranded them all here. When the ship went down Mauri had dragged him into the last shuttle off, having to cauterize the leg stump with a welding torch. Treasher still has problems sitting next to fires let alone trying to light one of them. The shuttles had jack all for prosthetic making supplies, so local materials with minimal skill meant he had to make do for a lower leg. Some days Treasher cursed her but not in the last 35 years.

Treasher bowed over Leah's body, whispering a small prayer, before turning to Yeara. Treasher's tail flicked twice before he knelt in front of the grieving woman. The two of them had butt heads over the years, on supply allocation but family, as odd as it was, always came together in times of need.

"Yeara." He took a deep breath, picking up a tightly clenched hand. "I can help if you let me." He said gently.

Yeara shook her head violently, not looking at the Katherian, her eyes seeing only her daughter's body. "I don't want to forget my daughter." She choked through her tears.

"And I would never do that to you." His blue eyes, only slightly dimmed with seeing two centuries of life, held sadness but hope. "I can, when you are ready, blunt the pain so that you take comfort in her memories, but the sorrow doesn't eat you from the inside out."

Yeara shook her head again. "No!"

Treasher looked to Nori standing behind her. Nori knew the pain of losing loved ones, so he knew the gift Treasher was offering. Nori nodded, mouthing thank you. He would bring Yeara to Treasher if grief became more consuming than life.

A screaming yowl broke the quiet murmurs of the villagers as Brother announced his return. Brother ran into the light, a beast of shadow and threat to half human half primitive animal. The hair on his body, stomach, spine, head, and tail stood straight out as he gave another scream in animal rage.

"Torithon! I challenge you for the death of Leah." Brother's growling voice rocked through the village. There was no place that his voice did not reach.

An ugly murmur ran through the crowd as they parted around the chieftain's brother. Brother's gold green eyes locked on the man, a hungry growl starting in the back of his throat as he stepped forward with the bloody thirsty menace of a nightmare.

Nathan stepped in front of his brother with a curled lip and a hand on his coral hilted knife. "You better have a damn good reason for calling out my brother when he was with me all day hunting."

"He was with you till you parted at the graveyard split path. He went down to the river falls where he met Leah, killing her there."

Nathan's spine went rigid. "We split and met up less than a finger of sun later when he had washed up from falling down…"

"The side of the mountain where the stink weeds and

goats are." Brother's eyes never left Torithon's. "His scent was all through the area where he went to the river. His scent and Leah's blood. No one else's."

"You've always hated our family. You will not kill another one of mine." Nathan snapped. "You have to lie this time to do it. You'll take my little brother over my dead body." Nathan snapped.

Brother gave a pointed smile. "I've been waiting to hear you say that you…"

"Stop!" Grenich's odd grating vocals cut through the tension. The Silver came into the light; his ghostly reflective bodysuit glittered from the dancing flames. His four foot nothing barrel-chested body had a commanding enough presence that all eyes turned to him and away from the violence offered.

"We are not doing this without checks and balances." Grenich looked at Brother then at Nathan. "You." He pointed the first of his six fingers at Nathan, "Will trust anything Brother finds because of the history of your family. And while I trust Brother's…research, there is strong animosity that questions what you say. Yes?" He looked between the two men.

"Yes." Nathan snapped his attention back Brother, who growled menacingly at the chieftain.

"I will take that as a yes, Brother." Grenich's bodysuit covered his entire body, from head to foot. Grenich body was too controlled to give anything away nor could anyone see through the silver mesh covers where his eyes would be.

"Treasher would you be so kind as to assist in this please." Grenich's treble vibrating voice carried back to the medic hut where everyone had emerged from. "We are in need for you to mind walk with Torithon and verify where he was and if he did indeed come in contact with

Leah and how they parted."

Treasher's ears went flat, his tail flicking at the very tip, but he nodded. "I'll need Torithon…"

"No fucking way am I having that head trauma cripple in my mind planting information that Brother's feeding him!" Torithon snapped backing away from the firelight. His jaw set in a stubborn line as he hunched his shoulders unconsciously reflecting his fear and insecurity.

"Why would you think he would be planting anything in your mind?" Grenich asked mildly.

"He's another fucking genetic experiment. They're all in it together." Torithon snapped.

"So all non-humans are genetic experiments?"

"Yeah." He glared at the Silver. "None of you have done anything but take up space and food since we've been here. Useless."

A murmur went up among the other villagers. This was an old argument, but no one actually believed that, really.

"So you are refusing to have anything to do with Treasher?" Grenich tilted his head for a moment. "Would you prefer a human telepath?"

"Fuck no. I don't want some joker in my head, survival sucking parasites." Torithon said with a curl of his lip.

There were louder murmurs at this, joker being a crude term for non-humans that had done much for the survival of all. The villagers were giving him more space, angry that this one person would speak for them all. Even Nathan was looking at his brother with eyes wide as if seeing him for the first time.

Torithon pointed at Brother. "That little bitch was starting to be just like you. What did you do? Sneak up on her mom and rape her? Threaten her life, so she never told anyone that you were the tail's father? How is it that Nori never killed you or her before now?" Torithon bit his words off savagely, heedless of the company. Brother's eyes narrowed, but he said nothing to refute the words spewing out.

Nori stepped out of the hut's doorway and into the light of the fire. "I can't father children. We asked Brother to help as he is built more like me, and much smarter than you could ever hope to be."

Brother looked up at Nori, giving him a slight bow. "Leah was always your daughter. I am honored that you asked me to be the genetic donor for your family." Nori gave a sad smile at the not so open secret the three of them had shared, now open for public gossip.

Grenich looked back and forth for a moment. "So was she doing something she shouldn't have been Torithon?"

"She should have let me have a chance to plow her fields." Torithon glared at Brother. "Instead of having a little monster that would kill us all while we slept!"

"She was starting to change," Brother said staggering ever so slightly. He went down on one knee, putting a hand on the sand for balance. "You found her mid-change. You didn't rape her, but you killed her for being a shifter."

"I…" Toithan stopped trying to back up his vile words. "I would never kill a child."

"You don't see anyone who's not human, as a person though," Nathan said through clenched teeth. The chieftain slowly deliberately slid his knife back into the sharkskin sheath to cross his arms over his broad chest and stepping back from his brother. "As Chieftain, here is my decree. You Torithon will submit to Treasher's scan or accept Brother's Challenge. Should you refuse either, I will personally put my blade…" he tapped the coral hilt for emphasis. "Through your heart and twist it till you are good and dead." The words were solemn, controlled and as empty of warmth as space.

"Nathan! You can't let these monsters kill me!" Torithon spun on his brother's words fear finally creeping through his thick skull.

Nathan took another three steps back, his voice thick and bitter. "Accept my words or die." Nathan's hand fell back to his blade. "This is your sentence."

Torithon looked at his brother blankly for a moment, before his face twisted in rage. "Joker! Just like everyone else on this filthy beast..." He was about to hit full screaming meltdown when he was smashed to the ground by 225 pounds of fury in the form of Brother's body slamming him face first into the sand.

"Challenge accepted," Brother growled, punching Torithon in the face with full force three times before bouncing back to let the man up. "I'll make you pay for her life."

Torithon was stunned but not without some cunning. He went for his knife, staggering to his feet brushing sand out of his eyes and nose. "You would have let the little monster live instead of protecting us." He tried to shout. Instead, he only managed mumble and spit out three teeth and blood.

Brother gave a cold smile. "Like that taste? Because you will be tasting your own blood more when I'm done ripping you to shreds. Like the lying mewling pisser your mother was."

Torithon screamed with rage, charging Brother head-down with his knife flashed in front of him. Brother twisted at the last second to the left, bringing his right fist down on Torithon's spine as he spun. Torithon went down with a sobbing grunt, but Brother did not get away without damage. Torithon's knife had found Brother's bare flesh and cut deep along his stomach.

"How does that feel you family-less joke?" Torithon spit out sand, rolling to his side trying clamber to his feet.

"You'll have to do better than that," Brother said, standing up. He let Torithon see his bare stomach, how the wound was already sealing. "Won't be more than a scratch in a moment." Brother gave Torithon an edged smile. It was the smile, without fear or pain that had Torithon feeling the first real threads of fear along his spine.

Torithon snarled but didn't charge. He turtled up as best he could. Arms close to his body, his knife held at the ready. He was going to make Brother come to him. Brother was ready to bring that fight down.

Brother didn't move so much as seem too bound from one side of the gathering area to the other in three steps. He came at Torithon head on, only to slop to the right in passing as the heavier man stabbed where Brother had been. Brother grabbed Torithon's left arm in his left hand, pulling the arm back even as Torithon tried spinning into the pull. Brother punched the taller man on the other side of his lower spine. The punch landed hard enough to bring the bigger man to his knees, screaming. Brother's second punch landed on the back of Torithon's left shoulder blade, hard enough to crack bone. Torithon fell on his face for a second time, his pain raw and loud.

"Ready to die Torithon? If not, we can keep going." Brother snarled down at the wounded man.

"She begged me to help her when I raised that rock." Torithon looking up, his face covered in sand, glittering like a diamond mask in the firelight. He stumbled to his feet, knife in his right hand, his left arm hung useless at his side. "Little aberration was midway through shifting. She was…"

As Torithon planned, Brother charged, he was even

ready for the offline attack. But this time Brother took the slicing blade, 14 inches of battle steel, through his hand, with enough force to push Torithon's hand to the side. The man would not let go of his blade, trying to shove it deeper than it already was. Brother shifted slightly. His hands elongated with the fingers ending in sharp curved blades sharp enough to dig out rock. Torithon's throat was easier. Brother grabbed the other man's windpipe, between his clawed right hand, ripping outward.

Torithon face held shock and disbelief. Blood gushed from the torn throat, coating skin, cloth, and sand in seconds. Only when he touched where his throat had been, did he release the knife to try and stem the blood loss. His knees buckling, as Death came to visit.

Brother let loose a primal scream, curling his right hand into a fist, pounding the dead man's face. The force shattering and fracturing bones. Torithon's brain leaking between the visible shards of bone and hair. Brother staggered backward when his hand sank to the wrist inside the skull. He dropped to his knees, pulling the knife from his hand as he regarded the body. Brother's mind flashing back to the building, with the deadheads and the dead man in the waste room. A different death, just as violent.

Brother took three deep breaths, then stood, turning towards Nathan. Brother hefted the knife, seeing the fear in Nathan's eyes. Nathan stood straighter. He was chieftain but Brother kept the peace, sometimes the two were not the same. A slight curl of the lip and Brother tossed the knife at Nathan's feet.

"We're done." Was all he said. Brother shifted slowly, letting the villagers see the skin, bone, and muscles, changing into his hunting form to stand on four feet with fur. With one last primal scream and show of teeth,

Brother turned limping from the village.

Silence reigned, other than the popping of the fire, for thirty seconds. Sister stumped over to Nathan, retrieving Torithon's blade.

"You'll be wanting this. It's too valuable to be letting sitting out." She said mildly as if commenting on the weather, holding the hilt up to Nathan.

"Brother…"

"He'll be back. Killing isn't that easy on him even if a body needed it." Sister looked at Nathan pointedly.

Nathan looked away first but asked, "Why didn't you see this coming?"

"Do you see every grain of sand on the beach?"

"No, but…"

"Hmph. I can't see every life and still see what will keep us all alive. Pick. You want every life till the day each dies, and I go insane or do you want us all to live including our grandchildren? Possibly able to teach the next Torch when they are born?"

Nathan had to consider for a moment. "Everything happens for a reason, and it still stinks of rotting corpse balls."

"Called life, child."

Nathan took a deep breath still shaken accepting the knife back from Sister. "Yeah." He turned to Treasher. Nathan bowed to the old Katherian. "Good gentle would you be so kind as to mind walk with me to comfort those in our village; I do not harbor the same thoughts as my late brot…family. Please."

Treasher touched two long fingers to his forehead. "It would be my pleasure. Chieftain."

Chapter 8

"Mommy!" Arie's wail in the dark room jolted Lauranya out of her deep slumber, like a live wire through her skin and heart.

"Shhhh..." Lauranya reached for her child, guided by the child's voice in the dark. Her searching hand found Arie's flailing arm. Lauranya followed the arm to Arie's torso. She pulled Arie close whispering into the child's ear. "I am right here baby. Right here for you." Arie flailed for another moment before her mother's calm words penetrated her sleep fog brain and she relaxed, clutching her mother's hand like a lifeline. The flailing stopped turning into a toss and turn then deep breathing as sleep found Arie once again.

Lauranya closed her eyes, Arie's hair against her cheek and smelling faintly of the rare scented soap, the child's body heat comforting against her. Lauranya's mind raced with things to do and things that might have been. She was trying to chase a few more hours of sleep though sleep was being elusive lately like sunshine through the clouds.

Lauranya took deep breaths the way her grandmother Kya taught her. "You gotta focus girl. If you can't focus then let go and let the moment be! Just let it be."

Lauranya remembered Noni Kya for those words and her hands. Noni Kya's hands had been large, strong hands with ropey pink scars against her dark skin from the arena. Hands with large joints and paper-thin skin that knew how to hold a child or smack an errant teenager on the head for something so stupid that words shouldn't have been necessary. Noni Niss would give a small, sad smile when she heard Noni Kya say these words.

Noni Niss's watery blue eyes and pale skin, yellow with age seemed to turn inwards when she contemplated her one good hand and the stump where the other had gone missing decades ago. Noni Niss was Kya's continuous companion and could sing better than any of the Gods hymn singers. Lauranya hummed a tune for calming that Noni Niss used to sing to her as a child. Her breathing calmed, her thoughts stilled, crystallizing to the "right now." Lauranya had not been very good at letting go. The second time an Overseer whipped her, leaving scars, Noni Kya and Noni Niss had taken her under their wing to keep her from being beaten to death. She cherished the memories if not the reason why.

She let out a sigh, missing her grandmothers and the care they gave, care that Lauranya was not going to be able to give to Arie for a few weeks or months. Lauranya already missed Nanny. Jacks had been very good at making machinery almost human. To good.

Lauranya shook her head slightly bringing her thoughts back to her immediate needs. Plants. She would need 16 hours of lighting per day for maximum growth. Generators run on solar for light, the problem being no sun for solar for the panels to generate the lights, which meant fuel for the generators until the fuel was gone.

She needed water for the plants, birds, rabbits, her and Arie. Again, solar panels to operate a generator but she would have to use fuel until the sun broke through the clouds. Drinking and shower water would need a filter for the pipes and hose filter connections.

The soil for the plants with worms and something for pollination. Were the plants self-pollinating? There were nectar-collecting insects. One made honey if memory served her correctly. This would be Korth's area of expertise but did he destroy the insects prior to leaving on the second shuttle or just let them drown?

Lauranya slipped from the bed to get her laptop from the living area. She stood by the door for just a moment, listening to Arie's deep even breathing. Lauranya closed her eyes in relief with a smile. She left the door open so she could hear if Arie had another nightmare. She found the small laptop on the middle table, fumbling by touch for the button to turn it on. The screen lit up the large living area with a dim light but did not pierce the darkness of the bedroom.

Switching off voice, she started to query the supplies necessary to answer the questions posed. The computer had been tracking which items had moved and which she had left behind. Seventy percent of the items for bare necessity were on hand already, but she would need to get the other 30% as well as backups. She could do this the day after tomorrow…no tomorrow, per the clock. Her list was smaller than when she first started her mad scramble for survival.

Chapter 9

"Menodisces! God Menodisces! Please, I must talk to the God!" The voice was young, not having reached vocal maturity. The dead guards did not move. Their leathery skin oiled in spices to cover up the slight hint of rot. Their eyes rolled in their sockets with glazed milky corneas, staring at the dark-skinned girl in the soft woven synthetic tunic in bright blue with woven bands of gold and green at the neck and hem, a free woman but not well off.

She knelt on one knee on the floor, bent over, with her right hand hitting the floor in a slapping sound to gain attention. Her agitation palatable as she vibrated in place, not yet risking an attempt to eel past the guards with crossed spears blocking her way.

A woman in her sixth decade, looking as if she were still in her middle third, came to the inner sanctum entrance. She stood three feet behind the dead guards, her face empty like a reflecting pool. There were no ripples on the surface; everything buried deep. The woman wore a beautifully carved jade collar. The jade showed how valued by the God Menodisces she was, while her scars were not quite hidden underneath her shoulder-baring peplos.

"Meera, child you are new here but your value is not so great you can…"

"Mistress! My father hasn't checked in in 2 weeks. There is something wrong!" The girl's voice was breaking from fear in her voice.

"He was being moved from an unprofitable colony to

another of course…"

"No Mistress! Even on the ship out to the research colony, he was able to keep in touch. We talked every day at least once. Even if it was no more than a hello! Something is wrong!" Meera's voice caught as tears fell along her cheek. "Please, Mistress please! I need to speak to my father's patron."

Menodisces could hear the entire conversation from the comfort of his inner sanctum. At the moment he was testing out the two new body slaves for muscle massage skill, an older slave, with white threads through the dark of his thinning hair, instructing the two newer body slaves with hand gestures and motions. Menodisces preferences and needs were now their only concern and thought.

The God waived off the new slaves, his other regular body slave, a pale-skinned woman with dark skin sister to the massage teacher, was ready with a spider silk robe as he rose from the table. Menodisces' muscles bunching and uncoiling like a well-trained athlete, still firm in his 3rd decade.

"Drinks in the main room," Menodisces said with no concern that his words would be disobeyed or render anything less than perfect. His servants moved on silent feet and no chatter. Each had their tongue removed once they were selected for personal use. Only a few servants kept their tongues the others were muted and readily replaceable, different only in looks but never in reliability.

Menodisces padded into the room behind his head Overseer, Korlah. The girl Meera was still pleading to be let in. A look from the God silenced the woman mid begging. "Korlah," Menodisces said with a nod to the almost hysterical girl. "Bring her into my rooms. I will hear this." He touched the Overseers shoulder with a velvet stroke as one would a favored pet. Menodisces voice was neither inviting nor hostile. His veneer smooth and calm. The same face he wore when overthrowing his mother for control as the top Dead God of this world ship.

Korlah nodded, her skin crawling from his light touch but hidden under her peplos. Too many years as a slave kept her face blank. She commanded the undead to move aside for Meera with a flick of her fingers. The guards moved their spears with a snap and rigidity the living was hard pressed to duplicate. Meera crept through the cleared path only to jump when the guards clicked their spears out, barring the way. Meera half crawled half walked to Korlah's side as her heartbeat in terror.

Korlah pursed her lips but shook her head a hairs width. Korlah knelt down to help the girl up, putting her lips so close to her ear there was no space and hissed, "You are not safe child! Do not show so much emotion!" Before stepping back from the terrified girl.

The two walked into Menodisces' room, where the God was already lounging on a velveteen half couch. The rugs and throw pillows placed strategically for either guests or favored free. Colors screamed from every surface that Meera had only thought might be possible, as used to being surrounded by steel grey walls and faded colors of plastic loincloths or tattered slave tunics.

"Sit child and tell me what it is that brings you to me." Menodisces motioned to the rug covered floor.

Meera was overwhelmed by the display of the undead and the riches surrounding her could only stutter.

"My father. He…he…we always talk. I…I haven't heard from him in days."

"Do you normally talk via regular channels?" Fragrant tea steamed around his face framing him in misty whorls.

"No Lord. He gave me a small communication phone." She said, hesitantly.

"May I see this?" Menodisces asked with peaked interest and soft voice. He leaned forward on his couch.

Meera reached into her peplos to pull out a small round disc of bright colors. Easily mistaken for a child's toy and easily hidden. A keepsake that was mostly worthless, unless one knew what it could do.

Korlah took the proffered item to Menodisces. He put his drink down and sat up with intent. He found the catch to unlock, and the disc popped open on a small steel hinge. The inside was a cross between a battle cracked screen and small multi-colored buttons in hard plastic that looked to be badly glued together.

Menodisces frowned, running a tongue over his teeth. "Your father is Jfess?

"Jhen Lord."

"Ahh. Yes. A very intelligent man." Menodisces looked down at the toy in front of him.

"Call your father please. I wish to see how this works." He smiled winsomely at the young girl, handing the toy back her.

"Yes, Lord!" Meera knee walked to the dais to where he sat, taking the small phone from his chilled fingers, that were warm only where they had touched the cup he drank from. She pushed three buttons in a set pattern. The upper disc sprang to life — the crackling facade fading.

"How clever. A low-level display to hide the clarity of the real screen. False buttons to hide the real buttons."

"Thank you, Lord." Meera beamed at his recognition. Her face fell as the screen remained on but blank.

"I keep calling, but nothing comes on." Her voice choked up, and she looked into Menodisces' eyes with large pale green tear-filled eyes. Menodisces touched her cheek with one finger.

"Did you help him to build this?" Was all that he

asked.

Meera nodded. "Yes Lord. He wanted a way to keep in touch and if he needed help." She bowed her head, embarrassed by her emotions in front of her God, wiping the tears from her cheek with the back of her head.

"I will see that we find out what is happening. Your father is valued, child. I would be very upset to see him missing." A dismissal.

"Thank you Lord!" Meera collapsed over her knees letting her forehead touch the floor in obsequies.

Korlah touched the girl on the shoulder to escort her out. When the Overseer returned to Menodisces, she found him contemplating the small toy like phone.

"Your orders, Master?"

"Jhen loved his daughter enough to give her something that would cost her dearly if found but knew I would be intrigued if necessity brought her to me."

"Yes, Master?" Korlah waited, still as the undead around them.

"How high does the child test?" An almost casual question.

Korlah pulled a tablet from the pouch sewn into her peplos. She called up the information he was seeking. "Top scores but not in the 2%."

"Hmm…average by genetics or by coaching from her father?"

"I…couldn't say, Master."

"Let's find out, shall we?" Menodisces picked up his teacup putting the small phone down on the wooden filigree table next to him. "Bring her to live here."

"She is a free woman, Master."

"Free is only as long as I allow." Menodisces gave the woman a chilling half smile with cold eyes.

Korlah tilted her head, acknowledging his command.

"As you will, Master." Swallowing acid bile in memory. She would have nightmares tonight and possibly the next few nights after that.

Chapter 10

Arie woke up with her mother next to her and her mother's turned off laptop lying on top of her stomach.

"Mommy?" Arie laid a hand on her mother cautiously. Mommy sometimes woke up cranky when she didn't have enough sleep.

Lauranya woke with a start, almost wild-eyed at the gentle touch and a soft voice in her ear. Dreams and memories of Maison's ghost saying good-bye with a slow kiss blended together in the moment vivid as if it were happening now. Yesterday flooded through her brain as the dream shredded with her daughter's voice.

"Arie!" Arie froze as Lauranya pulled the child close, hugging her tightly. "I am here," Lauranya whispered fiercely into the child's hair.

"Mommy. Mommy!" Arie hugged her mother back tightly, digging sharp elbows into the sides of Lauranya's shoulders.

Lauranya pulled back with a smile and dark bruises under tired eyes. "Are you ready to start connecting tubes and wires while we have lights?" She asked in a hoarse voice.

"Yep! But could we have breakfast first?" Arie asked with a bounce getting onto her knees in the soft bed.

"Of course. I think we still have some bars left."

Arie recoiled in distaste. "No mommy! Real food. From the kitchen." Arie was emphatic.

"The kitchen? Where did you go yesterday and got trapped in the freezer?" Lauranya's voice cracked with skepticism and fear.

"There were eggs and sausages in the freezer. They were frozen!" Arie had rarely seen frozen foods and eggs were a real treat. "I couldn't eat them." Arie pouted at her mother.

Lauranya had to laugh. Arie had almost frozen solid yesterday, but she was childishly outraged more by not being able to eat a rarity then by being trapped. "Babies bounce." Lauranya murmured. "Ok sweetie. Let us go and take a look at the treasures hidden in the scary freezer."

"It's not scary mommy! Just cold! And dark." Arie said with a deep breath a firm chin. She was going to meet her nemeses head on this morning it seemed.

"Sometimes, my love, those are very scary times." Lauranya yawned picking up her laptop so she could swing her legs over the side of the too soft bed. "Time for clothes." Another yawn threatened to crack Lauranya's jaw.

Arie bounced her way out of the bed, dashing to her room for clothes. Lauranya placed her laptop to the side, on one of the gorgeous inlaid wooden tables. She stretched for a few seconds then went looking for her own clothing, choosing soft pants and an old comfortable shirt, anticipating climbing under and over things for wiring.

When Arie raced back into the room, Lauranya was just finishing buttoning her pants. Lauranya looked up; blinking a few times at the garish combination her child was wearing but decided not to pick a battle over the electric blue skirt with a polka-dotted striped short dress over it. Sometimes clothing ruas as much learning what not to put together as what to put together. This combination had the advantage of being hard to miss anywhere in the line of sight, nor was there anyone else to care. She and Arie were the only people, so clothing had become however they wished. Even if the eyes wanted to bleed.

Lauranya held out a hand for Arie to take and picked up her laptop. Arie scooped up her stuffed rabbit then took her mother's freehand. Arie bounce the way only the young can be; she kept pulling ahead skipping and singing, dragging Lauranya along faster than she wanted. Lauranya could only shake her head while trying to keep up. All was right in the world today.

Lauranya approached the kitchen slowly like approaching a gladiator fresh out of a tourney and high on adrenaline and drugs, with extraordinary caution. Lauranya put her laptop down on the stone countertop, smooth but a warm buff colored with a mirror finish. Arie stood back from the door, her singing, and skipping stopping at the entrance of the kitchen. Taking a deep breath, Lauranya pulled the handle back, swinging the freezer door open.

The freezer was a mess with shelves toppled over and food scattered throughout the floor and under the remaining upright shelving. Nanny's body was crumpled under the third shelf. A large can had collapsed the head by a good five inches. "Damn it Jacks. Why could you not have spare parts on hand that I might have had a chance to reattach another head to?" She tapped fingers on the dented portion of the nanny bot's head. There was no way she would be able to fix this without more help than her daughter's.

She pulled the broken body out of the freezer setting Nanny into an out of the way corner. Walking back into the freezer, what Lauranya could see of the food labels, the freezer was filled with meat, legumes, grains, and eggs in plastic cartons. Lauranya's jaw dropped. There were more items than one glance could account for. She wondered what the inventory was, as she walked deeper into the freezer. Arie followed closely behind, almost walking on Lauranya's slippered feet.

How was she going to keep the freezer active once the generators were under water?! Solar until the fuel ran out. Lauranya would need to set something up and quick.

"Mommy?" Arie tugged on Lauranya's shirt.

"Yes…yes dear?" Lauranya was almost in tears over the unexpected bounty. She could not tear her eyes away from what the shelves held. Even the items scattered on the floor would be edible once picked up and reshelved.

"I'm hungry and cold." Arie had her arms wrapped around her midsection with a slight shiver, trying not to look too worried.

Lauranya bent down and picked Arie up. "Ok baby. Let me find something for us to eat." She stepped in a foot when she found a box labeled rabbit, showing a picture of a skinned carcass and six legs. She handed the box to Arie then grabbed a package of mixed grains to cook with the rabbit. She turned to the door, bumping the inside handle hard with her hip to open the door up. The door opened on well-oiled hinges. They stepped into the warm, dry air of the kitchen. Lauranya put all the food on the counter and plopped Arie next to the food. Lauranya looked at the raw food items with pinched lips and a frown.

"What's wrong mommy?"

"Umm…I have no idea how to cook this."

"Oh, we can't eat it cold," Arie stated the obvious as if her overly studious mother should know this already.

"Or frozen." Lauranya agreed with a slightly distracted smile.

Arie tilted her head for a second as if listening to something. "How about the computer mommy? Would it have recipes for rabbit?"

"Probably so, my smart child." Giving Arie a quick smile, Lauranya went to grab her laptop from the other side of the kitchen island and looked up rabbit and grain recipes. The search proved more fruitful than anticipated. Hundreds of recipes popped up. Each recipe calling for spices she did not have. She narrowed the rabbit recipes to roasting. No luck. Lauranya had not seen oil in the freezer. Lauranya almost broke down right there, a tear slid down her cheek. Here was food to feed both her and her child and she could not cook the bounty in front of her, frustrated and blocked at every turn.

"Mommy." Arie touched Lauranya's arm gently. "Mommy don't cry."

Lauranya wiped away the tears with the back of her hand, giving Arie a false cheerful smile that fooled either. "What?"

"There are things," Arie motioned to the other side of the kitchen, to large recessed matte blond wood doors with hammered steel hinges and handle. "Things in there. Are they for eating as well?"

Lauranya frowned at Arie then at the doors. Walking over she ran a hand over the smooth exterior. From the touch and a judicious tapping, she could tell the door was denser than the outer veneer led her to believe. The wood for the doors was three inches thick with very fine dense graining. Lauranya had never seen anything quite like it before. With a shrug, Lauranya pulled on one of the doors, lifting the metal latch releasing the door catch. The heavy door swung open, filling the kitchen with an exotic perfume wafted into the kitchen

The material for the door forgotten, as quickly as noted, Lauranya took a good look into what was on the four rows of steel shelving. The pathways were narrow, made for one person at a time, if that person were thin they could walk abreast otherwise they would be walking sideways down the long rows searching through the very well stocked shelving. The room was cool but not freezing so definitely temperature controlled, Lauranya noted as she tried to absorb the smells and sights of such rarity in one place.

Spices in various metal or rectangular plastic containers, the oils were in larger clear rectangular plastic jugs at the bottom. There were more spices in this one space then Lauranya had ever seen before.

"Oh Arie! You are my smart girl!" Lauranya said, turning to her child on the kitchen counter with a stunned voice and eyes wide hinting at tears.

"All better Mommy?" Arie asked with a huge grin at her mother's joy.

Lauranya wiped off a tear winding slowly down her cheek. "Mostly." Was her honest reply.

"Good. Is there anything to eat for breakfast?" Arie asked wistfully, resting her cheek against her stuffed rabbits head.

"I'll see what I can find." Lauranya went back into the freezer. She locked the door open so Arie could see her from the counter. The freezer layout was both efficient and methodical. The meats to the back at the coldest section, with everything else, depending on their freezing needs placed closer to the door. Most of the items were raw ingredients. There were a few packages of pre-made items. Lauranya stopped to look at the brown plastic box. It was a box of frozen bread. Opening the lid showed 32 loaves packed tightly in plastic bags. She chewed a lip and started to pull one package out to leave everything else as it was.

"Mommy!" Arie screamed.

Lauranya looked up as a can the size of Arie's torso

spun towards her head. Lauranya threw an arm up, ducking. The can corrected its course midair to slam into her arm and chin with a bruising impact, sending Lauranya staggering back.

Lauranya saw stars and a hazy cloud of a ghost. Tass, the biologist with a grudge, was a ghost now, glaring at her. A fury so cold Lauranya was sure she would freeze in the spot she stood. The ghost raised another huge can above its head to slam down on Lauranya when Arie started to yell.

"No! Do not hurt my mommy!" The ghost turned to glare at the small child with another chilling snarl.

"Arie! You have to dismiss him! He is not being controlled! You raised him so you can dismiss him!"

"Mommy?" Arie looked at her mother with huge frightened eyes. The ghost drifted towards the child with a snarled ghostly lip of anger.

"The words and the intent. You must say and mean, "Do no harm and leave this plane. Back to Obatala you must go."

Arie started to back up from the approaching ghost. Lauranya staggered to her feet screaming at the ghost. "Tass you will move no more!" The ghost's forward motion slowed but did not stop. "Arie, my love," Lauranya's voice shook in fear and effort. "You are a very strong summoner of the dead. This man's spirit was raised and is full of hate. We need to let him go to his rest."

"How did I…Why is he coming after me!" She whimpered pushing against the pantry wall behind her eyes huge as she clutched her bunny close.

Lauranya staggered along the other side of the counter, beating Tass to her daughter by a foot. Lauranya threw herself over Arie as Tass's ghost threw the can as hard as it could. She blocked his second kinetic throw with her body taking the can along her ribs. Pain radiated at impact, spreading both ways along her spine. The can rolled a few feet from them, stopped by the wall.

"Uuuuh!" She gasped at the impact. The ghost gave a psychic scream in anger moving like ice on cold steel slow as it went for the can again.

"Arie, we have to set Tass's spirit free. He will keep haunting us and doing harm as long as he is unbound." Lauranya gasped for air. Each breath hurting.

"How Mommy," Arie whispered in a calm voice. Her body limp and her face still. She was going into shock.

"We have to send him back to Obatala. Free his spirit. Say after me and think of him in Obatala's arms, love." Lauranya was trying for calm, her voice shook in pain and fear, trying to calm a child in fear and shock.

"Ok, Mommy." Arie was voice was soft and faint.

Tass's spirit had the can in hand again, rising for another blow. This one aimed at Lauranya's head.

"Repeat after me dear. "Tass Burntglass, Do no harm." Lauranya said slowly enunciating each word in her daughter's ear.

"Tass Burntglass…"

"Do no harm," Lauranya prompted

"Do no harm," Arie whispered touching her mother's face inches from her own. Tass's ghost gave another psychic scream that cut through their minds.

"Back to Obatala. Leave this plane." Lauranya finished the simple banishment.

"Back to Obatala. Leave this plane." Arie finished her voice stronger, firm with intent. "Do not hurt us anymore!" She said with a stubborn chin.

Tass's ghost gave one last wail, this time in despair instead of anger, which trailed off into nothing as the formed mist dissipated.

The can that had been held up by his energy dropped inches from Lauranya's head. Lauranya let out a gasp of pent up air, clutching Arie close.

"Bastard! I knew he hated me." She whispered. "I did not know he was a child killer." She pulled Arie into her lap rocking her back and forth, ignoring the dull ache of her ribs, singing softly into her daughter's hair until Arie started to squirm

"I'm hungry mommy." Arie looked into her mother's face intently, wiping away a tear falling from Lauranya's cheek.

"Of course child. Let us find out what type of bread we have." Lauranya sniffed wiping away another tear and letting Arie go so they could both stand.

"Bread? Oh, I love bread!" Arie perked up bouncing off her mother's lap. Arie stopped in her tracks to look at the large can next to them. "Momma the ghost…"

"We will discuss ghosts and the undead after we eat," Lauranya said firmly. "This is a subject best talked over on full stomachs." Lauranya staggered to her feet using the wall for support. "Oh, this is going to hurt."

"Pain meds are in short supply. You will need to find another derivative." Jacks said from in front of her. As in life so in death, his ghost was not tall, but his wiry, curly hair seemed to drift into smoke, giving the ghost the image of a pale curling halo around his head.

"Jacks?" Lauranya reached a hand out from her half-crouched position, to her dead friend. Jacks' fingers touched the tips of her own as he faded out of sight.

Arie stared from the sideline unsure. "Momma?" Waiting for her mother to direct her.

Lauranya dropped her hand. "No love. Jacks would not hurt us." Her voice choked as her stomach clenched in pain. She swallowed her grief again trying to bury the hot prickling of incipient tears. To many shed today she thought. She swallowed looking at the ceiling and shaking her head, sniffling. "He is gone but still here." She whispered continuing to pull herself up along the wall.

She took a moment to catalog the new set of bruises and soreness. Her breathing while hurting was not indicative of a broken bone; it may be cracked but not broken. Her arm, where the can had hit, was already forming a large bruise in a lovely soft blue coloring with darker purple spots. Lauranya winced. That bruise was going to be ugly when the full coloring came in a day or two.

"Ok. We need breakfast and to get dinner cooking." She said in a calm firm voice. Ignoring the violence of the morning, she slowly walked back into the freezer to grab the dropped bag of bread. The cold air was bracing along sweat-soaked skin. She bent down and collected the bag with her good hand and arm, hissing breath between her teeth. "Bending is now optional." She said trying for humor.

She stepped out of the freezer, closing the door behind her with a solid thud. Arie stood by the counter with wide eyes not seeing her mother but something else.

"Arie?" Lauranya said with concern.

"Momma, there are other ghosts." She looked at Lauranya with fear and wonder.

"Of course there are child." Lauranya placed the bread on the counter, undoing the tie. "Everyone has a ghost when they die. Most ghosts are harmless. Most." She emphasized as she pulled the frozen block of pastry out of the unmarked wrapping. "The lost ones, necromancers try to send on their way; however there are some ghosts that need to be banished."

"Tass."

"Yes, Tass." Lauranya frowned at the bread having reached the extent of her own cooking experience and there were no cooking instructions on the packaging. "He was becoming dangerous, needing to be banished or harnessed so his destructiveness could be curbed." Lauranya ducked into the freezer to look at the box.

"And Jacks?" Arie asked curiously.

"Jacks gave what advice he could." Lauranya gave a sad smile at the memory of her friend. The box did not show any cooking instructions either. The cook was supposed to know what this was and how to cook it. Lauranya glared at the box in frustration before exiting the freezer again.

"Do ghosts fade away?" Arie asked with a tilted head at her mother's odd behavior.

"Depends on who you talk to or who the necromancer is that raised them." Lauranya reached for her laptop and pulled up a query menu, answering in a distracted voice while concentrating on how to feed them, multitasking two diametrically opposite tasks.

"I don't understand," Arie said frowning up at her mother. Arie looked at the frozen bread. Slightly smaller than a small woman's fist with golden dome tops but frozen hard. Arie reached for one, but the rolls were still firmly frozen to each other defeating her small fingers questing for food.

Lauranya queried frozen rolls cooking instructions then sucked in her breath a long list of various types of frozen bread and cooking instructions scrolled by. Far more than just a few types Lauranya had seen in the freezer. Luckily, there were pictures of each type of bread with the instructions, not just the names. Lauranya searched for a few moments before finding the one that looked the most like the bread rolls in front of her.

"Sweet meat buns." Lauranya murmured.

"What Mommy?"

"The type of bread might be a sweet meat bun."

"But you aren't sure."

"We should cut one open just to confirm." Lauranya started searching through the various drawers before seeing the impressive collection of knives on the left hand of the stove. She pulled one; no larger than her hand, to the countertop where she placed the blade on the roll and pushed down with her hand on the handle. The selected roll sliced slowly. Lauranya's wrist wobbled on the hilt causing the knife to slide to the right, taking off the top of the bun and skittering from her hand along the counter then to the floor.

Lauranya and Arie looked at each other in shock.

"Don't think the knife is supposed to do that mommy," Arie said with a tilt of her head and a firm conviction that her mother wasn't doing something right.

"I don't think so either sweetie." Lauranya touched the exposed center of the bun. Small chunky bits of red meat that emanated a sweet aroma even though full frozen. Arie leaned over the counter and sniffed.

"Mmmmm. This smells yummy! When can we eat?" She looked up at her mother. "I am really hungry."

"Well, the directions say thirty minutes in the oven at 325," Lauranya said. "I think…." She looked at the video with a frown hesitating between what was shown and what she had on hand, "I need a pan to put them on."

"I'll get!" Arie ran to a random-seeming lower cabinet, yanking it open with the enthusiasm of a child, spilling out a multitude of metal pans of various sizes and shapes. "Which one mommy?" Arie asked crouching down, scrutinizing each pan with a fierce intensity.

Lauranya reviewed the video to the pans that had

spilled onto the floor. "Let us try the flat pan." Arie reached for a long rectangular pan sitting half in the cabinet and half out.

"The square one, my dear." Arie put her hand on a smaller square pan looking up at her mother for confirmation. "Yes, that looks like it will fit the buns nicely." Lauranya stopped for a second remembering the rabbit and grains. "We could probably use another deeper dish for the rabbit as well.

The pans were procured and the buns placed inside without room to spare. Lauranya put the pan with the bread in the oven. She scrolled through the instructions one more time. "Timer. Where is the timer?" Lauranya pursed her lips as she scrutinized the stove once more. "Ah! Here we go."

"How soon till we eat?" Arie said with pouting lips staring at her mother with large eyes.

"About 20 minutes dear," Lauranya said trying for cheerful to her hungry child; she continued scrolling for a moment this time on rabbits and grains. She found one recipe that looked promising and within her culinary skills. Lauranya left the counter area to walk into the spice pantry pulling out salt and a premixed spice the recipe had suggested in a square tin box.

Arie nodded at her mother, her attention caught by the video on the laptop screen. "Mommy, why is the man wearing a collar?"

Lauranya glanced at the video. The cook had a younger thinner pale-skinned man handing him various bits of cooking equipment. The slave's eyes were always downcast looking at the floor or the counter never at the camera. Well trained, Lauranya thought, dismissing the slave to concentrate on the deep cooking dish in her hand with curved sides that looked to hold a goodly amount.

"The collar shows that the person is property to another." She turned towards the sink to get water for the rabbit recipe, pouring in the grains then the water. The rabbit was rubbed with the spice mixture and salted. Once the spice mix was over the rabbit, Lauranya put the rabbit on top of the saturated grains putting a lid over the bottom dish and popping the entire thing into the oven.

"Dinner should be ready in a few hours now," Lauranya said with satisfaction washing her hands of spice and rabbit juices.

"How can a person be owned?" Arie's question stopped Lauranya mid-turn, her hands dripping water onto the stone tiled floor. "Micha never wore a collar."

Lauranya stopped to explain then stopped with her mouth open. It was. This had never been a question she had ever had to consider. People were owned, or people owned other people. It just was. Yet now there was only Arie and herself. No Overseers and no Dead Gods. They were free…until the ships came back. Lauranya's mouth went dry as her hands on the towel. If the ships came back. The thought was a whisper threading through her thoughts insidiously. If…when. Either could be dangerous.

"Micha was your father's body slave. She was kept the same way you have a teddy bear." Lauranya settled as an easy analogy. Trying for the simplistic without further detail. This was a discussion that Lauranya had never had to have. The boys had known Micha was property, as Lauranya had always known about slaves with the same thoughtlessness that came from growing up with slaves. Slaves were slaves, and not even the free were safe from becoming slaves again. "Micha was known as your father's body slave. She could go anywhere on the planet without permission or be considered a runaway. The punishment for running away is...very harsh." Lauranya did not feign the shudder. "Most ship slaves do not need collars. Just slaves on world colonies."

Arie thought about this for a moment then asked her mother "Why doesn't the man just take off his collar? He wouldn't be owned then."

"The Overseer would beat him very badly if he did so." Lauranya pushed out a breath of air hard.

Arie frowned thinking hard on this for a moment. "But if a lot did this there would be too many to beat."

This froze Lauranya in her tracks. "Do not talk like that!" Her voice a whisper of fear.

"But what if..." Arie said with the persistence of a child.

Lauranya crouched in front of Arie, grabbing her shoulders tightly. "No! Arie." Lauranya swallowed hard looking away for a moment. Her uncle dragged away in chains, beaten and gagged as he tried to fight the Overseers, flashing through her mind. "If we were on a ship, things would be different. You would have grown up knowing of slaves, of indentured servants, of free people, of Overseers and of the Dead Gods. But what you speak of right now could get us beaten or collared to be sent to the slave pens."

"But we aren't wearing collars." Arie said in obvious confusion.

"No. We are not wearing collars." Lauranya sat on the floor and pulled Arie into her lap. "Your grandfather won our family's freedom on the gladiator sand; however freedom is never, never, a sure thing." Her voice, a fierce whisper in her child's ear.

"But no one is here..." There was a frown burrowing between Arie's scowling eyes. "I don't understand!" An imperious child trying to make the adult world with weird rules more understandable.

Lauranya rocked her child back and forth. "It just is child. It just is. When you are older, I will try to explain life better."

"You always say question and observe. How can it just be?" Arie was not going to let this go easily.

"Later child. I promise you we can discuss this later. Right now we need food then to get generators and lights up."

"Are the buns burning?" Arie sat up sniffing the air at the mention of food, changing the subject in a mercurial shift only a child could do.

Lauranya sniffed as well. "Oh no!" She spilled Arie from her lap with a thump opening the oven and reaching in with her hand to salvage the buns only to snatch her hand back with burnt fingertips.

"Oww! Damn me." She hissed.

"Here mommy!" Arie handed her mother a square silicone pot holder.

"Thank you, love." Lauranya reached for the pan, this time with the potholder firmly gripping the side of the pan.

The pan clattered on the counter filling the kitchen with the smell of spicy meat and sweet bread. Lauranya rummaged through the upper cabinets for a plate while Arie looked for eating utensils.

The plates with two forks were found and put to use. They cut into the buns blowing on the steaming hot food before eating. The buns were flaky, only a slight charring on the very tops, while the meat was sweetly spiced with a little heat.

"These are delicious!" Arie chirped with a mouth full of warm bread and meaty goodness.

"Yes, they are. We'll have to learn how to make these

ourselves." Lauranya said with a smile.

Each bite was better than the last, melting on hungry tongues. Lauranya tried to savor each bite. Not tomorrow but soon they could be eating much less tasty fare.

They could have eaten another three easily; however, Lauranya stopped Arie from reaching for a fourth.

"We'll save these for dinner tonight dear," Lauranya said gently to Arie's pout. Lauranya put the plate and dishes in the sink.

"Where do we put the rolls mommy?"

"They are already on the counter," Lauranya said with a blank look at her child.

Arie's head tilted slightly. Lauranya saw a slight shimmer coalescing next to her, with a cry of warning Lauranya pulled Arie behind her to ward off another ghost.

"No mommy! It's Camdia. She said we need to wrap the food with aluminum from the drawers and put it in the fridge or we could get sick." Arie concentrated as the shimmering faded. "She said bacteria is retarded by cold on food."

Lauranya swallowed bile, the savory meat buns like lumps of lead in her stomach. "Love, can you hear any other ghosts?"

"No." Arie's head tilted again, thinking. "There aren't any others speaking."

Lauranya took a deep breath before talking of the dead. "Ghosts are the souls of people. Zombies are the bodies without souls. We do not keep ghosts in bodies nor do we keep zombies unless we have a great need."

"What's a great need? Why no souls in a body? Wouldn't the body want a soul if they had one before dying?"

Lauranya answered the last question first. "A soul,

once a body has died, should go back to Obatala. So that he might send the soul to its next life. Keeping the soul in a dead body would anger him."

"And we don't want to anger a God."

"Not if we can help it, no." Lauranya gave Arie a wan smile. "As for no souls in a body, would you want to wake in a body that is no longer your own and rotting?"

Arie tilted her head for a moment, considering. "That sounds really icky."

"Very."

"And a great need?"

Here Lauranya spoke slowly, thinking of life on the ships. How to give enough information without terrifying her child. "Zombie guards are loyal to the necromancer that raised them. Unbribable and very hard to kill."

"What are guards?"

Lauranya stared at her child blankly again. So many things Lauranya had taken for granted Arie had never experienced. "Guards keep people safe who are special or are in danger."

"Are we in danger?"

"No. We are very safe." Lauranya said firmly. She gathered up the leftovers from their dinner turning back to the mundane rather than talk of ghosts and zombies. "Love, I am going to put these in the refrigerator, and we will start working." Lauranya started looking through drawers for foil and said in an offhand manner. "Arie, if you hear any new voices would you tell me please?" Lauranya was trying for a calm façade and mostly succeeding in fooling the child.

"Sure mommy!" Arie said licking crumbs off the countertop.

Lauranya turned to catch her doing this and in an exasperated tone, "Arie, don't lick the crumbs, please. We aren't starving."

"But mommy!" Arie started to whine.

"No. Stop." Lauranya fixed Arie with a look. Arie pouted but stopped trying to lick the last of the crumbs up.

"Let us find out if we have enough lights and generators to grow a garden inside." Lauranya headed into the main area, Arie followed along skipping to a tune only she could hear.

The rooms where the supplies had been unloaded and crammed together were stacked vaguely in some sort of order. Lauranya put her laptop next to the first room on a small hip height decorative fragile looking table, native blond wood decorated in semi-precious stone mosaics.

Lauranya blew out a breath. "First thing first. We need to catalog all we have to what we may need to what is still to be collected from the warehouse."

"How do we do that?"

"We rearrange all the rooms into mini warehouses."

"Sounds like fun!" Arie bounced to the top of her toes clapping.

Lauranya laughed and shook her head. "Yes. Fun. The exact word I was looking for." Lauranya knew she was going to be missing having lab drones to do the hard work for this project.

Chapter 11

The first two rooms took less than three hours to sort and catalog. Lauranya's ribs ached, her muscles sore and not getting less so, but she felt under pressure to continue. The cataloging was almost done and she still needed to get more items.

Three hours into the work, a delectable smell began to waft from the kitchen. Arie lift her head from the laptop to sniff the air. "Oh! Mommy, that smells good!" Arie smiled with genuine pleasure.

Lauranya looked up from two of the generators she had pulled from the room and the cables entwined on the floor. She sniffed the air as well. Her stomach rumbled as her mouth filled with saliva, reminding her that she had been running on too little food for the last few days.

"Let us go and see how the meal is progressing," Lauranya said straightening up, wiping her hands along the sides of her pants.

They entered the kitchen where the smell emanating from the oven was almost overwhelming. Lauranya leaned against the doorjamb and inhaled with a smile. For the first time she had hope this surviving on a drowning world might work. Arie went to the oven doors to pull out the dish.

"Let me do this dear." Lauranya picked up the potholders "When you are a bit taller you can pull the meals from the oven."

"Oh, mommy." Arie only gave a slight pout for a few seconds that lasted only as long as it took Lauranya to pull the dish from the oven. Then Arie's eyes went huge, and her stomach growled loudly enough for her mother to hear as well.

The rabbit was crispy along the edges of embedded fat while the grains had absorbed the savory drippings from the six-limbed animal. The spices had melted both into the meat and the grains.

Lauranya found a large spoon to scoop out the grains and a carving knife to cut up the meat. She gave a portion of the side and a leg to Arie along with a generous scoop of the grains. She took a leg and a side for herself with a smaller scoop of grains. Arie got out forks and spoons.

Lauranya looked at the meat and the grains with hunger and trepidation, having never cooked, this would be a first for her. She picked up the intricately carved two-tined fork, pulling a small bite of flesh from her plate. The smell was enticing, but Lauranya still closed her eyes with the first bite in wary anticipation. Her eyes flew open as the spices and meat melted in her mouth, one spice giving way to another then combining in a heady intoxication.

Arie was gobbling up her meat and gains as if she would never see food again.

"Arie…slowly child," Lauranya said after the first swallow, trying not to emulate her daughter.

"It's delicious!" Arie said with great enthusiasm, dripping food from an overly full mouth.

Lauranya's smile was more relieved than happy. "Small bites, my dear and yes it is very delicious. The recipe is a keeper. I will have to get the remaining rabbits from the lab tomorrow so that we can continue eating like this."

They continued to eat with Arie taking a second helping. Lauranya stuck with her first meager portion in consideration of limited food.

"I'm glad you like, sweetie. We will eat the rest of this for dinner tonight."

"Ok!" Arie hopped down from the stool to put her plate in the sink. She hesitated for a moment. "Mommy, aren't we supposed to wash the dishes?" She asked looking at the now growing stack of dishes in the sink.

"Umm…yes?" Lauranya stopped to look at the dishes with a chagrined look. Laundry and cooking had never been something she had to worry about.

"I'll do the dishes mommy, you do the lights," Arie said in a voice firm in the conviction that only a small child could say to an adult.

Lauranya let out a small huff of laughter. "Ok, sweetie. Let me help you…"

"No mommy! I have this." Arie opened the cabinet underneath the sink to pull out a plastic bottle of pink goo. "I watched Micha do this all the time at our old home."

"Micha did…" Lauranya stopped with a shake of her head. "Of course she did." Out of curiosity. "Did you ever help her?"

"No. She wouldn't let me. Saying it wasn't good for me." Arie looked up from the sink plug she was trying to fit into the square opening at the bottom of the hammered sink before lifting an arched handle to turn on the water. "But we need to do it now don't we?"

"Yes, we do dear," Lauranya said with a nod. She mentally added house chores to her list of things on her to-do list and things she needed to learn. Lauranya watched the water running into the sink. Something tickled her memory about water, but no idea was forthcoming.

Lauranya gritted her teeth for a second before taking a deep breath. "That idea is just going to have to wander its way forward."

"What mommy?" Arie was finishing their meager stack of dishes, filling the cooking pan with hot water for later attention.

"Nothing dear. It is time to finish what we started in the downstairs room." Lauranya said with a smile as she rose from the counter chair. She moved slowly and stiffly letting out a soft hiss of pain as her ribs, and various bruised body parts complained of the unexpected motion.

There were a few stumbling missteps as she headed back to the rooms. The walk helped to stretch out the soreness, but only just, before she was back to lifting and cataloging.

She started in the main area hooking up the solar generators for the incubators and a second to the grow lights, except there was nothing to attach lights to other than the walls and balconies. "I am going to need a ladder." She tilted her head a moment looking at the wood covered concrete walls. "And a very strong set of drill bits." She made a moue of irritation. Drilling concrete for running computer wires had never been an easy job; in fact it was a real melter of a job. "Hmm…If I run the wires along the wall and used a little metal glue I could just use the existing light fixtures." She looked up at the vaulted ceiling, turning slowly in place with her head and neck at an odd bent back position. "That would be easier than trying to drill through. Still need more lights till the sun shows his face again."

She popped her neck straightening up, causing her eyes to cross shortly. "Still going to need a ladder." With a moment's thought, she chewed her lip. "Let us see how bad the freezer is going to be to hook up." With that, she went to the kitchen to look at the freezer's power panel.

The freezer's panel needed a power drill to remove the cover. Lauranya looked at the stainless steel freezer with disgust. "Well I knew I was going to have to get the power drill anyway. Just would have liked to have this one thing done before moving on to the lights."

"Will the plants still grow mommy?" Arie trailed behind her mother dragging her rabbit behind.

"Yes love, but not as well as natural light so we need to supplement as much as possible." Lauranya was staring out the arched windows over the kitchen sink into the dark rain clouds, thinking.

"Water will be an issue. Once the pumps are no longer working, we will not have fresh water until a hose can reach the water from the stairwell." Lauranya drummed fingers on the smooth cold concrete countertop. "That will not be for two maybe three months…need a water collection system and a pump."

Arie fiddled with her rabbits leather round ears, jumping from one foot to the other. She knew her mom was thinking and interrupting was not a good idea, so she waited as patiently as possible.

Lauranya turned away from the window with her mind firmly somewhere else, heading out to the living area again.

"Mommy where are we going?"

"Hmm…oh to the roof. I need to see if we can rig a water collection with all this rain. A cistern."

"Oh like a pool!" Arie exclaimed with great conviction.

"A pool?" Lauranya stopped to look at her child blankly.

"Camdia was talking about sneaking over to the building to swim before the Lords and Gods actually arrived," Arie said excitedly bouncing even faster. Her eyes wide, her voice dropping into a whisper.

Lauranya frowned slightly, having no idea what a pool

was. Even so, sneaking anywhere before the Gods arrived usually precluded a whipping. "Well, we do not have to worry about Gods or sneaking. So let us see what this pool is."

"Camdia said it was filled with water!" Arie's voice was still in a whisper ascertaining from her mother's frown and Camdia's comments that the pool was an off limit place.

"Like a bathtub." Lauranya shook her head with a slight roll of her eyes as she led Arie up the flights of wooden stairway. The bathtubs here were a decadence not seen on ships except for the Gods, a shocking waste of water.

Reaching the door, she had to push it several times to open. The first time was too timid as she tried not to aggravate the bruised ribs. The second time the door opened a fraction before thudding shut. The third time, Lauranya pushed with her shoulder opening the door wide enough so that the wind caught the metal door yanking it from her hands, slamming it against the stone covered concrete building, with water sweeping into the hallway soaking the two of them.

Lauranya cringed from habit, thinking of the damage done and displeasing the Overseers. No one cried foul even as the water soaked through the carpet and the scratch on the door barely a whisper along the metal.

"Wet!"

"Yes, it is. Now let us find the pool." Lauranya went back to practical, shielding her eyes with one hand and taking Arie by the other, they wandered on top of the roof looking for a large tub with water. Within the first three seconds, they were soaked to the skin, their feet gripping the sandstone tiles as the rainwater was pooling in odd places. Lauranya could see through the driving rain the blonde wood furniture randomly stacked in a sheltered corner. Even with the gusting wind, the heavy furniture had not blown away. There were tall planters, formed in stone concreted to the roof that were long and deep, the vegetation brown and rotting, from excess water drowning them. Lauranya was almost sick with the loss of dirt and plants but nothing she could do for the moment. Later, she thought to herself. She would come back for the dirt, but not now. She had to find the water storage pool.

There were several distinct areas. The area opening from the door would be a lush jungle with chairs and small tables. Stumbling to the next area there were tables and more stone planters this time with stone arches 15 feet high. There were round metal trellises. There was a large grilling area with fire pits under stretched dark green triangular awnings. Beautiful if not for the vining dead plants, withered and brown, in the stone planters. When the rain stops, Lauranya promised herself she would try to regrow plants up here for an outdoor oasis.

Lauranya turned left to an incredible view through the raindrops. The roof area could have hosted 500 people with room to spare. The large area in the center focused on a pool done in a natural stone waterfall towards the north side of the oblong pool. With all the rain, the pool overflowed with the waterfall rushing loudly enough to be heard over the pounding rain.

Lauranya walked cautiously to the side of the pool, water flowing over her ankles and out the small fist-sized circular portals on the side of the rooftop wall. Her mouth hung open for a second at the width and depth of all the contained fresh water. She had never seen water contained like this just for pleasure. The thought was almost beyond her comprehension, so drilled on water conservation from ship life.

The pool was mostly clear, the pump and filters still working, showing the deep end as very deep. Arie tried to get a closer look. Lauranya threw an arm across her daughter's chest.

Ari looked up startled. "What's wrong mommy?"

Lauranya's teeth chattered but not from the cold water flowing along her spine in rivulets. She swallowed a lump in her throat before answering in a hoarse whisper. "I do not know how to…swim." Her voice gained strength as she spoke her fear. "If you fall in, I would not be able to save you, love." Lauranya could see this happening, Arie falling in or Dead Gods forbid, jumping into the deep end, and she would only be able to stand on the sides helplessly as her daughter drowned.

The thought wound through Lauranya's brain, chilling her blood stopping all thoughts. Lauranya gasped for air, sinking to her knees, her hands clenching and unclenching as wave after wave of fear swept through her. Water around her. Water over her. She couldn't breathe. She would never escape the wet. She gasped for air, her lungs never filling fully, feeling light-headed as darkness closed over her.

It was Arie's warm touch that brought her out of her fear.

"I thought you could swim mommy?" Arie looked up wide-eyed at her mother's fear, wet hair straggling across her face, giving her an even more impish look than usual.

Lauranya shook her head unable to speak. "No. I cannot swim." She rasped out, gasping still.

"You can use the indoor pool to learn mommy."

"Indoor pool?" Lauranya looked at Arie blankly, not understanding the words used in the sentence.

"We can go inside and I can show you. We can even get dry first!" Arie was dancing in the water puddling around her calves, the thought of being dry trumped by playing in the rain.

Another round of racking shudders, tears falling at the thought of water so deep she couldn't stand. Lauranya swallowed hard, metallic bile taste in her mouth. Arie came to her mother, slipping her small hand into her mother's.

"I...I need to learn to swim." Lauranya stuttered. The wind whipping over the patio. Lauranya trying vainly to push back the occasional errant wisp of hair that the storm kept whipping into her eyes and mouth. Lauranya had a faraway look in her eyes for a second. Shaking her head, she was coming back to the here and now in the storm-lashed rooftop, holding fast to her daughter's hand.

"It's easy mommy! I can teach you and we can both swim like fishes!" Arie hugged her mother. "Don't cry. You're just going to get wet like you do in the shower."

Lauranya gave a grating humorless laugh. Arie didn't understand the fear. Everything was easier for a child. Always in the here and now.

She stood slowly stiffly, backing away from the pool, shivering slightly. "That we can baby. Let us get dry and see this indoor pool of yours." They waded back to the door. Lauranya yanked the door hard, bracing this time for the door blowing open further by the wind. The wind was almost polite, merely tugging at the door as she tried to close it this time, instead of ripping it out of her hands.

She locked the door from habit but breathed easier being further away from so much deep water. She knew the pool would take care of the water needs for them and the plants until the water had risen high enough in the stairwell for use, but she never wanted to imagine swimming or being in water so deep again.

She sank to her knees again in the stairwell. The

image of the water rising so fast and so deep that she and Arie were drowning inside overwhelmed her. She leaned against the hard metal door, gasping for air. The metal cold on fear and water slicked skin, nails clawing at the door.

"No more please Olokun. I honor you and your oceans." Lauranya shook as she prayed to her Gods. She shook and gasped for a moment more before her chest eased and her brain blanked for a moment, granting her the peace she needed to breathe.

"Feeling better mommy?" Arie asked gently touching Lauranya's cheek with her hand.

"Better. But I fear Olokun is too generous with his gift of water for us." Lauranya croaked. "Let's find this indoor pool of yours so I might learn to swim."

"Follow me!" Arie turned on her toes to bounce down the stairs. A wet trail easily followed if anyone else had been there to see. Each step away from the rooftop pool and the visibly climbing water eased the fear in Lauranya's mind.

"I need to dry off first, baby," Lauranya called as Arie was turning right at the second stair level.

Arie made a face but followed her mother's lead, turning left and running ahead of her mother. Lauranya and Ari went to the main bathroom and stripped down to get warmed up in the shower. The dirty clothes from last night giving off a vague wet sweaty stink that multiplied when the new wet clothes dumped into the growing pile.

"Ugh." Lauranya made a distasteful face. "Laundry is now a priority."

"How do we do laundry?" Ari asked swaddled in a clean towel, her skin pink from the hot shower, prodding the wet pile of moldering clothes with a toe. She made a face at the sour smell emanating from the clothes.

"I do not know baby, but I think we are about to find out!" Lauranya nodded firmly as she put this on her task for the evening.

They both pulled on dry clothing before starting to search for Ari's indoor "pool". Arie led Lauranya to the far end of the second tier on the upper floors. Arie skipped into the open-air room turning to the right slightly. The area she headed for was a section of native pale white and tan striped stone, raised off the main wooden floor by a couple of feet. The stone was almost gritty under Lauranya's bare toes as she cautiously stepped onto the platform.

Lauranya's cursory inspection had noted that this area, unlike the other floors, had hardwood floors and no furniture just training mats of thickly woven plant fiber filling the space with an outdoor green smell and sparse equipment. Today the windows, as prevalent here as in the other rooms, showed dark clouds and splattered with raindrops plinking against the thick insulated glass. The rain was coming down hard enough that the landscape Lauranya knew was now hidden behind a veil of rain. If the rain had not been so heavy, the view would have been magnificent, encompassing the valley and the tops of the valley ridge, a dominating view.

"We see all." Lauranya murmured. She quickly buried that thought.

"Here mommy!" Arie's excited voice broke through Lauranya's revere. Lauranya turned from the window's view to her bouncing child. The area, an opulently huge room was more of the same raised stone dais area where four padded tables for massage leaned against the far left wall. Where the bathroom would have been were two glass-enclosed rooms. One labeled heat and the other steam. Between the two doors was a stone tub 10 foot wide, 14 foot long, brimming with water that came within an inch from the top of the carved curving edge tiles. There were stone steps, of the same almost gritty stone, leading into one end of the clear water tub.

Lauranya leaned over the edge but could not ascertain the depth. She swallowed hard, feeling bubbles of fear floating upwards through her brain. She had to take a quick step back.

"Watch this mommy!" Arie had bounced over to the wall with a square-filigreed cover done in vines and cloisonné flowers. She opened the cover and pressed a button before Lauranya could stop her.

The water in the pool started to froth at the end without steps even as Lauranya held out a hand to stop Arie from pressing the button. Lauranya ended up hopping further back from the edge of the tub in startlement. Much to Arie's giggling amusement.

Lauranya was more entranced with the frothing bubbles then Arie's laughing at her surprise. The water rose in waves, bubbling, and foaming, always threatening to spill over the banks of the tub yet never reaching over the top.

Arie moved to the steps, stepping into the moving water, her dress hem getting soaked.

"Arie, no!" Lauranya rushed to make the steps before Arie had completely submerged.

"Watch mommy!" Arie moved deeper to her waist then kicked off the steps into the tub, paddling against the current created, splashing water on the stone tiles and onto her scared mother's pants as Lauranya stood on the steps, having just missed grabbing the child.

Lauranya stepped lower on the steps, up to her thighs, feeling a strong current pushing her back against the steps. Except for where her heel touched a metal grate, where the water entered for circulation, the steps were stone and slightly gritty to the touch.

"See mommy, we can learn to swim now!" Arie gurgled happily splashing about. "It's only a little deeper than the bathtub!"

Lauranya tried to swallow her fear not wanting to discuss with her child that anything over her mother's head standing was still deeper than a tub. She said instead "That we can baby."

Lauranya was still catching her breath unwilling and unable to go past her knees. Her breathing ragged watching Arie paddle around the small tub happily.

"We can't go outside but we can be active in here," Arie said clambering up the steps to hug her mother's formerly dry thighs.

"I do not think we can just swim baby," Lauranya replied sitting down on the steps, scooping her fearless child up.

"Oh no! There are things to work on in the other room too." Arie looked into her mother's face earnestly with great enthusiasm for the many other areas to explore and clamber on.

"I am sure there are baby. This tub…"

"Pool."

"Pool, will help us to learn to swim. Unfortunately, we can swim or we can have it double as a water source if we run out of water up top." Lauranya regarded the treated water for a moment. "The planet is drowning and we need to learn to swim. I will need to learn how to treat this water to keep it clear and keep our drinking water fresh."

"Tubs?"

"Yes, we are going to fill up all the tubs so that we have water on hand when the pumps fail."

"What about bathing?"

"We'll have to use it sparsely till we can get a new pump and shower working." Lauranya nodded firmly to her active water-loving child.

"But not today?" Arie looked at her mother with downturned lips in sadness.

"No, baby, not today." Lauranya squeezed Arie tightly, causing Arie to squeal in delight. "Let us find some dry towels and dry off again, and then we need to do laundry and perhaps grab dinner before we go to bed."

Arie tilted her head for a moment as if listening to something. "I am hungry. I can feel my stomach making noise."

Lauranya leaned over, poking her child in the tummy gently. The tummy growled loudly as if it were going to chew on the offending digit. Lauranya looked up startled for a second then both she and Arie started laughing.

"Dry clothes and washing, then we get food," Lauranya said firmly. There was a small shower room to the side of the glass door rooms. The shower room was half the size of the one in her room, not surprising seeing the amount of space taken for working out. However the lack of opulence was. The room was decorated with stone and steel, nothing flashing of gems or gilding. The shower made for two; at most, not the ten of her shower room, but the shower heads worked as well and the towels soft to the skin.

"A second cleaning for us both today." Lauranya teased Arie who just giggled in the shower enjoying the warm cascade and sweet smelling soap.

Lauranya packed up their wet clothes in a wet towel, draping herself in a dry towel with Arie in tow, naked as the day she was born. Arie seeing they were heading to their room, ran ahead flashing a cherry cheek butt. Lauranya smiled indulgently but her concentration lugging up to the washroom was on how much water she and Arie would need to survive the two months without pumping water. Two months equaling 1.5 gallons of drinking water per day. 43 days per month give or take. 129 gallons and there were 27 cubic feet would hold 7.5 gallons equaling 202.5 gallons per tub. This did not include the birds or rabbits or showers. Every tub on the upper floor, all 8 tubs, would need to be filled to take care of the basic water needs for those days. They could do this.

"And no filtration system for waste reclamation," Lauranya said in disgust at the lack of foresight of the world colonizers. "Hmm…I could make a dual chamber dry toilet. Pouring out the urine and keeping the shit for compost." Lauranya's thoughts began to churn with needed materials. She chewed her lower lip for a second, staring into space with her arms filled with damp clothing.

"Mommy?"

Lauranya shook her head coming out of her reverie. "Coming dear…was having an epiphany."

"Is that like when daddy makes the apartment stinky?" Arie asked with a hand hovering over her nose to pinch it close.

"No. Not even close." Lauranya said with a straight face and only a slight pinching of the lips in remembered distaste.

The weight room floated through her head. "An education of the mind and the body." Lauranya quoted from her grandfather. They had the body; she just had to ensure the mind now.

"Ok darling, we have things we need to get set up still. Let us get dressed."

"Why?"

"Because we do," Lauranya said in a firm voice that

signaled the end of the conversation.

Chapter 12

After dinner, Lauranya spent time researching how to wash clothes and dishes on her laptop. The methods usually showed a machine and a slave loading said machine. She had to go back to other colonies and read accounts from those documented tasks, with little more than basic medical and how they survived in primitive conditions.

"Mommy?" Arie asked quizzically from the doorway, her hands stained from markers.

Lauranya pulled herself from her report with a deep breath, like a swimmer from a deep dive finding the surface. "Yes, baby?"

"Have you found how to wash?"

"I think so; however I am going to have to go down to the bottom floor and get more soap." Lauranya stood, stretching her arms high over her head, pulling her shoulders back after hunching over her laptop for so long.

Arie clutched her rabbit a little tighter. "Are you leaving me?"

Lauranya went to the wide-eyed fearful child. "No baby. You can come with me if you like." Wrapping Arie up in her arms. "We are only going downstairs."

"Ok. I can do that!" Arie bounced back with enthusiasm for a new adventure.

They took the service elevator to the bottom of the hotel. Arie insisted on coming along, though her fear was plain as she clung tightly to Lauranya's hand.

"Shhhh. We're ok baby." Lauranya said as the doors

opened up on the bottom floor and no lights were on. The double moons were waxing, five days past full although the combined light filtered through the lobby windows. They shone for just a few minutes before the clouds veiled their faces again, a path of pale moonlight at the far end of the hallway, giving Lauranya a relatively bright light to head to.

"It's dark Mommy!" Arie whispered.

"It is baby." Giving her child a comforting squeeze on the hand. "Sometimes the dark is a good thing."

"What about…ghosts?"

"Ghosts are not scary." Lauranya stopped for a second and amended "Usually. They even cast their very own light, so in the dark you can see them easier." Lauranya started walking down the dark, quiet hallway with Arie close beside her. The rain was making a drumming noise on the lobby windows, loud enough that the sound was heard in the back slave hallways.

"Are we going to gather everything up in the dark?" Arie asked, comforted by her mother's lack of fear.

Lauranya let out a chuckle. "No baby. I am going to turn on the lights as soon as we find a switch."

"Is the switch close?" Ari whispered, looking up with a swish of her hair to her mother.

They reached the patch of moonlight; Lauranya walked the three steps to a slightly recessed alcove and pushed on the wall switch that showed lighter than the stonewalls surrounding it. Light glowed softly, gaining strength by increments, illuminating the magnificent front area of the hotel.

"Yes baby, not far at all."

Arie's mouth was open as she walked into the middle of the huge vaulted room, turning to see all the beautiful colors in the wall murals. Her feet made no sound as they sunk into the inch deep pile of hand-woven natural fiber rugs as vibrant as the walls.

Lauranya stood back for a moment, watching Arie soak in the visuals of the Gods tower. The crystal sconces done in skulls or dancing skeletons along the wall, the murals of the Gods on worlds as different from where they now were, to the different world ships themselves. She would see nothing like this again as the water would fill the lobby, yet the impression would last for a lifetime.

Arie turned slowly gaping at all the murals and unique sights. No details were too small for the artisans who had painted these scenes, seen in the fine laugh wrinkles of the Goddess Osun to the many folds of Ibeji's draped wrap. Small details exquisitely rendered.

Lauranya turned to the front doors. The doors, beautifully done in small pieces of colored glass from top to bottom that formed geometric spiraling patterns with a dull grey metal strip between each piece of glass. The overall impression was stunning, set within thick and heavy wooden frames, each door opening wide enough to allow three men to walk through abreast. The side windows were tall with only the upper arched portion done in the decorative glass. The wide windows allowed an almost unobstructed view of the valley below and the shuttle port.

Right now, the view was dark but with rain smeared streaks on the outside glass. Lauranya pulled on a door, testing its weight. The doors didn't budge. She peered closer for a look at how they were sealed. A small recessed panel, not quite hidden to the side of the doors camouflaged in the mural of a desert world showed it was a ten digit numeric panel with a thumbprint override.

Lauranya mulled over her options. She might be able to override the door panel code, maybe, but she was not going to be able to get through the thumbprint overdrive. The back door was going to be their only way in and out until the water got too high. She let out a sigh. The doors would have been closer to the warehouse to the left but only by a few feet, so not a huge loss. She was still glad the door lock was secure. The whiskered cats were dangerous, not to mention the whispers of other refugees on this world. She did not want anything able to push its way through the front doors while she was collecting supplies.

Nor, as unlikely as it was, the shuttle crew returning to finish what they had started. The reminder of so many dead caused her throat to tighten with emotion. A sob threatened to escape. She threw a hand over her mouth to stifle any others. After three deep breaths and her right hand clenched in a fist, she was not in danger of any other sobs escaping.

"Damn you to the other Gods Hell!" She snarled a curse that fell from her lips to the Gods ears in a whisper as she stared into the rain-drenched darkness.

"Mommy! Look!" Arie's excited voice snapped Lauranya's head around.

"Arie?" Lauranya could not see her daughter, only hear her excited squeals.

"Over here! You have to see this!" An odd thrumming accompanying Arie's voice.

Lauranya moved quickly across the plush rugs to where Arie's voice emanated. Lauranya rounded a wide square pillar of fieldstone to see her daughter entranced by a huge floor harp. Lauranya gasped at the floor harp her daughter was gently touching. The harp was of simple steel engraved with copper in a vining pattern along the spine and rib dominating the musicians' corner. There were several other harps, of differing patterns and size, yet it was the silver and copper harp that made Lauranya's hands itch to touch.

"Mommy, can we take these upstairs with us?" Arie asked, touching the gilt strings of a smaller, almost child-sized, floor harp.

There was no consideration of usefulness or space. Lauranya's response was made of equal parts desire and want. "Of course. We'll gather those up when we get the cleaning supplies and extras from down here." There was no hesitation.

"Can we take the drums as well?"

"Drums?" Lauranya asked with a slight frown. Her eyes saw only the harp, hearing the soft thrumming of songs lilting through her mind.

Arie ran to the side where several drums sat. They were shoulder high, narrow butt, with wide shoulder drums made of carved dark and blond woods. The drums caused Lauranya to do a slight double take. She was surprised that the plebeian dancing drums had made it to the exalted circle of instruments for the Gods. She chewed a lip but nodded.

"I know a few rhythms for the drums, and I know you like to make noise banging on things," Lauranya said with an indulgent smile then sighed. This was going to be at least two trips, maybe three. She would need the strings and drum heads not to mention the tuning forks for the harps. Where would she… "Ahh." She walked to the back of the musicians' area to see rectangular and flat square boxes. Opening the short flat box, she found spare drumheads with both a screw bolt for tightening the heads on a shorter metal doumbek and the glue for the larger wooden djembe. The gilded rectangular box held the bolt toggle and extra strings and tuning pins for the harps.

"There you are my beauties." Lauranya hummed

softly, the sound bouncing off the walls and instruments in beautiful echoes. She moved the box kits to the front next to the harps. There were a few other instruments, several flutes, of both wood and metal types along with two stringed instruments with wide bellied bottoms and a flat face. The neck of the instrument bent severely backward, looking almost broken if not for the fact Lauranya could see the jointing done purposefully, not broken in transit.

"Oh! Mommy, look!" Arie had opened a large plastic case where one more string instrument rested inside a cocooning bottom. The overall instrument stood only a few inches shorter than Arie. The neck took up 3/4ths of the overall length while the body more oblong than circular. Lauranya walked slowly up to the instrument, touching the wooden neck gently.

"Do you know what it is?" Arie spoke so excitedly her words were almost strung together intelligibly.

"I think this is a Chanthrak..." Lauranya stumbled over the odd word, then shook her head. "One of my grandmothers spoke of having an instrument like this she played as a child. The grandpas could never find one on ship or trade from other ships that would not have cost the amount of all family apartments."

"It's beautiful!"

Lauranya held up a hand, stalling Arie's next question. "Yes, dear, we will take this with us as well." She ran a hand along the neck, lovingly feeling the wood. "We will be very busy learning how to play these after studies."

"I'd rather just learn how to play these then do studies," Arie said sulkily. Her dream of living on sweet meat buns and playing stopped cold by her mother's words.

"And I would like to live like a God; however, we will have to make do with the life we have, which means learning the planet's watery secrets as much as possible while learning how to play these to keep ourselves entertained," Lauranya said archly to her almost petulant child.

Arie let out a heavy sigh with slumping shoulders. "Ok. If we must."

"Yes dear, we must. And speaking of must. We need to gather the supplies we came down here for."

"And the instruments!" Arie said earnestly to her mother, looking into Lauranya's face trying to impart as only a child could how important the instruments were.

"And the instruments." Lauranya amended with a small smile. Lauranya looked up for a moment before turning back to Arie. "Child, I need to go to the kitchen to gather up all of the cleaning supplies we need for the days…years to come." Lauranya looked at Arie. "Do you want to stay here with the instruments and play while I get everything together or you can…"

Arie stood up, but her shoulders were hunched and her hands by her side. Lauranya couldn't see Arie's face; the child's hair covered her face almost totally. Lauranya knelt down, brushing the hair from Arie's face. Arie's lower lip quivered and her eyes filled with tears as her shoulders shook.

"Shhhh…" Lauranya scooped her up, holding her close. "What's wrong baby? Are you scared?"

Arie shook her head but the tears were falling down her round cheeks.

Lauranya rocked Arie back and forth, humming a lullaby. Arie wrapped her arms around her mother's neck with her shoulders shaking in silence.

"Ok, we, both of us are going to go and get supplies and come back for the instruments." Lauranya pulled back from her daughter, tapping Arie's tear-stained face up.

"Better?"

"Yes mommy," Arie whispered.

"That's my brave girl." Lauranya gave her another tight hug, before letting her go. "Now before we fall asleep on our feet, let us get everything together!"

"Okay!" Arie bounced high on her toes, excited again.

In the back of the washroom next to the kitchen, Lauranya found a large laundry basket on wheels, the kind that large interconnected family apartments used to gather laundry and sheets in one easy chore by a domestic slave. It was easily wide enough to fit both her and Arie combined four times over.

The kitchen had been picked clean of anything edible, including the spices. Lauranya had expected nothing less, yet the loss still cut through her gut like a knife. Items not stripped included the laundry supplies, towels, soaps, shampoos, and other sundry personal hygiene items. Lauranya loaded those up with an almost giddy sense of gleefulness.

Lauranya snorted at the lack of care taken to make off with the female hygiene products. "I bet their wives are going to be really irritated." However, the amusement cut short as she remembered the bodies. Shaking her head she continued loading the laundry basket until the basket could hold no more.

The loading and unloading for all the downstairs supplies took four trips. Lauranya stripped everything even remotely useful from the kitchen and washroom supplies. Arie helped her by reaching the lower items, placing each item carefully into the basket. The items were carefully but hurriedly dropped outside the lift in the hallway. The gathering was more important than the organization at this moment.

"Are we going to do this again tomorrow?" Arie asked, noticeably tired on the third trip down.

"No darling," Lauranya said, muffled through a hand-covered yawn. "We'll strip the other rooms once we can no longer get out of the tower. Starting at the bottom rooms and working our way up."

"Okay." Arie yawned, echoing her mother's yawn un-muffled by a hand.

The instruments took only one trip. These she placed carefully into the basket, not allowing Arie to do more than hand her the smaller items. The larger harp went in first followed by the drums, then the stringed instruments, the smaller harps and wind instruments. There was room but just barely. The cart handled like a drunken gladiator fresh from rutting, unable to steer straight and bouncing into walls. By this time, both Arie and Lauranya were so tired that neither could speak. They could barely do more than yawn and try to keep the cart from running into walls. Lauranya placed the instruments by the stairs. She decided that carrying them to the second floor could wait until sometime in the next few weeks.

She looked at the shower and was about to comment to Arie about showering when she looked over onto the huge bed to see Arie snuggled on top of the cover with her rabbit. She had not even tried to get under the covers she was that tired. Lauranya stripped out of her own clothes, dropping them on the floor to crawl into bed next to her softly snoring child. She pulled the covers over them both. Lauranya closed her eyes to start her list of things to do when sleep wrapped her in slumber.

Chapter 13

"Ok, people! Get your arses in those seats!" The Katherian growled loudly enough to be heard over the marines' normal pre-mission din. Clawed feet clicking on the metal transport floor almost muffled the stomping of booted feet. Her voice rumbled out in a snarl that echoed along everyone's ear bones. The other Katherian and Wolfens lowered their ears in annoyance or gave a flick of an ear to acknowledge her, turning to get their weapons, packs, and helms to their seat. Several of the more alpha types lifted muzzles in reflexive snarls, but none would meet her eyes in Challenge. High Sarge would shoot first, roll the body out of the shuttle then ask questions.

High Sarge gazed out over her motley crew with a glower of icy blue-grey eyes with a battle rebar steel of a spine. Not even the six experiments raised either eyes or muzzles in Challenge. High Sarge glared at the six of them for a moment. She ran a hand through her shoulder-length mane of dark browns and golds, trying to ignore the siblings but it was hard. Something about the abnormal tentacled freaks made High Sarge's fur stand on end every time she walked by one of them. They were all being the soul of military conduct, had been for the last few weeks. High Sarge snorted like a dust popped Wolfen were they meek, she thought.

Their overly human eyes followed her, with twitching ears and the occasional finger motion. They looked more human than Katherian, almost like a fur covered human with longer than average limbs and four tentacles. And it was the almost human part that creeped High Sarge out. No Katherian should look human or have tentacles. Each tentacle was hairless and a body length as well as prehensile. Any of the six could stand toe to toe with the Katherian and Wolfen in the height of just the sheer amount of damage they could dish out and take. They weren't telepathic the way a normal Katherian was, but they could communicate amongst themselves easily enough with touch telepathy. However, since she couldn't find anything wrong with their manners, she couldn't shoot the sick freaks as much as she'd like to.

She waited for a moment before moving up to the shuttle, herding her company like a ragged, fur and clawed band of four-year-olds about to go on an outing. She had gotten the last of hers boarded and in their seats ready to be buckled in when she heard the side hatch open. High Sarge turned with a snarl to the latecomers when her snarled died mid growl as her mouth went dry.

"Redeyes." High Sarge breathed, her ears not quite flattening while her tail went very still. Not unexpected… not really but still a surprise when one of the Gods, herself, joined, and Redeyes was never the same person twice after a death. High Sarge was not sure how this Redeyes would be on a flight.

"High Sarge." Redeyes nodded to the company leader. The God's head turned to take in the seated boarding team. High Sarge couldn't tell where the God's eyes actually fell, as they were a solid red like freshly spilling blood. Where her head turned the Marines acknowledged her with a lowering of their heads and a hand to heart motion.

Redeyes was loaded for Undead God, High Sarge noted, as the God walked by her on feet, covered in toeless furred knee-high boots, that looked more

Katherian than human. She was up on the pads of the foot and toes with a longer extended arch and heel; however, since her feet didn't touch the ground in the first place, High Sarge knew she would never hear the God sneak up behind her.

Redeyes had a brace of disc pistols for the lower arms, worn like a Wolfen's. High Sarge knew from past painful experience and a lighter pouch on betting against Redeyes at the range that the God was also ambidextrous with all four of her arms. Again deceptive. The swords on Redeyes back weren't for decoration. Thirty-six inches of steel, the width one and a half inches that had split at least one Challenger in half on the dueling sands. Good with either sword or pistol, however unlike a Wolfen, Redeyes arms weren't the size of a human thigh, just normal well-muscled human woman that could split skull with her blades. Well, youngish looking woman, High Sarge amended. No matter how old she was or how many bodies, male or female, she had been in she always morphed into a short white-haired woman with four arms and the ability to walk on air with very dangerous nightmares.

High Sarge's eyes moved to the guardians flanking the God, guardians being a deceptive phrase.

"Leave one behind?" High Sarge said with a motion of her chin towards the two Guardians following far enough behind Redeyes to be out of sword range.

"He's prepping the rooms for tonight," Redeyes said in a low voice, her eyes shifting from blood red to human with green iris. Her voice wasn't quite enough. The marines close to her and High Sarge, with good hearing, took in a deep breath; a few hissed in displeasure.

"It's been three weeks since the last sleep and no nightmares." The short God said, floating 3 inches from the metal decks with her fur booted toes flexing cat-like in the air over the battle steel as she tried to quell the fears that came from her sleeping.

"Your last dream expanded the ship by 18 feet on the port side." One brazen Wolfen said; though he couldn't quite meet her eyes, clawed hands clenching the seat-strapping.

"And killed 21 civilians." Another voice, human male, said from down the line. Redeyes looked towards the voice, but no one met her eyes to claim that statement; however, there was only one human male in the row of jump seats where the voice had emanated from. She raised an eyebrow, turning towards the lone human.

"Stop." High Sarge barked, reacting without thinking, putting a hand on Redeyes arm, claws tips just pressing into the God's arm. "I need all of my people alive." She said in a sotto voice to Redeyes. High Sarge ducked her head to look the shorter God in her deep red eyes. Redeyes pulled back her lips over more Katherian like teeth than human in a silent snarl at the Katherian marine. A visible shiver went down the Katherian's spine.

"Then teach them when not to challenge unless they want to take one of my guardian's place for the nigh," Redeyes said acidly moving down the aisle towards the human.

High Sarge nodded her agreement then took a deep breath as the surrounding marines watched their officer stand up for them to the God. "The Gods are still with us and we are free." High Sarge's voice carried along the seated Marines with ease, her steely gaze caught and held the bravest one's eyes until they too looked away. "You will respect this! And do not offer challenge. We fight an enemy who would enslave us all. We do not need to fight amongst ourselves." No more voices were raised against the God's upcoming sleep and possible nightmares. Death came for them all. The nightmares were just another challenge. The marines were silent for the moment but not forever.

Redeyes turned facing High Sarge with a raised eyebrow. "Keep them from killing my guardians…or me for that matter until we get this little jaunt taken care of." She spoke with just a small flicker of a smile in a loud enough voice to carry through the silence.

High Sarge nodded, flicking an ear in acknowledgment, releasing the God with a rapid unclenching of her hand, only shaking a little after releasing the petite human God.

Collins picked his seat with more care than would have been thought after the slight altercation between High Sarge and Redeyes. Red would have won but High Sarge would have done some serious damage making betting on either one of them interesting. With a heavy sigh for lack of violence, he sat next to one of the experiments. Easy enough as the seats two on either side of the multi-limbed Marines was empty.

"Kill anyone today?" Morris asked Collins, the one sitting in the no longer empty seat, as the guardian strapped next to the experimental Katherian.

"Not yet but the day is young," Collins said, flashing an easy smile and bright blue eyes.

Morris touched the tip of his tongue to his nose. "You are looking forward to this aren't you?" Morris' eyes lightened up with belly tightening anticipation.

"Not enough killing on the ship and Redeyes won't let me challenge anyone for sport," Collins said, irritation lacing his voice. His eyes landed on Redeyes, fists clenching in an unconscious reflex of the emotional turmoil the God brought him.

"Not to your liking?"

"Eh." Collins shrugged focusing back to his seatmate and stowing his gear in the webbing, cinching it down. "She lets me kill when we go on field trips so I'm not totally bored."

"Thought the nightmares kept you five on your toes."

"Three." Collins corrected absently, running a hand along his sides and hips checking the various holsters and weapons.

"I thought there were…"

"Korik died seven days back from last month's dreams."

"Surgeries didn't help?"

"Complications afterward." He said with a shrug, looking into Morris' human brown eyes with down-turned lips.

"What about Jeria and Nero?" Morris asked casually as Collins adjusted the swords strapped to his back before he could sit comfortably.

"Nero's got room prep for tonight. Jeria decided to blow her brains out rather than go through another dream session." Collins slipped his scattergun in the harness next to his seat, easier to reach.

"Rads!" Morris didn't have to fake the surprise. Guardians dying weren't rare, committing suicide was. A Guardian's family benefited the foremost in added calories to their diet, when the person was added to Redeyes entourage. The longer the service, the better off the guardians' family was. No-one had so many calories these days that extras weren't welcome and the guardians knew this. They tried to live as long as possible not only for their sake but for their families.

"Yeah, had to clean up her shit and brains before breakfast," Collins said in disgust, sliding into his seat to buckle his own harness slipping the disc-gun into his arms. He liked to cradle the gun in flight. Only Redeyes' guardians had that privilege. It was never abused, at least more than once and a new slot opened for another guardian replacement. "Nero lost to Iarris for clean up." Collins nodded to the tall Katherian female, Redeyes' other Guardian.

"And you have to do a babysitting run this afternoon," Morris said, licking his whiskers with a very long Katherian tongue that was incongruous in his furry human face, flexing claws on his harness webbing, eyeing the other Guardian.

"The bright spot of my day," Collins said flashing a blade thin smile in pleasure.

Morris gave him a predatory smile in return, his eyes on Iarris, looking slowly over every inch of her 6'5" fur and uniform body.

Iarris gave a not so silent growl, fingering her multiple knives, glaring at him through narrowed eyes. Morris just smiled wider, miming crude sexual finger innuendos. Iarris's hand snapped sideways, blurring, before coming front and releasing. The two balanced knives stopped one inch from Morris' face but the first one was actually denting his nose. A drop of blood trickled down from the dent.

The ship's chatter stopped. Morris snarled a Challenge, trying to rip off his seat webbing while standing up. The webbing was shredding but he was still unable to stand.

"Iarris, you know I can't let you kill any of the Marines," Redeyes said amusedly from the side where she was standing talking to one of the pilots. The pilot, taking this as the perfect time to escape from her questions slipped back into the cockpit.

Iarris growled at Redeyes with a curled lip, but she didn't pack any heat in the snarl. "He's a waste of skin." The guardian snapped.

"He's useful waste of skin on missions like this," Redeyes said holding out a hand. The throwing blades glided through the air to nestle into her hand. The blades were oversized for her human hands but not so much so that she couldn't have thrown a killing shot herself.

"Shut up Morris." Redeyes snapped to the snarling marine.

"The Gods damn ship fucking…" His mouth shut with a snap as Redeyes shook her head, closing his jaw with a flick of her telekinesis. She walked slowly down the aisle to stand in front of him but out of reach for either claw or tentacle. Her telekinesis was good but sometimes there was a slip and Morris would feel justified to kill her even if he would have to face her on the sands next reincarnation.

"Iarris, you know you're not allowed to Challenge."

"It's not like you would have let me kill him." Iarris said with a shrug, giving a teeth-baring smile at Morris, sending him into an apoplectic frenzy. "I just wanted to bloody him. A lot." She snapped her teeth at him loudly, her fangs white and wet against her glossy tan fur.

"Stop teasing him, or I'll let him challenge," Redeyes said to her guardian, much like one would to a disobedient teenager. Whether it was Redeyes' voice or the implied threat of meeting Morris on the sand, Iarris clenched her jaw and locked eyes with Collins, who was viewing the whole thing with amusement. He did have his disc-gun under Morris' rib, more as a just in case, like Redeyes feeling particularly lenient and changing her mind about not letting him shoot his former fellow marines than thinking Morris was going to break the God's control.

"Morris." Redeyes turned to face him fully. Her blood red eyes locked onto his as he tried to snarl, writhing locked in his seat by her Power. "If you or your misbegotten siblings kill my Guardian, the person or persons who kill her..." She stopped for a moment to consider her words, "Or him, will have to take their place for twice the length of their sentence."

Morris stopped at this momentarily before trying to writhe out of the seat. The threat meant nothing to him for the chance to rip the Katherian female apart. It was Carris, his brother who put a hand on Morris' shoulder, claws extending into fur finding flesh to get his full attention.

"We understand the full implication, of any actions toward Iarris, Lady Redeyes." Carris said with utmost reverence, no trace of guile in his face or voice. Morris glared at him, but Carris ignored his younger brother's mental frothing.

"You have him under your control?" Redeyes asked mildly, her elbow bending in an un-humanly twist, backward to hand Iarris her blades back. The God never took her eyes off of the experiments.

"Of course. We are all under your province." Carris said with a smile that showed no teeth and no Challenge.

Redeyes narrowed her eyes for a moment before nodding. "Move your brother up to the front where there are still empty seats and keep him contained. Or the next time I will be adding new fur boots to my wardrobe."

Carris eyes dropped down to her boots, that were indeed furred and in the pattern of a Wolfen pelt. He swallowed but nodded his understanding. He released himself from his webbing then took his silently frothing hostile brother to the greenie seats to have a deep conversation for their ears and minds only.

Redeyes watched the two brothers walk away in their

leather harness and tan synthetic baggy pants.

"They are going to try and kill you, Iarris." She said softly to the Katherian.

"Would it be any different than if it were from them or your dreams?" She snapped at the God, glaring.

"No. I suppose not." Redeyes did not look away nor apologize for the danger of her dreams. "Though my dreams kill a lot quicker than they would." With that the God turned and found her way to the cockpit.

Collins leaned forward to put a hand on his partner's knee, his hair falling into his face. Iarris growled but knew better than to swipe a claw at his hand. Collins was fast with his hands in the most dangerous ways. The dangerous part making him fun to fuck. That comment wasn't idle, darlin'. They will try to corner and kill you at some point, making it look like an accident." He brushed the falling hair from his eyes, giving her his full regard. Collins concern was genuine.

Iarris lowered her ears, looking away, making no further comments. Collins pursed his lips but said nothing more, leaning back in his jump seat. She would either survive or die, nothing he could do except hope the next replacement was a bit smarter or less suicidal.

Chapter 14

Morning came but not heralded by a clock or the rising of the sun's soft rays through a window, but the pressing need of a bladder and the knowledge supplies had to be gathered. Lauranya woke to the soggy grey morning, thoughts forming slowly then more and more quickly. Lauranya crawled from beneath warm thick blankets. She counted her lack of dreams during the night a blessing.

Arie disturbed by the bed moving and the lack of her mother's body heat, woke with wide eyes and a bright smile, counter to her mother's sleepy eyes and slow step, she bounded out of bed, beating her mother to the toilet. Lauranya blinked as her daughter squatted then peeing like a gladiator. She shrugged in sleep-induced fog, stumbled to the sink to clean her teeth and brush her hair in long strokes down her back. One whiff of her armpit as she brushed was enough to convince her that a shower should no longer be put off.

The shower was cold by choice, making Lauranya yelp at the first spray but had the benefit of invigorating her faster than drinking a morning stimulant. Halfway through Arie decided to join her.

"Cold! To cold mommy!" Arie spluttered giving her mother a glare of disgust for such a cold shower.

"My shower, my choice silly girl," Lauranya said grinning at the indignity voice her daughter managed as she massaged frothing shampoo dribbling over her face and down her back.

"Warm please," Arie said staunchly standing as far back from the offending water as she could. Her lips pressed primly together as she warded the cold water with her hands.

"If you want to turn the temperature up you may. But slowly so we do not get burned." Lauranya said calmly.

Arie looked at the shower knob and started to turn slowly.

"Stop."

Arie's hand paused on the knob waiting.

"Every movement raises the temperature significantly, so slowly. Test each turn." Lauranya said facing the child against her legs with closed eyes.

Arie turned the water another notch and waited. Two more turns and the water was at an acceptable heat.

"Better mommy?"

"For you, probably child," Lauranya said with humor stepping into the cascading water to rinse the soap from her hair and body.

Arie reached up, touching Lauranya's hip.

"Mommy, why is your bone standing out so funny?" Arie asked frowning as her mother's body had changed and not in a good comforting pillow for a child's head way.

"My bones?" Lauranya looked down in surprise. She looked at her hips and the hollow between the two. She frowned with pursed lips. They had been on their own for not a full week and had only one day of food. "I am afraid this is what happens when food is scarce love. The body can only support so much and uses any extra."

"But you are all poky now!"

"I know; however until we are growing substantial food I will not be able to eat enough to have extra padding over the hips," Lauranya said.

"Micha had hips like that," Arie said innocently comparing her mother to her father's body slave.

"Micha had no choice in how much she was fed and at this moment neither do we." Lauranya's voice dropped a degree or two, trying not to bring the anger at her husband onto her daughter.

She and Tine had for years fought over how the remains of their meals should be disposed. Tine used food as a punishment against Micha for real or imagined slights, so much that Lauranya ended up feeding the girl when Tine left for work, and the boys were out of the apartment. By that point, Lauranya had given up on swaying Tine with reason but did not want to lose face in front of him or his family. The boys would have tattled knowing their father rewarded information on either Lauranya or Micha. Then Lauranya might have been censored for helping a slave over her husband's desires, possibly losing Arie.

"Perhaps we should break our own fast? Yes?" Lauranya asked, pushing the memory of old, and now dead, fights to the side.

"More buns!" Arie perked up excitedly waving her hands at the prospect of the tasty meat filled bread for breakfast again.

"I think we have the remains in the fridge," Lauranya said with a laugh at her daughter's enthusiasm reaching for towels for the two of them.

Arie was enthusiastically drying her hair when she stopped to sniff the air. She bounced across the shower room into the room with the tub before stopping with a squealing "EWWWW!"

Lauranya dropped her towel, running to Arie's side when she too stopped wrinkling her nose. The pile of dirty and wet clothes had started to ferment into a very smelly mess. "Well I guess I know what we need to learn how to do today," Lauranya said holding her nose.

"Stinky!"

"Yes, and we are going to make these less stinky now." Lauranya went to find her computer pad and soap.

The computer pad showed how to make an easy type of clothes washer using materials on hand. The only thing Lauranya did not have was the time to make it. She improvised by filling the tub with hot water and soap gleaned from last night's gathering expedition. The tub filled with enough bubbles to become an overflowing frothy mixture even with only half of the tub filled with water.

Arie squealed in delight at this new adventure. Lauranya was a little less pleased.

"Note to self, much less soap," Lauranya muttered, with hands on her hips and disgust in her voice, as she observed the wasted soap. The water covered the clothes tossed into the tub.

"I am sure we will have a lot of practice in the future," Lauranya muttered in a fit of dark humor.

"Now what mommy?" Arie looked into the tub with hands on the rim and large eyes, weighing the risks of climbing into the tub to enjoy the rare bubbles and risking her mother's ire or tossing care to the wind and swimming like a small, lithe wild thing.

"Now we are supposed to agitate the water."

"Agitate?" Arie looked over at her mother.

"Move the water around," Lauranya said absently, noting the bubbles burst on contact with the thrown in clothing but those bubbles not disturbed by the clothes left towering foamy walls on the back and sides of the tub.

"Oh, so we're going to go swimming in the tub?" Arie asked excitedly throwing a leg over the tub edge ready to start swimming and stomping.

Lauranya caught her daughter around the waist pulling her close. "Not this time dear. The water is far too hot. Once it cools down, we will agitate the clothes and the soap. For right now we are going to let them soak." Lauranya had an idea. "However later this morning if you like you can come and stomp and swim in the tub to facilitate the washing of the clothes in a more expedient manner."

"Help the clothes wash faster?" Arie asked to confirm the large words her mother would drop from time to time.

"Yes, my love. Exactly" Lauranya gave Arie a large smile and a tight hug, before standing up and releasing the child.

Arie squealed in delight as she was going to be able to run rampant through the bubbles a little later that morning. "What's next?" Arie asked excitedly running fingers through the soap bubbles clinging to the side of the tub.

Lauranya hesitated before speaking. "Arie, I have to collect more things today."

Arie looked up at her mother, her face began to crumble. "No!" She started to cry. "Stay! Stay!" Her speech reverting to a much younger age.

Lauranya sat on her knees, pulling Arie, bubble covered hands and all, into her lap. "Shhhh." She rocked the distraught child back and forth. "I do not know how safe this will be, my dear; however," She forestalled Arie's interjection. "I will be back every hour or so and spend a few moments with you."

"But something might happen!" Arie wailed, running a bubbly hand over her tear-streaked cheeks before wrapping her arms tightly around her mother's neck.

"Very true." She thought back to the day before.

Lauranya hugged her daughter tightly, feeling the prickle of tears behind her eyelids thinking of how close she had come to losing her daughter.

"I just want to know you're close mommy." Arie sniffled looking into her mother's green eyes, her lower lip quivering.

"I think I have an idea," Lauranya said gently. "I believe there are a pair of earphones we can talk on while I gather supplies."

"Just like Daddy, Kam and Kar?" Arie asked, sniffling. The earphones had always been a no-touch item unless daddy had been in a very generous mood then he would let her wear one, and they would talk for a moment in separate rooms — a rare and special treat.

"Just like daddy, Kam and Kar," Lauranya whispering in a conspirator's voice.

Arie squealed in delight at the proffered formerly forbidden treat.

"Will that work for being close and still knowing where I am while I work?" Lauranya asked her daughter in a serious tone.

"Yes mommy!" Arie kissed her mother on the cheek. "Now I can chat all day with you!"

Lauranya stood, kissing the top of her daughter's head. "You can talk all day but you will still have to do your lessons." She held up a finger stalling Arie's almost whine. "For every two lessons, you can have one cartoon."

Arie thought hard for a moment. "Ok mommy!" The bribe and the lesson plan accepted.

Lauranya found the earphones while Arie grabbed the cold meat buns from the fridge. Two for her mother and one for her.

"There are another five and one left, mommy. There is also leftover rabbit. Can we eat that for dinner?" Arie asked handing the buns to her mother.

Lauranya took the proffered bun with shaking hands. She knelt on the floor and took a slow bite savoring of the sweet, meaty treat. She swallowed before answering. "We can love. I will not have any time to make something for dinner, so buns and rabbits are perfect."

Arie tried to squeal in happiness but ended up spraying part of the bun she had taken a bite of.

"Arie, love, do not speak with a full mouth. Do not waste the food Oko has gifted us with please." Lauranya chastised gently.

"Who is Oko mommy?' Arie asked biting down into her bun with the hunger of a small child.

"The god of the harvest. The one who bestows his touch on the hydroponics on the ships and the sky garden's so we have food to eat." Lauranya said slowly weighing each word she spoke, feeling the time was right to talk to her daughter of new things. "We do not speak of the Gods to the Undead Gods or the Overseers."

"Why not mommy?" Arie asked looking up from her bun.

Lauranya licked her lips, trying to remember the words of her Noni. "We do not want to offend the Undead Gods."

"Why would they be offended?"

"The Undead Gods are like a jealous man or woman. They want all the attention and get upset if they think you do not adore them singularly. So we make them happy but only talking amongst ourselves about the other, unseen, Gods."

"That's silly!" Arie proclaimed, rolling her eyes like her father.

"It can be. However we still do not want to offend. We praise in private those who are unseen." Lauranya said firmly finishing off her first bun before taking the second one in hand to nibble slowly.

"What are you getting today mommy?" Arie changed the subject in her mercurial way while dusting off fingers on her synthetic shirt.

"The rabbits, the medicine and the last of the hoses and generator parts. Then anything I think we are going to need." Lauranya said licking off the last of the crumbs from her hands. She tucked the second bun into the front pocket of her shirt which could fit hands, card keys and small toys for small children.

Lauranya handed an earphone to Arie, brushing back her hair helping her to situate the small device, then slipped one into her own ear.

"How far away can these work mommy?" Arie's excited voice, exaggeratedly loud, carried into Lauranya's ear canal in a booming burst of sound.

"Ouch! Child please, gently." Lauranya winced. "I can hear you fine. You do not need to shout into the earphones."

"Oh! Sorry, mommy." Arie whispered. "I'll be quieter now."

"And that is almost too quiet." Lauranya's lips twitched in a smile. "Just talk regularly without shouting please."

Lauranya hugged Arie before heading down the elevator. She paused long enough to pick up a stun stick and turning on her laptop to access the main computer. She pulled the grav lift behind her, opening the door into a wet, dark day.

The driving rain was so hard Lauranya could barely keep her feet, there was no thought of even contemplating staying dry, the wind gusted around corners like a wall charge hell-bent on carnage. She had to hold onto the hotel wall to stay upright, ending up with more scraped hands and knees from being thrown into the wall or pulled against the wall from the gusting wind. The grav lift, stopped when she let go of the pull handle, the only thing that didn't seem to mind the rain, but the water was lapping over the top of the lift while the grav lift measured against the road not the water.

At the small intersection, she hunched her shoulders, lowering her center of gravity just to stay standing. The water had risen to mid-calf over the last 24 hours, still flowing downhill yet far more sluggish than before. The water was staying on the saturated ground and not sinking in or flowing downhill as fast as it was.

"Too soon! The water is too high too soon!" Lauranya whispered in horror, the water's slow meandering registering finally. She rubbed her arms as goose pimples spread across the skin on her arms and legs. Fear for lack of time and supplies crawling up her spine, spinning through her brain.

She tried to brush sopping wet tendrils of hair out of her eyes for better sight, but could barely see to where the fields should have been. Everything was under water rippling from the rain, covered in various flotsam and jetsam of dislodged foliage with the occasional bloated animal corpse. Swallowing hard, she slogged through the water a little faster.

At the warehouse the card reader was so slick it took three tries of her key card to get the door open. Her hands shaking did not help. Lauranya yanked the door open, letting in a low wave of water into the building before stepping through. The grav lift barely fit through the open door, scraping along the walls on both sides. She had to jump onto the flat of the grav lift to get to the door, pulling it shut behind her, using both hands before the door latch clicked, locking into place.

Lauranya walked to the front of the grave lift barely causing a dip in the grav's height, before jumping to the cement flooring of the hallway. She glared at the lift more in disgust with herself for bringing it to the building section instead of the warehouse doors.

"I will have to move you to the warehouse, no matter how much you tear into the walls." She said with a last glare before abandoning the oversized grav lift for the moment.

She trotted to the medical section, the stun stick thumping against her leg irritatingly, for the remaining supplies. Nanny hadn't found many medical supplies in the apartments; however, Lauranya was hopeful she could find a few stashes that might have been overlooked. All of the staff had a fear of being shorted supplies for themselves that they kept a few bottles of most things hidden in office drawers or cabinets out of the main line of sight.

The medical office had been thoroughly cleaned out from the obvious cabinets but Lauranya opened every personal drawer and cabinet in every office. There she found the supplies she was looking for, anti-bacterial, anti-viral, pain meds, bandages and everything in between. Not as good if the shuttle crew had not scavenged but better than she had any reason to hope for.

She gathered everything in a waterproof box. There were even enough supplies to fill another box half filled. She found a small rolling box trolley for the boxes with enough room for the rabbits until she could transfer everything to a larger hover lift that wouldn't tip over in the water.

"The Gods provide." She half sang, half whispered, trying to shut down any train of thought on what was going to happen when the supplies ran out.

"What was that mommy?" Arie asked. The sound of water running on Arie's end slightly muffled her voice.

"Nothing baby. Just gathering supplies and about to gather up the rabbits." Lauranya said with false brightness to cover the growing anxiety in her voice.

"Oh! Rabbits. Rabbits are yummy." Arie said with the conviction of a carnivorous connoisseur.

Lauranya huffed out a surprised laugh. "Yes my dear they are very tasty. We will not be able to eat any of these for some time till they have had a chance to grow and multiply a little bit."

"Drat. But we have lots in the freezer, yes?" Arie asked, her voice sounding anxious with the thought of not eating rabbit for a long time, which translated into forever for a young child.

"You will not be deprived of rabbit forever child. There are still a few in the freezer." Lauranya smiled thinking of the boxes of rabbits holding in the freezer.

"Mommy?" Arie's voice turned unusually solemn.

"Yes my love?" Lauranya responded distractedly as she rounded the corner to the children's lab. She breathed a heavy sigh of relief seeing the rabbits still active in their cages. A quick glance showed their water a little low, but otherwise they were fat and sassy.

"Thank you, Osanyin!" Lauranya whispered with a smile. She gathered each cage, stacking them carefully on the rolling dolly. She hunted through the cabinets and drawers for anything useful in this section of the labs. Rabbit food, bedding along with the occasional box of sweet bars, medicine and more than a few bottles of alcohol, both the very bad to the very good. Lauranya chuckled.

"What's so funny mommy?" Arie said, the clinking of dishes and the swoosh of a cloth replacing the sound of water.

"I just found the three lash stash the Overseers were hells bent to find eight weeks ago."

"Oh. Wasn't daddy mad about that also?" Arie asked, the swooshing stopping for a moment.

"Yes, yes he was," Lauranya said finding the largest stash at Jacks desk with a raised eyebrow.

"Everyone brought their bottles to me for safe keeping." Jacks voice whispered in her ear making Lauranya jump with a gasp. "The Overseers were cautious around me after Tramine died shitting himself for five days."

Lauranya stared at the ghost in shock for a moment before shaking her head. The autopsy had proven that phenothalene had been introduced into his system with enough toxicity to kill. The real killer had never been caught. Some random poor slave had been blamed from Tramine's household. She had been chained to the whipping stock and whipped until dead. No one believed she had actually done the killing but the Gods would want a body for a tidy ending to the expensive death of a scientist.

"Mommy?" Arie sounded worried for a moment.

"I am ok, baby." Lauranya glared un-mollified at Jacks' amused and un-repentant ghostly face. "Jacks' ghost was answering an unasked question, but on the bright side I found another source for killing bacteria when the rubbing alcohol runs out." He gave her another grin before fading away. Lauranya glared at the spot he had been at for another moment before sighing and shaking her head. Jacks was…had always been the joker, kind to her but with an edgy sense of humor. Lauranya gave a sad smile; she would miss him sorely. She did not blame him for killing Tramine but the slave had been an innocent bystander.

"You are always soft to the slaves." Came Jacks ethereal voice to the side, causing her to jump yet again.

"Probably. But I never had to worry about ground glass in any of my food either." She said softly gathering up the bottles and other supplies.

She continued to search through the cabinets in case there were any other useful items they would need. When no more items could be found, she gathered up the supplies on hand pulling the dolly slowly around to not topple the cages or boxes with fragile bottles, heading towards the grav lift.

The lights left on from her last trip showed the cement floors still dry without water seepage. The water was mostly contained outside other than what she let inside. Lauranya began to fret over the trip back. Any other trips were going to be more perilous due to the slower deeper waters.

She spent a moment thinking of the remaining trips. "Maybe I can do it in one?"

"Do what in one?"

"Get the last of the supplies in one trip." Lauranya moved the supplies from her small dolly to the grav lift.

"Is it raining too hard to make two?"

"A little bit baby," Lauranya said downplaying her fears, the rabbits making squealing noise at the unusual movement of their cages.

"Mommy, will I get pretty brown like daddy?" Arie asked with the random subject change of the very young.

Lauranya smiled at the question. "No baby, you will be pale like mommy."

"But why are Kam and Kor darker skinned than me?" Lauranya could hear the frown in Arie's voice.

"Hmmm…" Lauranya stopped stacking the boxes and cages to think.

"You don't know?" Arie's voice was incredulous that mommy didn't know everything.

"Arie, I did not say that. I am trying to frame this so that you will have as much an explanation as I had when I was your age." Lauranya said, putting hands on her hips trying to keep the exasperation out of her voice. This was a valid question and one she wanted to answer but carefully.

"Oh. Ok then." Arie was slightly mollified.

Lauranya tried to hide her smile but continued. "Noni Mia told me the story of when the first Undead Gods gathered how they decided that only those with necromancy powers…"

"Necromantic powers?"

"Necromancy, the power to raise and speak to the dead." Lauranya pulled the handle of the grav lift, moving the machinery slowly trying to get a feel for the small space with the oversized piece of machinery.

"Oh! I can do that! The undead cry a lot" Arie said.

Lauranya hesitated for a moment. "Can you hear more than Jacks or Camdia?"

"Umm…" Arie's voice got very quiet.

"What is it baby?"

"I can hear some of the scientists still crying from the shuttle port," Arie said softly. Lauranya voice caught, as her throat closed in pain. It took her two tries to speak.

"We need to send them on love. We'll do that tomorrow if we can." Lauranya shook her head firmly. "No tomorrow. No ifs." Lauranya amended.

"Oh thank you! They aren't very happy." Arie said

perking up at the thought of the crying stopping.

"I am sure they are not, baby. So the Undead Gods decided that those who raised the dead should be pale and distinctive from those who would be fighters, who needed to be able to hide in the shadows or under very harsh sunlight on unusual worlds. Fighters who could protect the weaker necromancer. The necromancer, in exchange for protection, would raise the ghosts of those passed to seek counsel when needed or raise the dead to protect the living."

"So Kam and Kor can never speak to the dead?"

"Possibly, but it is far more likely that they would be fighters if they weren't as smart as their parental genetics point to."

"So they will be a smart scientist who can fight?"

"Something like that baby."

"Will I be a smart scientist who can talk to the dead?"

"I will try to make sure you have all the education I can fill you with so that you will always have something to think about than just spending time with the dead," Lauranya promised Arie, while silently thinking that Arie would never be tested on a ship to be either necro breeding stock or an arena necromancer for entertainment. Lauranya would train her to be a scientist and how to fudge if the ships ever came back any necromancy testing.

"Is spending time with the dead bad?"

"No baby. It is just a tad one-sided though." Lauranya said straight out lying through her teeth to her daughter.

"I don't understand."

"Wait till you are older child."

"I don't like that answer mommy, let's try again!"

"Not this day dear heart. I still have to load the grav lift to get this load in."

Arie was quiet for a few minutes. Lauranya was

grateful for her child but the quiet was nice as she rounded the last hallway to the main doors of the warehouse. She pulled the lift a bit more, moving a few inches at a time. The walls she did not care about but the damage to the grav lift would unrepairable, so slow she went.

"Mommy."

"Yes, dear?" Lauranya stopped pulling the grav lift for a moment, looking up as if Arie were next to her.

"Jacks and Camdia don't think you have all the supplies we need." Arie sounded a little worried.

"Did either say what was missing?" Lauranya looked up from habit as if Arie or even Jacks were standing next to her.

"Not yet."

"Then ask them to tell you what and where things are. That would do more good than wailing." Lauranya said tartly, with pursed lips. She kept the comments on airhead ghosts to herself though.

"Good idea!" Arie said missing the sarcasm in her mother's voice.

Lauranya chuckled then sighed. Talent was both a blessing and a curse. Maybe being so young if untrained the talent would wither away so as to be undetectable when or if the ships came back. Lauranya chewed her lower lip briefly. Arie would need to be trained in science to be considered viable in another field then necromancy.

Lauranya jumped when she heard a crash through the earpiece. "Arie!"

"I'm ok. I dropped a plate." Arie's meek voice came across.

Lauranya's knees went weak with relief. "I think we can spare one plate. However, if you break more than that, we may have to eat out of our hands."

"That would be very messy!" Arie said with profound disgust.

"It would be." Lauranya smiled at the childish outrage from a child who loved getting wet but did not like sticky wet hands. "So make sure to be careful and not break any more dear heart."

"Okay, mommy. I need to sweep now."

"Yes dear."

Lauranya made it to the warehouse thirty minutes slower than expected, but the grav lift was in one piece as were the bottles and the rabbits still alive. She found the seed grains and several more boxes of pollinating insects. The sweet stingers, who made a lovely gooey golden liquid that they stored in community hives, adept at pollinating flowers another blessing by Oko. Their sweet nectar was a luxury on the ships and highly valued.

The other insects were large lovely blue, green beetles that were poisonous if eaten but good at eating the waste material of animals and humans to produce a lovely fertilizing waste of their own. Invaluable with the confined conditions she and Arie would be facing with few waste treatments available.

The plastic boxes of seeds and bugs stacked well next to the rabbits. The generators were a little bulky and heavier than the other items put together. Lauranya had to unpack the grav lift then repack with the generators and seed in the middle and the rabbits on top. Lauranya found hoses in tight coils of various sizes that she strapped along the sides.

She took one last look around the inside of the warehouse, chewing her bottom lip tasting blood from a raw spot. She shook her head in irritation at her own unintended self-mutilation.

"So much still left." She sighed.

"So much what mommy?"

"Supplies baby. Just supplies."

"Can you get them after this trip?"

"I can. I could probably get a second load if I gather everything together for fast loading after dropping these off at the top floor." She stepped back from her load to glean through the bits and pieces, sorting out what she might need, more hosing, plastic piping, more odds and ends for computers, putting necessities to the side awaiting her return. The pile was sizable enough to take up two-thirds of the grav list when she returned.

"Arie?"

"Yes, mommy?"

"I will be heading back to the building in a moment. We can eat a midday meal then I'll make one more return for supplies." Lauranya said with a smile walking back to the grav lift.

"Are we having more rabbit?" Arie voice rose in anticipation.

"We will be having whatever is still in the refrigerator."

"I like rabbit!"

"Good thing we have a few rabbits for breeding stock then."

Lauranya went to the grav lift pulling it to the warehouse doors. She stopped before opening running her hand down the tongue to find the lift setting. The knob was at the lowest setting. She narrowed her eyes at the piece of pinched metal more suited to larger hands.

Chapter 15

The marine's ship came up on the large transport running silent and blending in the emptiness of space. The black non-reflective radar absorbing paint job made sure of that. Redeyes had nixed the idea of putting a fanged mouth on the front of the transport, only because she wanted to sneak up on ships and the fanged mouth was conspicuous if there were exterior cameras. The grumbling was only minimal when logic was applied.

Redeyes stood next to the captain and his co-pilots, not in their line of sight. She was trying not to jostle their elbows at this part, which required a delicate touch.

"Matching speed." The human male said, to the right of the captain.

"Any radar?" The captain growled, in an almost whisper, swiveling an ear to the Katherian behind him, as his four arms were busy with controls.

"Not since the last venting time you asked." The female Katherian snarled softly, her eyes and ears glued to the sensors in front of her. Her tail lashed twice emphasizing her irritation with the captain.

"Time to reach out and touch some dead meat in 30... 29...28." The captain flicked an ear to Redeyes, giving her the seconds she would have to get into her own drop position. Redeyes dashed out the cockpit, springing up the stairs to hit the lower catwalk between the second and third tier of seated marines, emitting a piercing whistle calling for her Guardians. She ghosted through the catwalk feet first, solidifying inches above the floor of the ship.

Collins and Iarris unsnapped their webbing harnessing as fast as possible, grabbing their packs, slithering through the railing almost as fast as the God herself, meeting at the middle of the marine carrier floor with three seconds to spare.

"Go! Go! Go!" The captain's voice carried over the intercom, as a slight shudder went through the carrier. The shuttle had landed on the back of the Dead Gods transport, nestling belly to back, metal to metal. Redeyes grabbed the arms of both of her companions, ghosting the three of them through the hulls of both ships. With arms holding tightly, both guardians glued their bodies to hers.

"Try not to get us caught halfway between, eh?" Collins said, in a mocking tone to partially hide his fear. Iarris didn't even bother trying to keep terror from her face, her ears flat, wrapping one arm around Redeyes' waist, as they ghosted between ships. Iarris squeezed her eyes closed tightly.

"Pfft. I've only done that once and that was before you were born." Redeyes said before their heads disappeared between their ship and they showed feet first in the next shuttle.

"And I'd like to keep it that way!" Collins whispered, emphatically in her ear, lover close. His breath tickling the hairs on the back of her neck.

The three of them tucked up their feet until Redeyes could rotate them from parallel with the ship hull to horizontal. The ship seemed to be on a night cycle as most of the plush overstuffed chairs were reclined, filled with sleeping humans under various types of covers or coats. The slaves slept, stacked in bunks along the walls with only inches between and above the stacked bedding. One in three had covering. Those without blankets curled into tight balls shivering while trying to get some rest before the hell of a world ship life came to their new life.

"Guards?" Iarris asked. Her question was a whisper's breath in Redeyes and Collin's brain. Katherian telepathy was useful for stealth.

Redeyes shook her head, pointing her chin at the few men and women carrying whips. "No guards, only Overseers." Redeyes breathed back. "House and body slaves, no guards needed."

"Easy work today." Collins' voice held a smile, as he licked his lips in anticipation. The human was born for this job, more so than most other marines.

"Cocky men die as easy as stupid," Iarris responded, her mind's voice hissing in irritation at Collins' easy attitude, not taking deadheads seriously, even if they were only scientists.

"We have 90 more seconds before High Sarge's team starts cutting through. You two ready?" Redeyes wasn't really asking. Her guardians flashed matching grins waiting for mayhem.

The drop was swift, Redeyes and Collins landing in front of one standing Overseer, with almost Katherian fast reflexes. The Overseer started to draw back, raising a whip for a devastating overhand blow. Iarris, however, dropped behind him, prepared with a large dagger drawn, 18 inches of battle-forged steel slid between spine and shoulder blades as easy as a surgeon's micro-scalpel slicing genes. The Overseer dropped to the floor with a surprised look on his face — an inglorious death.

"Down! Down! Down!" Redeyes roared as Collins shot anyone who stood up or rose from their seats.

Iarris started a telepathic roar, echoing Redeyes message. "Get down and stay down, or by your fucking dead organ composting piece of shit Gods, I will show your brains the light of space minus your skull!" The ship's passengers clutched their heads, as Iarris' message bounced through their brains. Few deadheads could keep out a telepath, and these deadheads were no exception.

The scientist froze in their seats, the slaves curled up tighter in their bunks, clutching their knees and praying to their Gods to be overlooked, as the Katherian and the renegade God moved through the ship. Only the true Gods with their undead servants and some of their elite fighters could withstand such a barrage, but even that was the exception, not the rule, and this ship had no Gods, other than the escaped God Redeyes.

"Getting a bit graphic there aren't you, Red?" Iarris 'pathed to her. The God's eyes turning human green. Emotions turning her eyes from their normal red to human.

"Not even close enough for any of the corpse fuckers to be flinching. Yet." Redeyes snarled, her lips pulled back showing slightly fanged teeth.

"Collins!" Redeyes yelled to the fast moving human, who was shooting at seemingly random people standing in the way with a gleeful manic cheer, like a hot knife through warm suet.

"Already on my way!" He ran pell-mell through the corridor, trying to make the cockpit before the captain could break out the weapons. Bodies piled up in the hallway's open passage, marking Collins' path forward.

Some few, felled by Collins, were still writhing and alive but not for long. Their screams filled the halls with the warning that the invaders meant to kill. Between screams from the wounded and dying and the mental barrage from Iarris, it was an effective one-two punch. Putting military and civilians on their asses and stomachs fast. Children clutched parents; most cried silent tears too terrified to scream. Parents held children tightly, their touchstone for calm.

Redeyes nodded to Iarris. Iarris followed Collins, slower. She took the time to dispatch the wounded deadheads, who would only stress out their own medical staff and supplies, quickly and quietly. Redeyes moved to the end of her part of the corridor, alternating gun and sword in upper and lower hands. No one on the ships would look at the human God. The passengers, still seated, lowered their eyes and faces, refusing to meet those terrifying blood eyes of hers. Redeyes noted, in the back of her brain, the smell of shit and decay emanating from every angle, not just the slave horizontal pens. Whoever was in charge of this ship didn't care for the human cargo, slave or civilian.

"High Sarge got the ship secured. You ready to jump?" Iarris sent across the short space.

"We're already in suits and out the door. Tell Redeyes to have tea and biscuits for us." Iarris could taste High Sarge's adrenal surge as she pushed out into space from their ship's portal.

"You're on your bloody own for that one. I'm babysitting the bloodthirsty human." Iarris retorted to High Sarge. Iarris saw one of the passengers ahead of her try to sit back up while reaching out to another across the aisle. Iarris backhanded the reaching passenger, then kicking the one trying to hand off. The handoff person slumped in his chair, out cold or dead; she didn't stop to check, while the attempted receiver slumped, clutching a broken nose bleeding profusely. He made no more sound than coughing whimpers.

"The one that's been trying to jump your bod for a bit?" High Sarge 'pathed back, as she led her team to the deadhead shuttle on a short spacewalk.

"Fuck you and yes." Iarris could feel her mental blush bloom, even as she scanned each row in front of her.

"Gods! You did sleep with him!" High Sarge said, almost stopping mid spacewalk, surprise flavoring her words.

"Not talking about it!" Iarris said, wiping the blood off her dagger on a convenient body's shirt.

"We'll see about that." High Sarge said, smugly closing the connection that lasted less than ten seconds total.

"Iarris!" Redeyes roared, from her end of the ship.

"Passenger end secured!" Iarris roared back through the short shuttle.

Redeyes put up the gun and swords from her upper arms, so the hands could tap into the computer at the shuttle's hatch.

"Cockpit secured. Message sent to High Sarge." Iarris said. Collins was finishing a brutal assault on the two pilots remaining, with his fist and the butt end of his own pistol.

Sixty seconds in and the ship was effectively immobilized. Redeyes allowed a small smile, showing teeth coldly, her hands flying over the flat screen in front of her. She was relying on Iarris to catch anyone moving out of their seats towards her, as the God bent over the arrays to open the doors for the marines.

"Blood," Iarris growled loudly to Redeyes.

Redeyes looked up with a scowl of concentration. "Pilots?" The software was booby-trapped, making navigation tricky. The pilots hadn't been able to blow the information but that didn't mean the information was easy to find.

Iarris flicked an ear at the one pilot who had tried, a tall dark-skinned man with blood red hair. He had been shot twice in the chest and once in the head. Collins was unstrapping the body, to toss into the hallway out of his way. The other two pilots were a bloody mess.

"Just one. Mostly the passengers." Iarris took the deadweight from Collins to toss to the side where the other bodies were piled up by luck, not design.

"Deaths?"

Collins was sliding into the open pilot seat, ignoring the whimpers of pain from the sole conscious pilot, her blond hair matting on her face with blood and snot. Collins reached for a series of buttons close to her, causing her to throw bruised and broken hands, toward her face and chest in a vain attempt to block a possible blow. Collins snorted with disdain, as he continued to get control on his end of the ship.

"Other than current?" Iarris said, with an unabashed grin, leaning against the cockpit door jamb.

Redeyes looked up at her guardian, with a less than amused look, splitting her attention between the door and Iarris.

"A few, but not enough for the bleed out smell I'm getting."

"Check the passengers for whip marks, broken bones and split skins. The ones with whips are Overseers, they can be spaced."

"Really?" Collins yelled, from the front hopefully.

"For you, that's a maybe." Redeyes snapped back.

"Killjoy." He muttered, hands floating over the keyboards. Redeyes too far to hear his words.

"Think kill is more the word you want," Iarris said, in a sotto voice for his ears alone.

"Hence the pleasure," Collins said with a grin, wiping his lower lip with the edge of his left hand. A trace of blood smeared on his hand, which he licked off with a smile and a twitch of an eyebrow to Iarris.

"Sick fucker for a human. No wonder you like the experiments so well." Iarris said, with a roll of her eyes, as she turned back to the passengers to look for Overseers.

"No, not really that sick, but I do understand where they are coming from." He said, softly knowing that she would still be able to hear him.

"Are we confirming all passengers as keepers?" Iarris raised her voice for Redeyes to hear.

"Yes!" Redeyes yelled down the aisle, her mind clearly not on Iarris anymore. "Ahh! There you are, my love." Redeyes breathed, working through the final trap before hitting the payload of information.

"Hands up!" Iarris growled to each sitting row of passengers she stepped to. The slaves would have to have their pens opened before she could check them, but they weren't a threat locked up. The seated passengers' hands went up with various levels of ease. Most showed signs of abuse, no matter the age, fear, pain or just apathy showing in their eyes. Those who did not have obvious signs of abuse or have the empty eyes the others showed, she marked as possible Overseers.

Iarris worked her way down to Redeyes again. "We aren't giving them a scan choice to stay or go?" She asked.

"No. Scan them but try not to do any more damage. We have enough trouble with the mental issues, on top of any scanning damage we do. So try to tread lightly." Redeyes was watching the Marines' progress, marrying the space locks together.

"Just weed out the Overseers?" Iarris said, annoyed that she'd have to go through the passengers again, her hands fondling the pommels of her knives longingly.

"And Gods but I don't think there are any on this ship.

Manifest was wrong." Redeyes said, putting three hands on the ship's portal lock. Redeyes looked up at Iarris, her eyes turning human. "If you find a God, I'll question them before I space them." Her body, wire tight, belied the easy words for the amount of hate contained.

"Locked and airtight." High Sarge said, pushing into the middle of the conversation on Iarris' side.

"You're good to go," Iarris said. Cold was all she thought about her God, with a shudder as she turned back down the aisle. Shaking her head, she swallowed hard but kept her mind on the task. Knowing you were helping someone didn't mean the help wasn't damaging, for her it meant doing some damage to free another. Iarris kept this firmly in mind as she started her mental probe. She delved only deep enough to determine if they were anything other than a slave or civilian.

"Iarris," Redeyes called out.

Iarris looked back at her God, with a questioning frown between deep-set brows. "If and when you ever read the mind of a God, you'll begin to understand. Don't think I'm heartless until you can read one of their minds. Then go speak to Meagin." Redeyes said, eyes still green and voice of such quiet rage that came from hate so pure it could only be cold as the ice forming on an unpowered space suit.

"Yes, Lady." Iarris swallowed hard, turning back to the passengers, her hands not as steady on the back of the chairs as they were originally.

"Mits, Claft, Tree." Redeyes barked at the incoming Marines, who were lining up in the open area behind the seated Deadheads. The three Katherians stepped forward as if their tails were on fire. "Help Iarris, scan all their minds. We're looking for Overseers and Gods." Mits opened his generous mouth, white surrounded by tortoiseshell orange-brown and black. Redeyes cut off his question, having heard it from him before. "NO!" she snarled. "No images to the minds on what is next."

"But the creed." Mits was stubborn on insisting on mental rights for non-telepaths, to the point of being stupid in arguing with the God in a temper.

"Isn't being applied here." High Sarge growled, from behind him. Mits jumped three feet in the air, spinning to face the threat. However, a finger pushed into his chest by High Sarge overbalanced him, causing the tall Katherian to stagger backward into Tree.

"Good execution, bad form. Going to cost you on the mat tomorrow, kitten." High Sarge growled, in pleasure. Mits ears went flat against his skull. Tomorrow was going to hurt.

"You three have the best neutral touch with humans, now start using it!" High Sarge snapped her teeth together loudly at the three Katherians. They looked at each other then nodded as one to High Sarge. They didn't want High Sarge to rip their ears off with her teeth. They edged by Redeyes with her human eyes, focused coldly on their throats.

"I think we're all going to be on the mats tomorrow." Claft 'pathed, moving up the aisle to the left slowly as she scanned the scared humans.

"I'm just hoping to survive the day, let alone tomorrow," Mits said, morosely. He took the middle aisles. He could tell Iarris had been through; there were overly active and painful neurons still firing. He tried to soothe those active ones while coaxing the human's own body to produce endorphins of pleasure. The best he could do to help, under these conditions.

"Then stop arguing for the deadheads till they are civilized!" Tree said, with exasperation. She took the slaves in the pens on the right. Iarris hadn't hit this side so they weren't in pain, yet. She delved skillfully and quickly looking for key memories or associations with whips, beatings, and death by the slave's hand to another.

The three worked quickly going through the entire scientist, slaves, and others. Iarris and Collins rounded up those who were identified as Overseers. Their fate was already sealed. Overseers didn't transition well onto the runner's ships.

The Overseers found were brought to the front bulkhead, before the cockpit.

"Ok, this will tickle for a moment…" Iarris said, tying down the straps with a savage twist on the six humans. Four men and two women, each one with eyes colder than the last. The smallest woman had a free-flowing cut on her forehead, dripping blood over pale skin. Her straight lanky brown hair kept falling over the cut. Each flip to keep hair from her eyes, throwing a little more blood on herself and others. This did nothing to improve any of their overall looks.

The Overseers clothes were disheveled and torn. All had fought with the Marines after being scanned and ousted as an Overseer. One of the men's jaws was broken. His dark skin, puffy, turning a darker shade of brown. He had sunk his sharply chiseled teeth into Mit, taking out a chunk on the Katherian's shoulder, missing the artery by a millimeter. Claft and Iarris had beaten the human down, in a blur. He lived, but just. The other five had been sent small stunning mental blasts, after the biting incident, rendering the Overseers unconscious till the other humans could be removed and these six safely bound.

"No Gods," Iarris said, admiring her handiwork with the straps. The glares from the angry humans just made her flash sharp white teeth wider.

"Too bad," Redeyes said, gliding up behind her. Redeyes lower hands brushing the backs of the reclining shuttle chairs, her upper arms stretching out. A loud pop as a couple of joints cracked back into place. "Everyone else removed?" Her gaze fell over the mostly empty shuttle. The last of the humans, being removed in bags, floated out the door.

Iarris tilted her head for a second sending out a broad questioning pulse. Tree and Cleft responded in kind. "No one left but us. All the deadheads are aboard the ship in stasis bags."

"Tell the Marines we aren't waking them till we are on the main ship. We don't want a damn "sleeper" blowing up our ride home. Keep them asleep and easily stacked till we're home." Redeyes nodded, distractedly her memory on another mission. "Let's be about this then." Her smile was as sharp as her chopping hand motion.

"Lady," Iarris said, with a nod and a flick of her tail. She padded out the door, gathering the two remaining Marines without looking back.

Redeyes walked to the front slipping a small data clip into the shuttle's system port. The program began to glow green, a few keystrokes later and there was a beep as the systems synched up. Redeyes' program cozied up to the original program, making course suggestions outside the original programmed parameters.

"Heading over in three." Redeyes pathed, to High Sarge.

"Bringing the Overseers or leaving them?" High Sarge was able to path, while still barking at her troops. "Get those damn bodies hung up so we don't step on them. Nothing like opening a damn stasis bag and finding gooey bits instead of human! Makes dinner too damn gross and I hate being put off my feed!"

"They are staying." Redeyes' voice was malicious, as she eyed the glaring Overseers. "They can survive for three days without water but they might be able to break free of the straps and find substance on the ship."

"Pfft. We stripped that ship of everything but the insulation." Came Iarris's sly response as she caught the tail end of the 'path.

"Lazy Kat." Redeyes teased fondly.

"Damn straight woman! You keep us going like a damn high and mighty god or something."

"You'd do nothing but lick your fur and cough up hairballs if I didn't." Redeyes pathed back, as she slipped into the transfer tube between ships, unhooking their tube from the dead ship, without a glance at the Overseers she was leaving behind. "Water won't be their problem though. They'll run out of oxygen in less than a day." Redeyes' smile was pure evil.

"Ewww. You are such a barbarian." Iarris rolled her eyes in disgust. "Not saying they aren't worth the death, but we should have just shot them." High Sarge listened to the telepathic banter with amusement before turning to the two marines nearest her. "Get the tube back here! We're leaving as soon as Redeyes is on deck." Her voice barked out, causing a fresh scurry among the troops not already strapping in bodies or strapped into their seat. No reason to be slow now.

"That's God Barbarian to you!" Redeyes said primly, as she floated almost serenely back to her own shuttle and people. "For what they do, no. They can suffer the same uncertainty and pain they've given. The circle is a bitch."

"Uh huh." Iarris wasn't going to naysay the God, but there were days Redeyes was very bloodthirsty. Today was one of those times.

High Sarge's nails clicked on the metal flooring as she

touched one of the hanging bags. Largest to the back while the smallest were to the front. There were going to be a few extra medical issues among the deadheads from prying the small ones from their parents' arms. High Sarge grimaced, hating the separating part. She reached a hand to one small bag, her nails carefully retracted. "Soon enough child, you will be with your mother." She whispered so softly that her voice was but a breath from her lips.

Chapter 16

The first drop off went smoothly. The day was still young and Lauranya was still fresh. She and Arie would be able to have a good but quick lunch after the initial unloading. The rabbits they moved next to the chickens, everything else was stocked piled in the hallways and rooms. Lauranya did a scan of the incubators. All was green still.

"Mommy the hallway is filling quickly," Arie observed as she eeled between the boxes, bags and sundry items.

"Are you saying we're becoming messy?" Lauranya said with a teasing smile, moving a couple of the larger seed barrels so the lift could maneuver between.

Arie stopped for a moment, contemplating. "Messy yes and not very origami."

"Organized." Lauranya laughed. "If these were origami we could fold them into different shapes and hang them from the walls for decoration until needed." Lauranya stood up, putting her hands behind her back and bent backward then forwards then twisted. A subtle popping sound accompanied by an "aaaah" of relief. Her ribs still screamed but it was to be expected.

"Why can't we fold these up?" Arie was curious, pressing her hands to the plastic sack of one container.

"Besides the fact we are running out of time and that many of the materials are actually stronger than we are physically?"

"Yes." Arie looked up with the confidence and

whimsy of a child's perspective but without the physics of an adult's world.

"We" Lauranya motioned to herself and Arie but encompassed more "are not supreme beings who can control the physical realm, such as this barrel's shape, with our minds. We have to use machines or brute force. However, until the time when matter bends to our minds we make do with shapes and sizes we can easily or mostly manipulate into the space provided."

Arie's brow crinkled as she contemplated the seed barrel her mother was using for a demonstration. "That makes sense." She looked up at Lauranya then. "Can we have lunch now?"

"Yes, my growing bottomless pit. We can go and have the remaining yummy rabbit!" Lauranya's stomach growled in anticipation. Lunch was eaten quickly yet there was time made for snuggles and a few tickles.

Lauranya left with the grav lift and a smile. Things were not as bad as they could be; she thought to herself exiting the elevator.

The day was still wet and gloomy, but the sun managed to illuminate some of the street and warehouse. Lauranya heard the rumbling cough of whiskered cats. Their rough territorial calls coming from the forest. Closer than before. She shivered picking up the pace, pulling the empty lift faster to the safety of the warehouse walls.

Once inside she leaned against the wall, with her heart thudding in her chest. Water dribbled down into her face, mixing with the hair in her face and tears on her cheek, puddling on the floor, squelching in her shoes. She gave an angry swipe to the falling tears with her hand, flinging the droplets to the floor. She gathered her sodden hair in her hands, tying the hair up into a crude knot at the back of her neck to keep the wet mass from blinding her in a curtain of wet tendrils.

"Again to the sands, my family, to the sands!" Lauranya muttered to herself as she headed to the warehouse for the final list of items. Ties, tools, another barrel of seeds and a box of small fruit tree seeds and roots gleaned from the lab. The last of the rotgut bottles of alcohol from Jacks desk and the other lab offices. A bag of small medical supplies syringes scalpels, needles, sutures gauze strips and adhesives. Another bag of tools for fixing computers and one for fixing larger furniture issues, hammers, screwdrivers, pliers, two crowbars and several pairs of sharp scissors. She found a bonus bag of worms, more valuable than a fur blanket on a world ship. Each item precious for the coming years' survival.

Lauranya found several sets of training swords. Nothing with an edge but the hard plastic could do some serious damage if swung right. Lauranya gathered these as well, more on a whim then need. "Arie would like to know how to use these at some point I am sure." She grinned, thinking of her own free range run time on the training sands when the gladiators were on break, and her grandfather was feeling magnanimous. She could do a few katas but not the serious training. Not that the two of them would have need of sword fighting. They too went on the pile of gleaned items.

Lauranya found a half pallet of paper left behind. She chewed her lips, contemplating use versus practicality. Not as precious as food sources but the paper would be invaluable as she did research and wanted a hard backup copy just in case. "And I have the room. So it comes with us!" She nodded firmly, justifying her want.

Lauranya stacked everything next to the warehouse door. There were three piles of items for loading. She looked around the warehouse anxiously. So much still left and only so much room and time.

She had to shake her head. "When I am done with today's items then we come back for a final gleaning. I cannot be distracted." She spoke firmly. The sound of her voice was more to ease the anxiety than to note she might actually be missing something important.

The second load went quickly and smoothly, without tipping or crushing the items on the bottom of the lift. Having several days of practice packing, Lauranya was getting very good at packing with more items then she would have thought humanly possible prior to this experience. The lift hovered 2 feet off the concrete and was packed as high as her head. Lauranya grinned like Arie with a piece of candy, as she admired her handy work. The day was already looking good.

Tomorrow might see the end for gathering supplies. Lauranya gave a wan smile at this thought, brushing a stray strand of hair from her face. A day without moving or racing the rain, what would she do? "Chase a child and organize what we have." She huffed in humor at her own musings, opening the warehouse door to a fresh drenching for this load.

"Ufff!" She exhaled as the water caught her off guard as she had been daydreaming of a non-packing day. She pulled the lift out a few feet then closed the warehouse door behind her. No sense inviting wildlife to explore where she might be back later.

The water was almost up to her knees. The short time in the warehouse had seen the water table rise precipitously in a very scary way. Lauranya bit her lip. "Nova. Will there even be time to get the last two loads?" She hissed out, sloughing through the water with the hov lift in tow. The lift wobbled in response to her tugging, responding sluggishly. The water interfered with the lift hovering. The water giving way to the gravitational push, instead of resisting as the stone or roads would.

Lauranya's tugged the lift through knee deep water and thrumming rain coming down in sheets. Everything was slippery. Her shoes were no better than if she were in bare feet against the flowing water. Keeping upright was as much an effort as moving forward.

The unstable footing and sluggishly responding lift kept causing variations in movement and lift height. A low growling snarled pulled Lauranya from her fearful reverie of what still needed to be done. Lauranya froze, then looked up slowly. A whiskered cat was in front of her. He…no she, heavy dugs but no kits in evidence, was low to the ground, belly close to the water, her ears flattened to her head and a lashing tail, fifteen feet in front of Lauranya. The cat kept tossing its head side to side, giving a low rough yowl or random snarls either at Lauranya or the skies deluge. The cat seemed upset and disoriented, not able to fathom the water displacing disaster the world had become.

Lauranya went still; the water at her knees tugging her downhill, as she observed the prowler. They weren't her world specialty however she did know this behavior was not typical. The whiskered cat should have three or four cubs with her, Lauranya thought as she stood frozen, waiting, her mind working where her body was just now registering flight or fight mode. Even frozen in fear, she wished for her tablet to observe this phenomenon as a footnote to several other papers already done by other researchers.

When the lift dipped for the third time, almost touching the water, Lauranya missed the tug of the handle going down as she watched the cat in front of her.

Another whiskered cat screamed from behind

Lauranya. She jumped, turning her head enough to see the cat up on top of the lift, heavy enough to cause the lift to drop almost a foot so that he was only slightly higher than eye level. The lack of flight instinct and scientific ivory tower mentality saved her life, as she tilted her head and her body slightly to the left to admire the large beast. The feline aimed what was supposed to be a stunning blow to where her head had been. The whisker cat missed her head by inches, but the claw swipe took her on the meat of the scapula and part of her bicep. The sound of ripping flesh audible over the rain. Lauranya tried to give a terrifying pain filled scream of her own, flailing backward into the water, but her voice refused to come.

She landed on her back, flood waters flowing over her pushing her down the road a few feet. The prowler pounced to where he had last seen his prey go under. He came up without his prey from the deep water; snarling in frustration. The whiskered cat cast around for his prey that had temporarily escaped. He saw Lauranya as her head and shoulders came out of the water. He bounded over to her in a floundering splash to finish off his still living meal.

Lauranya's tumble backward, left her sucking in a mouth full of water and fumbling for the shock stick at her side with her right hand. The left arm was not registering pain yet, but Lauranya knew it would be any second. She sat up, coughing out water. She made it to her knees bracing to sit up, as the water flowed over her shoulders.

Lauranya saw a large dark shape looming over her, rising for a final pounce. She threw herself to the side, going under the water once more while still keeping ahold of the shock stick. The whiskered cat hit the spot she had been missing her as the flowing water pulled him down the road. He did manage to hook claws into Lauranya's calf, as he went by. This time the pain was not delayed, as the cat's claws ripped downward into the meat of her leg, pulling out as she continued to roll away and the water pushed him downhill.

Lauranya choked on the tepid rushing water as she opened her mouth to scream. She started to panic between the pain and the drowning breath. She stood up trying to cough and breathe at the same time. The cat saw her stand as he found purchase on the man-made road. He bounded, in splashing leaps towards her, snarling his displeasure at the work required to catch a meal in the rain.

Lauranya reacted without thinking, adrenaline coursing through her veins. She lunged at the cat, activating the shock stick. The shock stick connected with the whiskered cat's wet fur and flesh, sending volts of electricity over his entire body, not just the contact spot.

The cat opened his mouth wide, trying to give voice to the agony as his muscles spasmed and his legs collapsed, toppling the great beast over. The scream worked to Lauranya's benefit. The cat went under the knee-high water unable to move and drawing breath through jaws locked open. Had the water been less deep he would have survived, as it was his head fell under the knee-high water filling his lungs in a matter of seconds.

The electricity though was no tame pet. She heard the zzzpt as the shock stick crackled on but did not see the whisker cat go under as the current flowed from the cat over the wet stick and up into Lauranya's arm. The volt of electricity was less than what she hit the whiskered cat for but only because the cat had taken the brunt of the energy bolt. She fell to her knees, her own muscles spasming as the lesser charge covered her body. The force which she had hit the cat had caused a minor cracking in the plastic casing. This would not have been an issue if not for the torrent of rain and the flowing water creeping into the device causing it to short circuit, saving Lauranya's life in the process.

"Mommy!" Arie's voice in Lauranya's ear cut through the fog of pain.

"I am here baby." Lauranya's voice was no more than a whispering cough as she found herself on her knees in the flowing water up to her chin.

"Get up! Jacks says more whiskered cats are coming!" Arie's whisper was high pitched and breathless with fear as she relayed the information to her mother.

"Ok baby." Arie's fear cut through part of the fog and pain clouding Lauranya's brain. Lauranya's knees wobbled, as she tried to stand again the injured leg collapsed underneath her, pitching her forward into the water. Lauranya caught herself with her good right arm, scraping the palm. She moved forward slowly, crawling through the water on one good leg and one good arm. The injured leg added some stability, but her left arm was too shredded to do more than hang at her side. She half crawled half staggered to the lift's tongue, trying to grasp the handle.

"Leave the lift Mommy!" Arie's voice was demanding in her fear.

"I cannot baby. This is the last of the medical." Lauranya said through gritted teeth. She managed the tongue of the lift in her right hand, turned to face the tower, only to come face to face with the other whiskered cat.

"Osanyin, please protect me," Lauranya whispered as the smaller female cat moved towards her. The cat shook her head, giving one more yowling cry before it too bounded up-stream towards the hills, ignoring the strange two-legged creature that had killed a stronger male.

Lauranya leaned back onto the lift, breathing hard as water cascaded over and around her, trying not to cry or blackout, but it was close. She staggered forward pulling the lift one step at a time. Distance measured by each limping step and pain filled breath.

"You're almost to the door mommy." Arie's voice was encouraging.

"Thank you baby," Lauranya whispered. She stumbled to the back of the building, ashen-faced, her limbs trembling with every step, to find Arie at the open service door. Lauranya did not have the energy to scold her child of the dangers, so grateful of the ready door to fall into. Lauranya pulled the lift into the elevator then slid down the back wall to slump against the floor.

She did not remember reaching the top floor until Arie roused her. The child had moved the lift into the main room before going back for Lauranya.

"Mommy? Jacks says we need to get your wounds cleaned." Arie leaned over her mother with a worried look, as Arie patted Lauranya's face.

"Ok love. I am getting up." Lauranya staggered up. Arie slipped a metal rod, to work as a cane, into her hand for support. Lauranya took the stairs slowly, leaning on the gleaming banister heavily. Each step was excruciating, but Lauranya gritted her teeth and let the tears pour down her cheek as Arie offered encouragements.

Finally, Lauranya pushed through the double doors of suites designated as the medical lab, moving towards the medical supply counter. The supplies she needed were already laid-out next to a longer table.

"Arie…how did these get here?" Lauranya asked, numb with pain, her brain vaguely noting the laid out supplies.

"Jacks told me where you had put the medical supplies and what you would probably need."

"Ok love, I need to…" The room was starting to blur around Lauranya.

"You need to have the wound swabbed then sealed then bandaged." Arie said with a serious look on her face.

"Yes…that." Lauranya was fading fast. "Jacks talking to you now?"

"Yes! So I can help you better." Arie said with a proud smile puffing out her chest on a job well done.

"You did very well baby," Lauranya said, her words starting to slur.

"You need to have the wound swabbed then sealed and bandaged." Jacks voice came from her left side. She turned her head to see Jacks but the edges of her vision were going dark.

She turned back to the laid-out supplies, reaching for the swab. "Yes…that." Her voice was becoming distant in her own ears.

"I got it mommy!" Arie's small hands darted to the correct medical supplies.

Lauranya looked at her bright-eyed blonde child with a slight frown. "Arianya, you have never done a swab or a flesh seal."

"Nope, but you're shaking really badly." She looked at her mother solemnly.

Lauranya looked down at her hands. They were shaking, shaking like loose plastic sheeting in a windy ventilator shaft.

"Need to get the wounds closed, Jacks." She said to the ghost who faded out of view again.

"Noted odd bacterial and viral growth in the fur and under the claws, possibly from saliva or scat. Something internally derived." Arie intoned, slightly cross-eyed, channeling Jacks.

Lauranya stared at Arie, who was blinking to uncross her eyes from the channeling. Lauranya swallowed hard and was very grateful they were not on a ship. Her daughter would never be free if they were.

"Make sure Jacks guides your hands," was all she said instead.

"He said it should be fairly easy. You have good veins." Arie tilted her head, knowing there was a joke the adults weren't telling her.

Lauranya smiled faintly at this. Jacks had told her this many times when she had come to him for medical help on the side.

Lauranya eased onto the floor before she completely lost the use of both legs. Arie laid out a clean sheet next to her and a pillow. Arie then got all the supplies she would need to tend her mother. Arie cocked her head to the side a few times, asking questions out loud, looking serious when she wasn't talking as if someone were talking to her. Lauranya smiled faintly; someone was talking to her.

"Thank you Jacks." She whispered, starting to fade, the pain increasing to the point of tears. Arie came over, with a filled hypo from one of the small ampules, then pressing the hypo to Lauranya's neck on the non-damaged side of her body.

"Jacks says the next part will hurt." She stopped for a moment, listening. "A lot," she said sadly.

"I know, baby. Cleaning a wound is never pretty. And the claws ripped through the skin and muscle, leaving the edges ragged." Lauranya agreed, trapped in her haze of pain. The pain medication hadn't taken effect yet.

"Jacks says I should get you to talk while I do this, in case something goes wrong or he misses something." Arie hesitated, the hypo in her hand still as she looked worried.

A small wrinkle forming between her brows.

"I will, dear." The pain was starting to blunt the edges. "Jacks will walk you through everything and I will try not to squirm too much."

"Ok, mommy." Arie's eyes filled with tears. Her voice got rough as her throat started to close, choking on her emotions. "I don't wanna hurt you!"

"You are a brave girl, love. And I need you to be mommy's hands for just a little bit please." Lauranya asked in a calm voice, the one she pulled out to instill confidence for dangerous projects.

Arie grabbed a small square of absorbent synthetic sponge, dipping it into the cleaning solution. She started to daub the wound on Lauranya's shoulder.

"Baby, you'll need to help me take the shirt off first," Lauranya said gently even as the astringent brought tears to her eyes, as she started to tug on the top, she forgot and tried to move the left arm, hissing in pain.

"Oh! Right!" Arie started to pull Lauranya's shirt up before stopping. "Jacks says it would be easier just to cut it off."

"He is probably right." Lauranya quit trying to move for a moment, letting her arms slump to her side.

"I'll get scissors!" Arie bounced to the counter with the sponge still in her hand. She started to hum looking for small sharp surgical scissors. "Here they are!" She exclaimed excitedly, holding up the shiny pointed instrument.

"Good for you, baby," Lauranya said with a pained smile.

Arie trotted back to her mother's side, putting the sponge on the sheeting while she bent over her mother and carefully began to snip off the shredded shirt she was wearing. The task took only a few minutes, but those few minutes were enough for the pain medication to take effect. Lauranya still felt some pain but she was not inclined to cry nor really move if she did not have to.

"What should I do with the shirt?" Arie asked holding up the offending garment for Lauranya's inspection. Lauranya noted that the shirt, even after being in the rain and runoff was coated in a lot of blood. Her blood. "Throw it into a trash can."

"Ok!" Arie ran over to a carved trash basket lined with plastic, throwing the useless garment inside.

"We will need to do the same for my pants love," Lauranya said, as her brain finally processed that the leg would need to be cleaned and closed as well. She tried not to think of the blood loss from the leg wound.

"Will do!" Arie trotted back and started at the top of Lauranya's pants, working her way down with surer snips after having done the shirt without mishap. Lauranya's eyes started to close as a comfortable narcotic fog wrapped around her.

"Mommy, Jacks says you can't sleep yet. You gotta talk!" Arie scolded pulling the ripped pants gently from around her mother and taking them to the trash basket.

Lauranya chuckled slightly and let out a small whimper of pain as Arie moved to clean the shoulder wound.

"Sorry mommy!" Lauranya couldn't see Arie's face but she could hear the tears in her voice.

"Shhhh…it is ok. It hurts more than I want it to." Lauranya said soothingly. "Have I ever told you how your uncle won his freedom from the slave mine?"

"We have an uncle who was a slave?" Arie stopped, startled that she had family that wasn't free.

"He wasn't a slave at first." Lauranya started. "The family was free at that point, had been for about eight years when uncle Ager was born as a free person. Grandfather tried to instill into every child born in the compound that being free was an earned privilege not to be taken lightly. Ager had a middling talent for the arena and a small talent in necromancy - talking to the dead. Not enough to make a living, so he was trained in welding ship steel inner and outer hulls. He made decent wages, but Uncle Ager got caught up in thinking "free" meant no consequences."

Lauranya's eyes crossed for a moment at Arie's ministrations. "He never knew the everyday lashing that his parents received as gladiator slaves or the hunger of withheld food as punishment. He was allowed the freedom of the ship and allowed to travel between ships with his job, but he grew careless. Became spoiled with his freedom."

Arie placed the sponge back to the sheet and reached for the sealant for the shoulder as her mother talked. Pulling one edge of torn skin to its matching opposite side, while gluing the edge down, holding the skin in a pinch until the sealant dried enough to hold without tearing. She continued slowly as the skin was taut and torn, rendering it hard to hold onto and squeeze sealant at the same time.

"Uncle Ager would go out with friends drinking and gambling. He did not worry about his work or if he owed from his nights of debauchery. "'Til his debt was sold up to a Lord who wanted control of grandfather's training ground. The Lord told grandfather he would sell the debt back for controlling interest or the Lord would take his grandson. Grandfather knew what this would mean for the family so he told the Lord to take the grandson. Grandfather always said 'Family looks after family, not after self.' Lauranya took a moment, sucking in her breath, as Arie pulled and pinched a very deep cut.

She continued with a voice threaded with pain till the edges were sealed together and the skin relaxed a little. "Uncle Ager was pulled from the family apartments screaming. Stripped of his clothes, whipped and chained." Lauranya stopped again.

"Were you there, mommy?" Arie asked after a longer than normal pause.

"Yes, baby, I was. I was a few years older than you." Lauranya's voice went soft. "I saw the blood and the whipping. The terror on his face as he realized none of them would save him. Esu had taken an interest in his life and he would never be the same."

"Which god is Esu?"

"A trickster. A god who appears in a person's life at interesting times when there are hard paths to take." Lauranya said softly, still lost in distant screaming.

"Oh! Like in our life now?" Arie stopped applying a bandage the shoulder to ask.

Lauranya stopped and blinked for a moment. "I had not thought of our life being at a crossroads, but yes, Esu has a hand on our shoulder occasionally here."

"You don't like him?"

"Esu, like most Gods, is neutral. It is how you respond or are affected that makes actions good or bad." Lauranya tried for a light tone on Gods. Scary stories could wait till she was a few years older.

"So what happened with Uncle Ager?" Arie asked almost impatiently. Almost. Her hands busy putting her mother back together again.

"The Lord sold Uncle Ager, to a mining world to punish grandfather."

"Why would it punish grandfather?"

"Mining worlds are very hard on their slaves. They

take any slave, but usually only the slave's people do not want or those slaves that need excessive disciplining are sent to the mines. Poor food, with harsh conditions, leads to a very high death rate." Lauranya shuddered. She had been stationed on a mining world for six months, in the labs studying the water microbes for potential ship protein. The attrition rate of the slaves was worse than she was letting on. "Noni followed the auction Uncle Ager was sold in, and where he would be sent." Lauranya's eyes teared up for a moment. "Noni cried for weeks. No one could comfort her."

"Was she mad at grandfather?"

"No. If grandfather had made the deal, the family would have gone from being stable to borderline starving, having to sell children to feed the remaining members."

"If he was a mining slave how did he get free?" Arie was getting caught up in the story even as she moved to seal up the arm wounds.

"Impatient child." But Lauranya smiled as she said this, floating slightly above the pain now. "The mines were violent. Most people were out for themselves. Ager bought favors for his crew with his power of talking to the dead, who knew where pockets of poison gas were or weak tunnel structures were, where the veins of metal were the best. Small things like that, which helped everyone. Ager was an exception, but his crew valued him for his necromancy. It was his prowess on the sands that earned him true favors that he could distribute among those who helped him as much as he helped others."

"I thought necromancers couldn't sell their power or the speech of the dead." Arie had a frown again at this contradiction of rules she had learned in children care.

"Yes and no. Trained necromancers, who are in the employ of a Lord or a God, either as a speaker, a reviver or for the arena, are not allowed to employ their power outside of these areas. Those who have middling talents and are employed in different ways, the Overseers and Lords look the other way if they earn coin on the side unless their side job becomes too…obtrusive to ignore."

"And Uncle Ager's undead help wasn't noticed?"

"It benefited his crew of other slaves and an Overseer who benefited with bigger mining loads than others, so she did not punish him for his necromancy. Uncle Ager's other talent was not only surviving the fights that broke out between miners, but also the Pit fights the head Overseer staged for entertainment. Uncle Ager always won. He may not have been qualified for a gladiator but he did have full training that grandfather gave to all his children. "

"So was this how he won his freedom?" Arie asked as she finished her mother's torn arm, moving the medical supplies down towards her leg.

Lauranya rolled over very carefully to her stomach, using the pillow as a support for her chest as she laid her head down on her right arm and gently tried to move the left in a neutral, relaxed position over the pillow. The arm elicited a yelp, but no tears.

"Mommy?" Arie looked up from the deep scores on her mother's calf.

"I am fine dearling, just had to move the arm and it was not happy," Lauranya whispered through her tears.

Arie stopped for a moment, listening. "Jacks says it's too early for another shot mommy."

"I am not hurting that badly, dear." Lauranya lied to her daughter. "Keep going please."

"Ok mommy!" Arie bent down to swab away the blood from the ripped calf muscles.

Lauranya sucked in her breath, at the swabbing's first

touch, but continued her story. "No, Uncle Ager didn't win his freedom, until a young Lord came down to the planet, inspecting her newly won mining world."

"Newly won?"

"Lord Neferra had been challenged by an older necromancer and lost. When Lords or Gods fight, the winner takes all of the loser's possessions. Including all property. The family of the loser is considered part of the property to keep as newly made slaves unless the winner is feeling magnanimous and lets the survivors leave to live with relatives on another ship. This usually keeps fights to a minimum, as very few people want to see their children as someone else's slave."

"That doesn't sound nice!" Arie looked up from the wound with a child's outrage at the injustice.

"The Lords and Gods aren't always nice. That is why both free and slaves try to do the work as best we can and keep any recognition positive."

"Still doesn't sound nice," Arie grumbled bending back over her mother's leg.

"I know baby, but it is how it is." Lauranya took a moment to gather her thoughts before continuing. "Neferra had come to the planet because she wanted to maximize production but had noticed no matter how many slaves were used at the mines, production and profits were not rising."

"Isn't there supposed to be more work with more workers?"

"Exactly, this is why Neferra was not in a very good mood when she arrived planet side." Lauranya let out a small chuckle. "What's so funny mommy?" Arie looked up from the leg wound with a curious look that her mother would be laughing when Arie knew she was in so much pain.

Lauranya smiled at her daughter even though she knew Arie could not see. "Uncle Ager always said the moment he laid eyes on Lord Neferra; he knew this small, dark-skinned woman with the fierce expression and two undead bodyguards would change his life." Lauranya shook her head. "Uncle Ager was betting again, but this time he gambled with his life."

"Did he win?"

"He won, but it was a very close call. He almost never met her. The night before her arrival there was a pit fight. He was part of the main fight. The other Overseers were pissed off at Ager's Overseer for always winning when she entered him, so much so that they stacked the deck with 5 to 1 against him."

"Oh no!" Arie looked up with huge eyes, her hands stopping mid-motion.

"Oh yes. He won but he was barely able to stand or see he was so badly beaten. When Lord Neferra demanded to see all of the slaves, Uncle Ager stood out. Not only because he was so badly beaten but he was also surrounded by ghosts. And the ghosts had much to say to Neferra."

"Mommy?"

"Yes, baby?"

"I thought necromancers were usually pale skinned."

"Yes and no."

"That's not a very good answer," Arie said frowning at her mother's obtuse answer.

"Most necromancers are pale, but not all. Just like not all of the best fighters are dark skinned. Lord Neferra was also unusual like Uncle Ager. She could fight and actually had some training, but she could control and even heal up to 12 zombies at a time. I suspect she was actually much stronger than that as the Lord she beat, was noted for controlling 20 zombies at one time, even though he was starting to hit his waning years."

"So what did the ghost say about Uncle Ager?"

"Lord Neferra stopped in front of him, and listened for a moment, before asking Uncle Ager what had happened to his face. Now at this point his Overseer was terrified, as fights were forbidden and it was a death sentence for any Overseer caught wasting a Lord's assets, the mining equipment or slaves. Uncle Ager told the truth, that his Overseer had been forced to put a fighter into the pit or risk having her crew's rations cut or poisoned which would cause a lower percentage in productivity and ultimately see the crew broken up and herself taking the dead slaves place in the mines."

Lauranya stopped her narration for a moment. Longer than expected as Arie had to prompt her with a "Mommy?"

"Sorry, baby." Lauranya apologized. "I…the videos of the fights from the pits were gruesome. I hope you never have to know how to survive like that." Lauranya shuddered. Not all of it induced by memory.

"As long as we are here, Mommy, I don't think I will," Arie said firmly, reaching for the flesh glue to seal up the now cleaned wound.

"From the mouths of babes." Lauranya murmured. "Lord Neferra did not trust the living, so every word Uncle Ager said was weighed by the ghosts for truth. They supplied the details to his short answers."

Arie looked confused. "Why wouldn't she trust the living?

"Some Gods die from old age but most from challenges from younger Gods or Lords. Becoming a Lord starts a path to become a God unless one walks a tightrope between useful but non-threatening and too dangerous or costly to challenge."

Lauranya sucked in a breath as Arie pulled too little skin over a large section of raw flesh.

"Mommy, Jacks said this will scar. You won't have the beautiful skin he first noticed…Oh! I'm not supposed to say that part."

"That's ok baby, I was pretty sure I would scar anyway," Lauranya said through gritted teeth and tears. "Jacks has always been kind." She managed for Arie's benefit.

Lauranya took a deep breath continuing the story. "Lord Neferra knew that most people could be bribed, threatened or were swayed with sweet words. So she asked him again but this time she asked "why" not "what.""

"Is that important?"

"Usually the why will tell you what or how something came about, like in evolution of a certain species to their surrounding environment."

"Oh!" Arie filed this information away for later examination and use.

"The fights that he had been in had cost three of the regular Overseers dearly. Uncle Ager's immediate Overseer knew she had to keep Ager alive so she slipped him medical supplies and pain meds to the crew chief directly countering the demands of managing the Overseers. Ager knew his Overseer saw him as her ticket to a better job if she won enough to curry favor with the next round of upper levels. When asked how his Overseer knew the managers would be replaced he said it was only a matter of time before the Lord found one was siphoning from the top and the other selling drugs to fuel the fights."

"Did this make her mad?"

"Very. She summoned ten zombies from the earth

right there and slew every Overseer except Uncle Ager's. Ummm...Tythy, Rythy I think her name was."

Arie gasped. "That's mean!"

"They were stealing."

"But what about those not stealing? They didn't need to die."

"They knew about the skimming which made them just as guilty." Lauranya dismissed the idea of innocence in an Overseer.

"Did Uncle Ager know this?"

"Not at the time of the inspection but he would later."

"Lady Neferra's shuttle came to the inspection..."

"Aunt Neferra?" Arie asked in awe as a name she had heard bantered at the table as family now had a title attached.

Lauranya gave a weak chuckle. "Yes but she wasn't aunt at that time."

Arie began to cut tape for the dressing, hanging the sticky part on the edge of the table. She wasn't strong enough to tear the wrap section so she had to get the scissors.

"You can do this Lauranya." Jacks said in a whisper. "You have to survive for her."

Lauranya was hanging on by the skin of her back, yet Jacks' voice sent a shiver down her spine. "Good thing you could not read the future."

A humorless chuckle, just whispering in her ear. "Would never have had the drink if I could have." Jacks flashed Lauranya an edged ghostly smile. "Not to worry though, the captain and his crew have gotten their just rewards."

Lauranya swallowed hard. Jacks was a sweet man but he could be a vicious son of a God when he had cause.

"Do I want to know?"

"Gods found them."

"Their families?"

"To the miners on Teshrin."

Lauranya winced; Teshrin was a harsh world where gas leaks were common and always lethal.

"Mommy, what happened next?" Arie asked finishing cutting the bandages. Her attention back to her mother.

"This part of the story was gleaned from several dinner conversations and family gossip." Lauranya's smile was wan but there as she remembered the thirty plus who gathered for these meals. Lady Neferra went down the line noting the many injured workers, some who had to be held upright. She stopped at uncle Ager and asked him what happened. Uncle Ager said that all he remembers of this meeting is a goddess with beautiful dark skin and warm biting green eyes that graced him with her look. He also admits to being high on stolen painkillers the mining crew had just fed to him so he could stand.

Lord Neferra stopped in front of the unusually beaten but bandaged slave miner. "Was there a mining accident to cause such damage?"

"No Lord. Well, there was a fight you see." He amended.

"It looks like you were not very effective," she said dismissively, with pursed lips and a wave of her hand.

"True, but you should see the other eight," he said, with a lopsided smile.

"It was the smile that caught Lady Neferra's attention. Even beaten to a pulp he could smile and laugh at his own pain and possible death.

"The other eight?" She asked with her head tilted to the left looking through him. She was consulting the ghosts that surrounded him, most of the other slaves could not see. "I hear there were only five."

"I might have been seeing double towards the end. But I kicked all eight chests." Ager said with a lopsided grin.

Lady Neferra's lips twitched slightly.

Uncle Ager took that as a sign to keep talking, afraid the lovely lady would leave. "Oh yeah…the Overseers wanted some sport so they pulled some of us from the dinner line after we finished to have a bit of blood sport." He leaned forward with a conspiratorial whisper. "But shhh…we aren't supposed to tell anyone about this! It's not to be mentioned to anyone higher up!"

"I see." Came Neferra's response, her eyes flashing. The Overseer closest to her, hearing what Ager said, raised his whip, yelling "Liar!" at Uncle Ager. A flick of Neferra's hand and both of the Overseers' Doorn arms were ripped off by her undead bodyguards. She let her undead guard drag him to the very front and break his neck so that his screams were stopped.

"Please do tell me more?" She turned back to Ager.

"You have very good control of them!" Ager said to the tiny woman in front of him, too far gone in pain meds to be afraid.

"But my patience is not so great." She replied.

"Oh yeah. More. My Overseer is good to us. She tries to protect us and feed us as much as she can but the managing Overseer is trying to squeeze all the under Overseers for extra cash so he can buy a petite lordship on a world ship instead of here. So please don't go ripping her apart." The danger of who he was talking to finally seeping in through the opiate haze.

Ager's Overseer was standing at the front of her men, looking straight ahead knowing her moments were being counted but refused to beg for her life.

"Bed companion?" Lord Neferra asked eyeing him up

and down.

"Me?! Oh hell no. She likes men like Sager there." He moved his hand from round Corinth's shoulder to point to a rather large man with thick facial bones with no body or head hair; facial hair was fairly thick though. The man in question blushed bright red at being singled out for the Overseers favored sex toy.

"I'm too damn scrawny for her taste." Ager continued motioning to his almost emaciated lean muscled frame. Like all the slaves, male or female, their muscles stood out in pale contrast underneath whip-scarred skin, as all the fat had been long since stripped with hard labor.

"I...see." And so she did. Three of the dead men around Ager were talking to the necromancer. Each demanding she hear them. She turned to Uncle Ager's Overseer, silencing the ghosts surrounding him.

"See this slave is well tended. Bandages and pain medication."

The Overseer swallowed hard, taking two tries to speak. "Yes, Lord Neferra."

"How long have the slaves been fighting for the Overseers?"

"Since before I arrived."

"That is?" Lord Neferra asked exquisitely politely giving the Overseer her full attention. Her pale lime green eyes never leaving her face.

"Over five years."

"Who has been getting you the medication to treat your workers?"

"My foreman has a black-market lead. I let him steal small items from my rooms so he can trade for them."

This caused a stir in the slaves. They knew her lover was the black-market dealer, stealing for supplies but they hadn't known she was leaving stuff out.

"Was he only buying medical?"

"Extra food supplies."

"How do you know he was stealing for them all?"

"I placed ears and eyes in the quarters with night vision and on a different wavelength, then the regular jammer they stole from the last Overseer."

"So he feeds them all. Why?" Lord Neferra tapped her lips thoughtfully. "I can't see common mine slaves stealing for a whole crew when they could steal and charge for extra food."

"I told him if I ever caught him hiding food from the others or selling it when his own crew needed, I would let Jorge have dibs on him."

"Jorge?"

"The main Overseer. He likes to skin his humps." The Overseer looked Lord Neferra in the eyes. There was serious fear and horror there. "His sex slaves might survive three nights but no more than that." She shuddered delicately. "If any of them survive, they kill themselves before the fourth time."

"And did the foreman steal the supplies this time for this fighter?"

"No, I did." The Overseer stood up straighter, waiting for the zombies to approach.

"Why did you steal when you could have requisitioned such supplies?"

"Jorge didn't allow anything extra to the slaves over what he deemed necessary. This included food, medicine. The basics." Her voice was bitter; her hands clenched unconsciously into fists. "All the while demanding a 10% increase in production every quarter."

"10%. Every quarter?" Lord Neferra asked carefully. Her head tilted thoughtfully as she listened for confirmation.

"Yes."

"How…odd." Was all she said. "So you stole to help your slaves?"

"Sick and starving workers, can't meet the damn quota. And I sure as black hole nova don't want to be a slave on this planet if I don't make quota." Was all the scarred hand Overseer said to her Lord.

Neferra considered the comment before continuing down the line, consulting each Overseer. The one dead Overseer was dragged to the side with the mining refuse. He would be cremated later that evening with several other bodies that were thrown on the pile.

Lady Neferra continued down the line, talking with each Overseer. Sometimes she would cock her head to the side as she listened. Sometimes there was just a smile and a quick laugh.

The entire inspection of her slaves took less than an hour, where they were dismissed back to the barracks. Dinner time was almost intoxicating as enough extra rations were sent down from the kitchens. There was enough for each slave to go to bed with a full stomach. For the first time in many months.

The next morning, the slaves were once more summoned up to the main entrance. The first thing every slave saw, as they walked into the open area was a much larger pile of bodies in the refuse. All of them could see Jorge's head sitting on his ass, mouth open in a frozen scream. There were pieces of eight other Overseers' bodies, mixed in with his own torn apart bits.

Lord Neferra walked into the open area, with an extra two zombie bodyguards, former Overseers. Uncle Ager said that the rumor was that the hall where Jorge had set up with an eye to his new Lord's predilection for young men, had been so awash in blood that those same eye candy pieces took four days to clean up all the blood and viscera from the walls and floor. Lord Neferra had been very unhappy at the state of her new mines. The change was not unexpected, the gratuitous violence of ripped apart bodies was.

Even more surprising was that Star, Uncle Ager's Overseer, stood next to her.

"There have been a few changes to the way the mine is going to be run." Lord Neferra's voice carried through a speaker so all could hear. "There will be two weeks rest period, while I and my accountants go over the books." The slaves didn't cheer but they did look at each other as if they had never heard of such a thing. "Rations will be increased. All slaves in need of medical attention will be attended to in the barracks." Lady Neferra took a moment to look over her much-damaged slaves. Her lips tightened at the obvious misuse and damage of her property. "There will be an influx of new slaves." There was muttering.

"The new slaves will not take away from any rations — food, blankets or beds. However, there will be rotating shifts so that production does not fall. Without further damage to machinery or labor." The slaves were open-mouthed. Her words, enunciated, were not being comprehended completely.

"There is a new main Overseer." Neferra nodded to Star. "This Overseer is the one I will hold responsible for all further production, machinery and labor issues."

Arie interrupted, mid bandaging 'Why not just use zombies to mine?" She asked

"Raising a zombie and keeping it animated, moving, takes Power. This power comes from the necromancer. Some necromancers can only do small short bursts, requiring new bodies every time, while other necromancers can keep one body moving for…years."

Lauranya paused for a moment. "No necromancer wants to show all their power at once."

"In case they are challenged?"

"Exactly. That and if you need new bodies every time you animate, you soon run out of slaves and start making inroads on your free population." Lauranya shuddered, digging nails into her palm as Arie finished with the last of the bandaging. "Eventually the Power runs out or the bodies run out. So Undead Gods and Lords only flex their powers when they need to while keeping the bulk of their Power in reserve for a challenge."

Lauranya hesitated, looking over her shoulder, through damp blond strands. "Does that help explain why zombies are not good for menial tasks, sweetie?"

"I think so." Arie had a frown, as she sat back on her heels. "It's like when playing Go-Ships. You don't want to show all your cards, just one at a time."

"You have it in one, my love." Lauranya laid her head back down, trying hard not to dig nails into the palms of her hands.

Arie began to pick up all the bandage scraps and creams, putting them on the shelf. She reached for the hypo needle. "Mommy."

"Yes dear." Lauranya's voice was faint.

"Jacks said it's time for your next shot." Arie hesitated. "Are you ready for another one?"

"Yes love. I am in a bit of pain." Lauranya's voice was breathy, pain a heavy shadow that she would not show the full darkness of her daughter

"Okay mommy!" Arie carefully filled the needle with the correct amount of pink tinted fluid Jacks guided her to, and then pressed the needle into Lauranya's good arm.

"Thank you, Arie. And thank you Jacks." Lauranya's voice became softer as the narcotics hit.

Arie checked to make sure her mother was sleeping before putting everything away in the correct spot.

"You will need to set an IV for her as well." Jacks misted to the side, where the fluid was kept.

"I don't know how to do that," Arie said solemnly, looking at him the same way as when he was alive.

"Then it is high time you learned." Jacks said with a smile and an even tone that would calm even the highest strung slave working with corrosive acids in a laboratory setting.

"You're going to need to show me other things for both mommy and me to survive," Arie said, sticking out her chin defiantly to Jacks' ghost.

A pale grin encompassed Jacks' face. "And I see where the power source has not fallen far from the world ship."

Chapter 17

"Water's rising," Pogue noted, blinking up into the drizzle.

"Tell me something useful, whelp." Sister snapped, clutching a shawl of soft woven fiber closer over her bony shoulders with aged hands. It wasn't the cooler weather the storms brought that got to her, but the added humidity seemed to pool in her joints. Swelling them painfully.

"Going to need Morren to kill any of the prowlers who come close. We can only support one land-shifter. Any more will go through our meager stock and then start on the breeders." Caramina looked down at her notes. "Brother could always eat the whiskered cats, for added meat, saving some of our stock from being butchered for him."

"He's not going to eat those kills." Sister snapped with a curl of her lip in distaste. Unlike these children, two generations removed from their space-faring kin, they had no recollection of the first few years where everything was eaten until better could be found. Nothing but extreme hunger would ever make Sister choke down another bite of Whiskered again.

Pogue made a face. "Can't blame him there. Those things are damn gamey."

"How much land will be submerged, Noni?" Caramina asked, changing the subject, to keep them all on track. She was in charge of feeding the village and was notably nervous that the usual bountiful harvests were about to be ruined by the weather.

Sister looked up at the hut's ceiling, not seeing the tightly woven reeds shedding water like skin, but the heavy dark clouds above. A different bounty in both weather and future events. "We'll need to move about three miles inland. The beaches here will be replaced eventually with higher beaches of mud that will be covered in sand and shells in a few years of storm. No fertile fields will be spared except those at the base of the mountains."

"So we will have to tier more of the mountain and hope that we can transplant the reeds in the new ocean shallows," Caramina said with a sigh, blowing heavy, honey-colored curls out of her eyes. She started writing on her wax and board pad. The notes would be safe through the rains until she had everything finalized and put into action.

"Birds and some invasive will be a problem," Pogue said, popping a handful of nuts, from a hip pouch, into his mouth. He didn't bother writing anything down. His memory was good enough to dispense with wax writing tablets.

"Aren't they always?" Caramina said with a wry look in his direction.

"We may actually want to walk back the idea of only one land-shifter." Pogue started his thoughts taking another 90-degree turn. "The game will move up with us as well, getting into the terraced gardens."

"And after the shifters have gone through the game, eating the wildlife down to the finches, what then?" Sister snapped glaring through old eyes, rimmed in red. "We decide which shifter lives and the other or others die because we can't feed them anymore? Are you going to be the one to suggest that?"

Pogue opened his mouth, before closing it with a snap

and a flush, shaking his head. Good idea bad execution.

"Think child, before you speak." Sister rolled her eyes at the 40-year-old man across from her as if he were a stripling of 12. Full of ideas that were never completed to a logical conclusion. "Flights through the stars do not equate to what we face on the ground."

"Yes, Noni." Pogue said meekly.

Sister shook her head, pressing her lips together. "Brother has been unwilling to make another shifter. The doctors can't guarantee a survival percentage without a submerging tube.

"If we were on the ships…" Pogue started again.

"If we were on the ships we wouldn't be having this conversation to start with." She snapped at him. The fire popped expressing her very real irritation. "We will have another land-shifter but not for years when we can actually support more than one."

"We will?" Caramina asked looking up startled.

"Yes. Now back to the issue of growing on hand." Sister looked back over to Pogue, tapping her fingers against her leather pouch. "Pogue has a good idea." She held up a hand stalling him asking about his "good" idea. "We will have an increase in game till the land/water situation resolves. We will need everyone setting traps for the increased game without wiping out everything." Her eyes misted for a moment before clearing. "This will go for the plants as well." She nodded to Caramina.

"I'll take care of figuring out rough estimates." Caramina nodded, scribbling furiously.

"I'll get us moved and get us moving towards culling the native edible game as we move up so that we don't lose too much of our harvest to their foraging." Pogue opened his mouth then closed it again.

"Out with it. Might as well let the idea see the light of

day at some point." Sister snapped at him.

"Will we have problems with other islanders? Will they try to steal or kill for what we have?"

"No," Sister said dismissively, a curl of lip to show her opinion of his idea.

Pogue sat up stung. "Why shouldn't we prepare for fighting? We will have made preparation, have stores still…"

"No. There will be no war among us."

"But…" Pogue had his thrusters going.

"I said no. And before I rip your tongue out for wagging while the elders speak, you will listen." She glared at the others. "And don't think to go behind my back and stir up the hotheads, grandson." The weight of her eyes laid heavy on Pogue.

"Yes, noni." Pogue lowered his eyes in submission, speaking for the first time.

"Good. We are going to reach out to the other villages. Those who want can help and share equally with us: land and all harvests. We help the ship survivors as they would help us. We need to get this message out to all."

"Just fruit?" Pogue said with a sardonic grin. He stopped poking the fire to look up at his grandmother.

Sister tried to thank him with her cane, but he shifted to the side, easily avoiding her swing. "Smartass." She said with a smile. The smile died slowly as her face filled with shadows. "We were at war in space. The Undead Gods who wanted us, both body and soul. The war, bloodshed." She shook her head in memory of the fighting in the corridors as the ship had been boarded. "We fought like demons to never go back into bondage. We fought together. Together." Her cane thwacked the ground in emphasis. "Too many died giving the survivors a chance to make it to the world. Three months in shuttles to the one planet that could support life. Shifters, non-shifters. It doesn't matter. We all live together, so there will be no fighting."

Sister looked around at the council, pinning each person with a fierce glare. "We'll need to start moving next week," Sister said ending the night's meeting, reaching for her cane and levering herself upright.

Both Pogue and Caramina shared looks of dismay. "Well, what are you two waiting for?" Sister shook her cane at them, clearly in dismissal. "We have work to do!"

"Holy Gods. Next week? How…" Pogue whispered.

"We'll manage but it's going to take us starting to pack and move tomorrow," Caramina said grimly.

Pogue swallowed hard. "Tomorrow is an understatement." They left, with less confidence than their arrival, hurrying to their prospective targets on the inundating water and imminent move.

Warrick stopped, with a hand on the huts woven door frame, the handwoven cloth pinned to the side with one large hand. "I'll tell the water-shifters our plans."

"A good idea," Sister said but her thoughts weren't on him or the water dwellers. She was already lost in her sight, seeing what might happen — twenty variations for each small change they would do affecting the years to come.

The flight back to the Union was mostly uneventful. The main ship had cleared space on the flight deck in anticipation of rescues. The hold doors were open with a deluge of marines ready to tag a sleeping body bag. Each bag was laid out carefully large to small, largest upfront. General Cratt was already directing medics and marines to various areas of need.

Redeyes walked out with her Guardians down the line with 18 bags floating behind her. The Marines stopped for only a moment, but many of the nonmilitary stared at the show of power by Redeyes. Usually, a display like this was more for the other Gods, but this time it seemed Redeyes would be happy to allow word of mouth to carry back how strong her telekinesis was this time around. She deposited the bodies with a nudge here and there, to make room in the line of bags for the ones she was carrying.

Medics went to the largest bags first, unsealing then applying a hypo to each person. The hypo also contained a small but carefully gauged dose of something Kimma called "Don't give a shit". The newcomers would be fed this cocktail for a few weeks. Kept the newly freed from freaking out over the non-humans and made everyone easier to work with, until therapy for the new lifestyle and close proximity to not-completely-humans could take effect.

As the deadheads woke up, stretched then eased into standing positions, they were herded into the middle of the deck. Several other medics would set up medical records and notations on medical needs.

The undead segregated themselves. The free or upper caste stood, while the, now former, slaves sat or squatted at the feet of their former owners. Redeyes lifted her lip in a soft snarl.

"Easy girl. They'll learn soon enough." Cratt said, coming up to Redeyes' side.

"How the hells are you the only one to call me girl?" Redeyes snapped at the human general. He cracked large scarred knuckles on large ropey muscled hands. The hands went with the square body. Solid muscle, but svelte and General Cratt would never be used in the same sentence. He could fight a Wolfen to a standstill and outmaneuver even Redeyes on special tactics.

General gave her a sly smile, only saying "Spoilers."

Redeyes jumped as if pinched and gaped at the other human. With a shake of her head, she started to chuckle. "I taught you that didn't I?"

"Yes, you did." With a tilt of his head to the deadheads, he re-directed her attention. "I think you're up."

"We will cover when and where you get to call me girl," Redeyes said with a quick nod, was all she gave him as she stepped past him, closer to the newcomers. "Compassion, compassion." She muttered to herself walking away. The General shook his head. This part wasn't easy on anyone and he sure as hells didn't want to be the one who had to do it.

Redeyes was obviously agitated, as her feet touched the ground. Without preamble, she started. "Listen up!" Redeyes' voice drilled through the hold, vibrating along spines and through jaw bones. All eyes swiveled to the four-armed God.

Redeyes stood with her lower hands on her hips as she cradled one of the long guns in her left arm. Her right arm motioned to the deadheads in an open-handed gesture "As of this moment you are now with us. Your work determines your food allotment, your quarters and any extras you might want." Redeyes' voice tried for neutral to upbeat; though the tightening jaw muscles made it hard not to chew off each word she spoke. "There are no slaves; there are no Overseers. What you see is what there is." She pierced many with her eyes, causing more than a few of the rescuers a bit of alarm and fear. A few almost hopeful. Most too numb to think any more. Broken pieces of human effluvia.

Redeyes walked up to one kneeling girl, offering a

lower left hand. The girl looked up startled at the very scary four-armed God with vivid red eyes. She turned to look at the tall slender, dark-skinned man who stood next to her. The two younger boys, standing next to the man, shared similar facial features.

"Not him. You aren't property anymore." Redeyes snapped glaring at the rumpled man with a stiff spine and a haughty look. This is the part that made her want to tear off heads — the slave owners.

"You can't talk to my father…" One of the two boys started to say but was cut off when a Wolfen marine bent down to growl in the boy's face.

"You're not a fucking prince here. You're nobody special until you prove yourself." The marine growled to the stripling.

The boys shrank back behind their father, who had reached to pull both of them behind him as he stepped forward. He wouldn't have lasted thirty seconds against the Wolfen and yet he still tried to protect his children. The Wolfen gave the man a wide grin for having balls, if not necessarily brains. Neither boy cried or shit their pants, which were the usual first reactions when confronted with a seven-foot living nightmare.

Redeyes took the girl's hand in her own pulling her up. "No slaves. You earn your place by what you can do, not who or what you were." She motioned for the kneeling slaves to stand. Hesitantly, a few did, then a few more, until there were no more kneeling humans.

Redeyes nodded with a smile, which did not show teeth. No need to scare the children. There was always hope for most and redemption for a few.

This gesture did not sit well with all the newly arrived. "And if we preferred our lives before you kidnapped us?" A heavyset woman snapped. Her clothing screamed upper caste, wearing a disheveled blue peplum of natural fiber and richly embellished with gold brocade trim, flashes of gems at the hem of her dress. On her feet were sandals of leather, while her toes had rings, also with gems that glinted. She moved forward with purpose, pushing through the others, free and slave. She was not a God or a Lord but probably a Petite Lord.

And someone who would never fit in. Redeyes moved so fast her hands were barely seen as little more than a blur. The gun went off and a whistling pop, heard four times. The woman's chest and face were pocked with small flat lines of the disc gun in Redeyes hand. The discs went in flat and expanded on contact, lodging inside a body, usually halfway through, maximizing damage. Rarely would a disc not expand.

The woman grunted as if she had been punched in the stomach, a surprised look on her wounded face. She fell to the ground like a puppet with cut strings. This was not the response she had expected.

"You die." Redeyes voice carried throughout the hold. Her right hands holstered her gun even though her eyes were on the deadheads. "You live or die by these rules now. No slaves. You earn your spot among us." Heads swiveled between Redeyes and the dead woman, horror to glimmers of glee in those eyes. There was little sympathy shown. The well-dressed woman would not be missed by those from the ship it seemed.

A low rumble vibrated through the deck as if in counterpoint to Redeyes' words. The rescued looked around wildly muttering to each other on what fresh horror might visit them. One or two screamed. A couple more fainted. The former slaves, dropped to their knees their foreheads touching the cold metal deck, falling back on a lifetime of training, complete submission and abasement. This pose, ingrained into them, as the only safe posture to take when an Overseer or God raged.

The rebellious were looking around, slightly less wildly than the newcomers. They glanced over at Redeyes and the General. However, those two were looking just as out of sorts as the regular marines.

"Attack?" Redeyes shouted as the noise grew louder.

"Not that I know of!" General Cratt yelled back. His voice echoed loudly as the noise stopped as quickly as it started. It was the forming mist to the side of the hold, along the right-hand wall that gave Sanctuary away.

"The columns are new. So is the noise" Cratt said, almost amused. Almost. His voice carried through to those on the deck, relaxing them as it was obvious the God and the General were no longer worried.

"That they are." Came Redeyes' bland comment. She gave the forming image a glower, her hands running over her gun.

"Know why they're here?" asked Collins edging closer to the God, his hand on his own disc gun.

"Not a clue. Decoration perhaps?" Redeyes snapped in irritation at the solidifying apparition.

"You don't know?" Cratt snapped his head around, looking at Redeyes in disbelief.

"I was on a ten-day bender after Roland took the Carnival." She growled at Collins, glaring with human green eyes, either in irritation at the structure in front of them or at the memory of Roland. Cratt couldn't tell which and he wasn't going to ask. 'I have no fucking clue what this damn thing does other than showing up randomly over the last 22 years."

"It's not vanishing after the first few moments of misting, either. Think we're about to find out why." High Sarge said in a deep growling voice, the hairs along her spine were standing straight out, increasing her size by a quarter. Something was setting her and the others on edge.

Redeyes didn't ignore the warning of her marines. "Arms to the ready!' she barked out. Her voice barely carrying to the hold's marines in the back. The front marines pulled out disc guns or swords, whichever they were more comfortable with.

The doors opened slowly, showing only a dark emptiness behind the hammered metal doors. Then mist flowed out and down the stairs like water, not warm air. The marines closest to the mist backed up slowly, uneasily, but controlled. Redeyes stepped into the mist, testing it for acidity or poison. Her skin did not peel from the bone nor were there blisters of excruciating pain forming on the open skin.

With a shrug, she knelt into the mist and took a deep breath. Cold but…sterile? She could detect no scent — neither recycled air nor fresh. The air held no scent of who or where the air was from.

"Red!" Collins shouted from the side, jumping forward to pull her out of the heavy mist. A lighter mist floated on top of a thicker layer. Shadow forms could be seen darting in and out, defying gravitational normal for speed. No one Human, Wolfen or Katherian could follow the shadows' movements for more than a moment without their eyes watering as if glaring at a too bright spot. The shapes flowed through those gathered on the hanger hold like smoke across a mirror.

Redeyes tried using telekinesis to stop one of the forms. That did not work. Redeyes kept trying, causing a nosebleed for her effort.

"Damn." Redeyes snarled frustrated, trying to watch one shadow for more than five seconds with little luck. "Whatever spell they are using, is stardust good." Two of her hands on her swords, a third on a pistol while the fourth wiped away the blood from her nose. The blood crystallized within seconds, forming small perfect faceted teardrops. Redeyes, used to the oddity of her blood, shook her hand cleaning off the dried blood gems from her hand, concentrating on the shadows while ignoring the headache from her Power usage.

One shape stepped from the mist and slowed to form into a…human. Dark pants and a dark tunic. The woman had long red hair, thick with almost frizzy banana curls. The violet eyes were bruised under the lower lids, emphasizing the deep purple iris.

"Lady Redeyes." She said, in an oddly accented voice, making a short bow to the God.

Redeyes and the surrounding guardians gaped at the woman, but only for a second. Redeyes snapped out of the surprise first. She yanked a disc gun from her holster, pressing the barrel to the woman's temple. The woman responded by…ignoring the gun, looking not at Redeyes but at her own hand. She held up a hand forming strands of light. The strands formed patterns with every changing position of fingers or thumb. Sometimes the woman would shake her hand as if it were cold, a new pattern reforming on her upturned palm.

The words from the redhead's mouth were almost as disconcerting as the woman herself. "Holy shit! We came that far back?!" The woman's eyes went huge as she looked between Redeyes and the web of light on her hand. "No wonder you don't know who the fuck we are." She said, shaking her head with a downturn of her generous lips.

Redeyes and the other marines recognized what the threads from the woman's hand meant. A precog, and probably insane or heading down that path quickly, if the woman's lack of fear with a gun to her head was any indication.

"Start talking, Torch. Now!" Redeyes didn't have a lot of use for ambiguities, especially the crazy ones.

The response of "Of course." Nonplussed the God just a little.

"She's gotta have antifreeze in her veins." Iarris breathed to Collins. Iarris had a throwing knife out and ready for use in one hand, the other on her sword. Collins' hand was on his pistol but he was waiting for a more definitive floor show.

"Think she'll live?" Iarris asked

"Working. And no." Collins snapped back in a sotto voice. Redeyes had a nasty backhand if she thought you were going to get her or someone else killed by not paying attention.

Iarris took the hint, snapping her jaws closed with a click. She sucked in a breath but made no other noise as she bit down on her tongue with the snap of her teeth.

"We are from Sanctuary." The woman started.

"I know what the fuck it's called. The name is on the damn archway." Redeyes growled.

"You named it for the refugees that enter."

"Refugees? Enter?" Suspicious.

The woman shook her head, her hair flaring out magnificently. "Let me backup for a moment."

"You." She pointed at Redeyes "made this, while very drunk. You won't have a clue of how it works ten millennia from now as you do this moment. The best anyone can figure is that the construct is somewhat sentient and anchors a pocket universe." She paused for a second, letting her words sink in, combing locks of hair out of her face, watching this rather mercurial Redeyes as she explained Sanctuary 101 to the God.

"Sanctuary shows up when most needed by heroes or military and civilians." The woman swallowed. "Sanctuary does not always show up every time something goes wrong in history, just those times that historians have thought it was at the most opportune time to save a very important person or persons to ward off the Undead Gods for the final battle years."

"You're not making sense." Redeyes snapped, easing the gun back from the woman's temple. Redeyes didn't think the woman was any more of a threat than one of the deadhead children, just from the brief moments of the lecture. Irritating and confusing, but not a threat.

"How can it show up for those in need but not show up when needed?"

The woman shook her head. "I don't know. I can't see what makes the damn thing work any more than any other Torch." The woman's lips pressed together in agitation. Her hand motions disrupted the webs in her hand, for a moment. The web reformed into the same configuration as the last time. The woman's eyes fell to the web. She spoke to the forming threads and not Redeyes. "Shut up! I know, damn it, I know. This does not get any easier you know!"

Redeyes nodded. Full blown insanity soon, the first sign was always speaking to the threads as if they were speaking back. "So what are the threads telling you?" She asked gently, cautiously. Sometimes speaking slowly to the incipient insane helped.

"Atlanta."

Redeyes looked at the woman uncomprehendingly.

"My name is Atlanta. We will meet more in the future. Very far in your future and my very near future." The threads of light pulsed on her hand, in time to a heartbeat. Atlanta took a deep breath. "I need to leave one of my companions...sure as hell isn't a friend, with you." "You need his information and training coming up."

Redeyes frowned. "You'd leave one of yours behind?"

"Not just anyone!" Atlanta said indignantly. "You already know him. Mostly." She hedged that statement. She ran her hands up her arms as if cold — the threads disappearing for good this time.

As if drawn to the statement, a shadow separated from the mist to stand by the Torch. It didn't unblur visually nor were the words any more comprehensible before Atlanta had been unveiled. The shadow stood to the side of Torch, putting her between it and Redeyes, while animatedly waving a blurring arm. Atlanta ignored it for a moment, then with a shrug, stepped forward as if going back with it to the mist. She pulled her gun in one smooth motion and shot the apparition in the leg. With a scream, the cloaking shadow dropped to the ground, exposing the Katherian in the bone mask. With a bow, Atlanta stepped back into the shadows and mist, giving Roland one last pitying look.

"No! Do not leave me here!" He yowled, trying to crawl back to Sanctuary's steps. "She will kill me!"

Too late. Torch's movement signaled the end of the mission. The mist stopped as the last shadow, presumably Atlanta's, misted through the closing door. With a solid thunk of metal on stone the doors closed, leaving the wounded Katherian clutching at evaporating mist.

Redeyes took a deep breath. She knew this scent. Lips peeled back from slightly more elongated eye teeth of a regular human; Redeyes walked up behind the Katherian, who was clutching his profusely bleeding leg. She grabbed him by the scruff of his neck and pulled him upright, his legs dragging on the metal deck. "I've wondered when we would meet again, pussy Kat." She purred at him.

Roland's ears went flat and his tail spiked out in sheer

terror.

"Get him patched up, so he and I can chat after this." She snarled to Iarris and Collins, tossing the Katherian at their feet as if he were nothing more than a pair of old socks to be washed.

"Do it now!" She snarled at her Guardians, pointing her gun at their head.

Iarris and Collins exchanged looks. Redeyes never threatened a Guardian, even when ready to rip skin off.

"I'll get the kit," Iarris said, with a flick of her tail, which was fluffing slightly in growing concern.

"Leaving me to babysit the insane," Collins muttered for just her ears, referring to either Redeyes or the bleeding Katherian. Iarris' fingers brushed his shoulder as she moved towards one of the medics, in sympathy and concern. He touched her hand, just as furtively.

"Let's have a look at you, boyo," Collins said as he slung his rifle over his shoulder, bending down to the wounded Katherian. Collins pulled out a knife to cut off the Katherian's pants leg to be used as a makeshift pressure bandage till Iarris returned. The Katherian had obviously had enough battle training to keep his hands out of Collin's way while keeping pressure on the wound. Every second counting. The Torch had missed shooting the disk anywhere near a major artery but the disc had done maximum damage. Collins wasn't sure if that had been by luck or design, the damage to the leg was going to be crippling without major healing work.

General Cratt tied the legging pad and strips, not too tightly. "That'll have to do till the medic gets here." He nodded in sympathy with the Katherian before standing up. Cratt wiped his sweaty brow on his forearm. Getting Redeyes to calm down was going to be a voiding pain in the engine.

"Who's missing?" Redeyes yelled this time her voice carried to the back. It was her human iris green eyes staring out of her face that froze the marines in place. "Damn it, answer me!" She strode forward to High Sarge, wading through the freed deadheads. General Cratt close on her heels.

Collins looked over his shoulder surreptitiously as Redeyes walked back to the deadheads. "It's now or never if you want to die by your hand or hers." He said softly, looking the Katherian dead in the eyes. Collins touched the knife he carried in his boot with a finger. His left hand reaching to put pressure on the bandaged wound.

The gold-green eyes, pupils in vertical slits, looked up startled. With a shake of his head. "Torch did this…damn her, for a reason." He gasped in pain as Collins put on more pressure. "I will accept this fate. Alive."

Collins shook his head, a mirthless half smile. "You're either dumbest ship Kat ever born or the bravest."

"My wives used to say the same thing." A huffed laugh, breathy with pain.

"We need to get you to medic. This shit isn't going to keep you from bleeding out or keep the leg if docs don't see you soon." Collins sat back looking at his handiwork. "You won't have to worry about her in that case."

"Tease."

"One of the best! Now let's get you moving." Collins reached down when an anguished voice rose from the deadheads.

"My sons!" The dark-skinned man who had spoken just moments before was frantically searching through the freed. The boys were no longer at his side and Redeyes suspected not in this time line any longer, she ignored him for a moment continuing towards High Sarge. The man turned towards Redeyes, trying to intercept her, as she continued through. Two Wolfen were at the man's side halting his momentum with an overkill of arm ratio and force of holding for one human.

"Redeyes, Tress is missing as is Jonnis." High Sarge said with a voice growling in anger, her ears flat against her skull again. Her tail was thumping against her leg in anger. High Sarge didn't like losing one of her own.

Redeyes snarled something obscene, reversing her course, heading back to the Katherian in the bone mask. She got within two feet of him. "Where are they?" Her voice shook in a rage, which few had ever seen. Her hair spiked out in a white curling halo, her toes touched the cold metal floor of the deck. The air smelt scorched from the waves of anger generating from her.

"In Sanctuary." He replied. Fear threading through his voice as he visibly tried to keep his ruff and spine from standing straight up as his adrenaline kicked in for flight or fight. He swallowed metallic tasting spit as the flight portion was winning over the fight response.

"Can you get into his mind?" Redeyes sent to High Sarge.

High Sarge tried to scan then pry into his mind. "No. Shielding is damn good. Can't you get in?"

"No." Came the short neuron burning reply.

"Will they be returned?" She asked, squatting to be face to face with him, giving Roland a very close up of the human green eyes. Roland's bladder clenched once but he did not embarrass himself, yet.

"No. This was supposed to be a grab and go." Roland swallowed. "In and out. Take the targets back to Sanctuary for training and evaluation."

"You're good at stealing others away, aren't you?" She snarled, standing up and pulling a disc gun to put to his head.

"Your invention summons the survivors in Sanctuary and sends us to pull others out for the final battles!" He yelled, ears flat against his skull, throwing a hand with extended claws up to ward off the incoming shot.

Redeyes pulled the gun up to her shoulder, ready to drop it down to his head again. "Survivors? Final battle?" The Torch had said something similar.

Roland swallowed. "When a person is brought into Sanctuary, they go through an…orientation. The do's and don'ts. No killing, raping, stealing. Violate the rules and you will be sedated by the inner workings of sanctuary stone guardians to be placed in a cryo chamber."

"How the fuck does it have Cryo chambers?" She snapped. "We only have prototypes that keep killing black hole worm fodder like you." A not so veiled threat, chills went down the spines of those close enough to hear.

"I don't know! I keep getting summoned to bring in people who need to be rescued." Roland hyper-ventilated. Death would come, it always did, but he wasn't that anxious to meet Death in person just yet.

"Who decides who gets to live?" Redeyes squatted down in front of him once more, tilting her head slightly, exposing her neck.

Roland could see the vein pulse with her heartbeat, but he wasn't falling for this false weakness. He had seen her interrogate before. If he attacked, she would make things really hurt to break him down, cracking his mental shield. From there it was a quick scoop for her or another telepath to turn him into an empty shell.

"I don't know that either. Sanctuary is, as far as any of us can tell, semi-sentient fueled by whatever you put into it. Those who go on the rescue missions are woken up with a lightning mark on their hand. We go to the meadow where the stairs are and any extra supplies are needed."

"Such as?" Redeyes tapped the foot of his injured leg with her pistol.

He hissed in pain but kept talking. "Once we had to retrieve cryo units from a ship that had been damaged. There were spacesuits in our sizes at the steps. We pulled the units and took the cryo units and several of the crystal statues."

"Crystallized statues?"

"You develop a way to turn people into crystallized statues. A type of hibernation, which you can undo at a later date. But it's iffy."

"Who told you this?"

"Sanctuary."

"A fucking construct of metal and stone told you, I can turn people into statues and you believe it?" Redeyes gave a snort of disbelief and a shake of her head, sending her hair fluffing further out in wavy spikes.

"I've seen the statues. Regular and minis."

"Red if you want to keep talking to him till he dies by all means continue but he should see the docs if you want more than five minutes of useful information from him," Collins said in an annoyed tone, standing nonchalantly to the side. Iarris had returned and was clutching the med kit tightly. Tensions so high, her claws were denting the metal covering.

Redeyes glared at her Guardian. "What do you care if he lives?"

"Me? We need another to pick up the slack as your Guardian. He's obviously judged by you and those scars on his hands and arms says he's done sword work." Collins said with a shrug. "You're not exactly low maintenance or safe."

Redeyes drummed her fingers on one knee. "Fine. Take him to medic." To Roland. "You and I will be spending some time chatting later." She glanced at him through narrowed eyes, red again; he took her "orders" as a stay of execution. The Katherian nodded, past hoping for clemency.

Collins reached a hand down to help the Katherian up. Roland bent one leg underneath then stood, shakily on his good leg. Iarris handed the medical kit to Collins as she slipped an arm around his chest, letting the injured Katherian lean on her. Iarris brushed against High Sarge by accident. She flicked an ear at the other Katherian, touching her tail against High Sarge's hand in apology.

Redeyes turned back to High Sarge. "How are we doing other than the missing?"

"Par for the flight." High Sarge said with a snap of her tail, arching her whiskers forward. "Mental and physical trauma are...Watch out!"

A young child, less than 13 if her underweight frame, and stark facial features and shaved head were any indications, had stood up during the exchange between Redeyes and the injured Katherian slipping closer to the talking knot of grownups. As Collins helped Roland up, she was within feet of Redeyes. As Redeyes became absorbed in High Sarge's report, the child finished the last few steps between herself and the God.

Redeyes didn't see the trap. She reacted as if the child were a runner's ship child, putting an arm around too thin shoulders in comfort without consideration for herself. The child turned into the hug offered, the monofilament blade was as small as a pinkie but slid into Redeyes as easy as one of the marine blades into processed meat. Under the rib cage and to the heart, the child pushed, ending with a twist of the wrist. The child's face was blank when Redeyes dropped to the hold's cold floor as when she had walked up to the God.

Redeyes felt a pinch at her side; it was the fist pushing into her that shocked her that she was dying, again.

"Damn it." Redeyes gasped blood pouring from the wound in her side; a hand thrust out cushioned the fall to the floor for only a moment. The swiftness and the cut took her by surprise, unable to utter a warning to High Sarge or the General. Her emerald green eyes closed. The movement on the deck stopped for a brief moment, noticing something odd as their God fell to her knees then to the deck.

High Sarge, gave a roar grabbing the child's head and twisting to the right, hard. The snap was audible; the child's body slumped bonelessly into High Sarge's arms as if she were sleeping, her head at an odd angle. Her left hand coated in crimson crystals from the God's blood.

Collins ducked away from the bone masked Katherian, rushing to Redeyes side. He ignored the dead child, pushing his hands to her side to stem the gush of hardening blood. Her healing of any wound was legendary, but even this wound would need time, more time than the injuries had.

Iarris and Roland turned towards the commotion.

High Sarge dropped the body; put a hand to Redeyes neck. She started swearing vehemently. "Gods be damned, woman could you not see this?"

"Child," Redeyes whispered. "Didn't think they used Screamers so early."

"Shh, …we can get you to medical." High Sarge said trying for calm as she too knelt by Redeyes, ripping off one of her sleeves, handing him the impromptu bandage.

Collins looked up to the officer. He shook his head.

"Keep trying." High Sarge snarled in a not quiet whisper.

"Stop.' Redeyes whispered. Her redeyes going dull.

"Won't survive. Lay out the bodies."

Her voice so soft that Collins could not hear her but High Sarge could. High Sarge reached for her phone.

"She's dead, we need to lay out the bodies now!" the wounded Katherian said, leaning forward trying to drag Iarris back the way they had come.

"Sod off you bleeding piece of..." High Sarge growled, her ears flat, back arching as if ready to attack.

"You have a 12-hour window, for her to return. Unfreeze the bodies now." He said in slow even tones. "You need her to return. There can't be a hundred-year absence." He reached a hand out to touch her shoulder, an unconscious gesture of support.

High Sarge let out a snarl, snapping at the proffered hand. The Katherian judged the movement, keeping his hand out of range of her predator-sharp teeth by only a whisker. Her tail lashed, with lips skinned back over her fangs.

"It costs us all if she doesn't reanimate." Collin's eyes were tight with worry. He, like Iarris, was stunned.

"You just don't want to go to the fuel chain gangs." High Sarge snapped at him accusatory that he might feel more than self-preservation.

"What's not to like? Little sleep, less food and backbreaking labor in dangerous conditions." Collins gave High Sarge a hard look. But it was Iarris who shuddered. Two of her family was down in the lower levels. "Not the glamorous death by Redeyes hand or her metal shearing nightmares. Either way, all of us lose if she doesn't return."

High Sarge stood, staggering from loss and even grief. "Get the Captain on the line. We need bodies now!" She snarled. This Redeyes had been difficult almost unstable, but the next one could always be better. Please, she prayed wordlessly, a less deadhead kills crazy Redeyes is what they needed.

High Sarge was handed a phone. Small in her hands but huge in a human's. She dialed the bridge by memory. The captain's image came up small on the phone screen, belying his actual dimensions.

"We need bodies." High Sarge swallowed her pride by admitting the next part. "One of the rescues slipped through our guard and put a shiv into Redeyes." She stated without preamble.

"How the nova fucking black hole did this happen?" Captain Curiss growled into the phone, his gold and dark brown ruff haloing around his Wolfen features in a glorious mane that made many Katherian males jealous.

"I don't know yet but I will." High Sarge snarled back. Her back beam straight with the incipient dressing down that would come from this fuck up.

Captain Curiss' growl made even High Sarge's fur slick down in fear. "We will discuss this death later, we sure as hells won't survive without our Gods." He ran his upper right hand over his face. "I'll have the bodies sent down immediately. Think medical has two or three." He stopped for a second gathering his thoughts. "What about the one who killed her? Is that body of any use?" He pierced High Sarge with a look and a curled lip over one fang in disdain that made her feel 5 feet tall. "I assume the killer is a body now yes?"

The bridge crew heard the part of the conversation. A couple drifted closer. Redeyes was always a topic of whispered fears and hero worship. Sometimes both depending on the stories being told.

"We can lay it out but the neck is broken and the blood vessels to the brain…umm…not all connecting." High Sarge said sheepishly, her chin coming up with a tilt to her head. She had meant to kill, really.

"Who's kill?"

"Mine, Sir."

"Yes, good job on that but perhaps we could kill but leave the body slightly more viable next time?"

"I'll work that into my repertoire when taking down children assassins." High Sarge's sarcasm was not wasted on the Captain.

Captain Curiss snorted. "See that you do. Captain out." He flicked off the phone with a thick short trimmed nail. "Ensign, get medical. We have a situation."

The petite human ensign scrambled back to her seat, "On it now sir!" She replied breathlessly. Everyone else on the bridge tried to look busy as the captain's attention was no longer distracted by the God's death.

High Sarge threw the phone to another marine. "You." She stabbed an extended claw to the new Katherian, "will wait in Redeyes' rooms till she returns or we get this sorted out if she doesn't."

He looked down his long muzzle at the younger Katherian female with pulled back lips. "Guardsmen wait for their God where the God is." He said coolly back.

"She'd fucking skin you. She's not your God." Collins said, with a cold intense look. Any trace of comradery and help gone.

The Katherian looked away for a moment. "I ...she was my God long before you were born."

"But not always or you wouldn't wear a mask." High Sarge snarled, rising from her knees.

"No. Not always." He narrowed his eyes in challenge.

"Challenge me old Kat and I will wipe the fucking floor with you." High Sarge showed fang. Her arms loose at her side ready.

The Katherian stepped forward, forgetting his leg,

only knowing his pride and anger, claws out ready to take down an upstart mewling kitten. Iarris let him go. He collapsed a half step towards High Sarge. The surprise was evident in his wide eyes and open mouth as he ended up on the hard flooring and not ripping fur from the kit in front of him.

High Sarge moved like the well trained killing beast she was. She had a knee on his chest a clawed hand wrapped around his throat the other arm up with her hand in a fist, ready to pound his face into a pulp as she ripped out his throat.

Roland could feel her muscles shake with the need for violence. She wanted to kill him, or another, it didn't matter. She wanted that release of a good kill.

"Your choice." She growled barred teeth only a foot away from his face. Pupils wide in hunt mode. High Sarge had him dead to rights, and she knew it, could feel his pulse under her fingers. He knew it too.

Roland tensed but only for a second. He was defeated again. "Quarter." He snapped, with flat ears. His green-gold eyes glaring up into High Sarge's' huge pupils, almost no iris showing.

High Sarge's hand tightened around his throat. "Your life is mine. You ever fucking step out of line or Challenge me again and I will have your ears for a necklace."

"Get in bloody line. Redeyes has first dibs on my hide." He growled back, tension tightening his shoulders at the thought of the God, but he knew High Sarge's threat was good. She would kill him. Good to know if Redeyes decided to skin him alive, he could always take an easier death.

High Sarge eased back, her tail lashing, as she stood yet ready to pounce again if she needed.

Roland rolled to his right side, hesitantly. He had no clue if his leg would hold him, but he did not look for help. Collins and Iarris traded looks. She rolled her eyes to the ceiling. "Fine but you're on point if he fucks up again."

"Gladly. I always love taking out the dangerous ones, but his mangy old hide will do." Collins said with a toothy grin, almost worthy of a Wolfen. Iarris snorted in humor as she reached down to help the wounded Katherian up.

The bone masked Katherian, looked up in surprise with a flick of his ears, as he registered the Guardian's hand to help him up.

"We still need to wait for her to animate her bodies." He said looking up, grabbing the hand with his both of his, using his core to stabilize on his tailbone while trying to leverage up on one leg.

"Aye," Collins answered, standing back from the two of them. "We'll be getting front row seats." Collins jerked his chin at the wound. "You'll need to have that looked at still."

"Medics in the hold still," Iarris said. "Think we can snag one for our use. Guardians have to have some small perks, free medical being one of them."

"Not like we don't need it more often than not." Collins shook his head. "I'll see if Phisher is good for a once over."

It was Iarris turn to laugh at her partner. "She still won't give you the time of day other than medical." She called after his retreating back. Collins gave her a three finger wave over his shoulder.

"You're having a human look at me?" The Katherian was trying not to sound sulky but failing, the very tip of his tail twitching sporadically.

Iarris gave him a sidelong look. "Wolfen and the only

reason you're getting any medical is that Redeyes said you were going to have a chat with her later...which means dead or Guardian." A wide smile, her lips curling in amusement, arching her whiskers. "We could just let you die. Want me to call High Sarge and tell her we need to have you put down?"

"Cruel cub. You bit your mother's tail a lot didn't you?"

"Nope." Iarris laughed, arching her whiskers at him. "Just my father's. How I ended up being very good at running."

Medical had four bodies. Two humans, one Wolfen and one Katherian. Three male one female. Two of the deaths had been from the fall of scaffolding; broken bones ruptured internal organs, one death from electrical fire and the final body, old age had claimed in his sleep. Neither the gender nor the race would matter once Redeyes had taken over the new body. In a matter of days, the body would morph into a white-haired, four armed, red-eyed young looking human female. Any innate Power of the body's original owner would be magnified as well as any Powers that Redeyes might bring over. Sometimes she could shift into a wolf, and sometimes she couldn't. No one, not even Redeyes, knew how or why just that it was.

Redeyes was want to joke that she should discover lycanthropy at some point, increasing the furry population and human population at the same time. Her bad sense of humor was usually met with laughter and thrown objects of the pointed variety depending on how low the company was.

The deadheads were still being examined when the new bodies were brought down. The Marines set up between them and the bodies, just in case, but the deaders could see what was happening. The medics had answered questions bluntly when asked in whispered voices why bodies were being laid out. For people used to watching undead bodies reanimated, they were uneasy about an actual soul reanimating a new body. Souls leaving but animated by someone else's Power was ok, but a new soul seemed to unsettle most of them. A few were worried they might be donated to the dead body pile. None of the medics were in a generous enough mood to dissuade this thought.

The Guardians had a front-row view of the four bodies. Nero had come down from the rooms after a quick call from Collins. The Wolfen was edgy. Collins tried a brush of fingers on the Wolfen's arm offering solidarity. Nero's skin flinched as if brushing off an insect; he was too absorbed in his thoughts and the bodies to pay attention to the other Guardians.

Collins bumped Iarris elbow to get her attention. She turned with a frown. She had been watching Phisher's elegant fingers deftly work through the torn flesh of the other Katherian, pulling metal bits out and re-gluing torn pieces back together.

"You'll need to go to the hospital wing after this, but you won't bleed out any time soon. Twenty-four hours though or this won't heal for shit." Phisher was saying to the sweating Katherian. He had been given only a local numbing shot, which did help a little but the sensation of fingers in deep tissue where they shouldn't be made things...interesting.

Catching Iarris' attention, Collins pointed his chin towards Nero. Iarris gave him a once over then shrugged. "None of us want to see her dream again." Nero had years to go on his sentence still and had not become used to the idea of dying yet. If he survived, which Iarris didn't give him high odds, he might never recover. Guardians never came out of their sentences with Redeyes the same.

"Want to hit him with a dose of calm?" Collins suggested sotto voice.

"Nope. He'd get addicted and it slows his timing." She said with a shake of her head. Her braid twitching over her shoulder. "You could try your contacts for glowers."

"Pfft, now you're just trying to get him killed."

"Glowers work about as well as a mental fix." Collins rolled his eyes for just a second but he didn't dismiss the idea out of hand. There were ways to grind up the small luminescent fungi so that the fragments could not be visually seen in food. Though the best way to ingest was to just eat the damn things raw. Collins wasn't sure if he could talk Nero into taking any. Better to slip him some and see what happened. "I might be able to make something happen."

"I never had any doubts." Iarris quipped. Iarris hesitated for only a second before leaning closer to whisper into his ear. "If he goes berserk, I can only hold him for a few seconds. You'll have to do the shooting."

Collins opened his mouth when a body took a breath. The room went quiet. A second breath but not a third. Each body's chest rose twice, being tested but it was the burnt body that kept breathing. The jaw opened with coughing shrieks, no louder than that of an anemic human newborn mewling, escaped from burnt, blackened skin.

Phisher tried to go to that body but could get no closer than four feet before clapping her hands to her ears. She dropped to her knees, her muzzle opened as if to join the body screaming but nothing came out. Collins jumped forward to pull her back. He made a grab for the collar of her scrubs. The psychic screaming coming from the burnt body caught him as it had Phisher, staggering him.

"Ayieeeee!" Collins went down to one knee, but his hand had Phisher's tunic. He threw himself backward pulling the medic with him. Collins kept kicking along the floor, kick pull kick pull, refusing to go down with Redeyes screaming in his brain.

Iarris and Nero grabbed his arms pulling him further back out of range. The older Katherian started to pull himself towards the body, ignoring the others coming out of range. He was stopped when Cratt's Second in Command, a Katherian named Curiss, put a boot into the small of his back and the click of a disc pistol loading.

"We aren't going to have another dead Redeyes." Curiss growled softly, his voice carrying only to the bone masked Katherian's ears. The human put Wolfen level menace in his voice.

"Mind walk with me! She's stuck in a loop and if we don't get her knocked out she won't heal but die again!" Roland turned his head, snarling in fear and anger.

"How do you know this?" Curiss didn't bother hiding his disbelief. His gun never wavered from the Katherian.

"Seen it twice." Roland snapped trying to inch forward. He could mentally shield blocking her psychic screams but couldn't induce sleep with the shields up. The medic, Phisher, had dropped her kit next to the burnt writhing body. He needed to reach the bag for a sedative. Curiss boot lifted but Roland felt a mental touch, like a hammer from the human. Roland rolled over in wide eyes surprise. Humans were almost always nulls.

"Almost but not all! Now link, you damn Kat." Came the mental curse. Roland let Curiss in.

"Death's door you ARE Roland! No wonder she wanted to kill you." Curiss thought with shock.

"Not helping," Roland growled, digging claws into the centimeter ridges of the plate that helped boots and bare feet grip the occasional slick metal plates. Finger pads and claws inching him forward slowly.

They both tried to ignore the flowing data of any other personal information that was difficult to block at the linking. Difficult and there would probably come a long talk later but for the moment, Curiss helped with an extra level of shielding as the screaming got stronger the closer Roland crawled to the body.

He pulled the bag next to the body, opening up the kit. He looked at the syringes silver bodied ampules with banded colors. There was no lettering, no numbers. Roland had no clue which one would knock her out or cause an adrenaline rush that would magnify the mental screaming.

"Which one! None of these look familiar!" Roland wasn't panicking yet but he could feel his shields bowing in even with Curiss helping.

"Dark purple band with blue is what you want."

"A guess or for sure?"

"For sure."

Roland grabbed the correct ampule from the bag, pushing the needle into the God's arm. The writhing tapered off and the psychic screams a whisper till she opened her eyes. The opaque eyes were clearing with brown iris turning green and the whites becoming red as Roland watched. She saw him than past him and screamed "Monsters! No no no, monsters." pushing through mental barriers in terror so primal causing rapid heartbeats and elevated adrenaline rushes.

Roland pushed the ampule again then once more. Till the terror subsided. He panted in terror and pain, falling onto his back sucking deep breaths in through his open mouth. "Voids. What the fuck happened?" he whispered.

General Cratt came next to him, squatting down by the now sleeping God. "About time this one showed up." He looked up at Curiss. "Good job."

Curiss motioned to Roland; "About this one…" he let the sentence hang between the three of them.

"Oh aye, we'll get to that reckoning in a bit. But we have more important things." Cratt rubbed his hands together almost gleefully.

Roland looked up at the barrel-shaped human. "You expected this today?" Dismayed at the General's lack of concern.

"Not today boyo, but sometimes it was bound to happen. You're just the unlucky sod who gets to be babysitter and punching bag for the next few years."

"Why do I have the feeling you're going to be telling me that you're a Torch now." Curiss reached down helping Roland to stand on his good leg. Curiss turned to the other three Guardians, whistling and motioning for them to come over to him and Roland. Phisher was looking dazed but okay with Collins kneeling by her side. As one they turned to the General, walking to their God.

"Nope. But Redeyes did tell me when I was fresh shorn and still horking up a lung at the sight of blood, that when she was screaming and shitting her diapers at monsters, I had helped her learn how to navigate ship life and how to fight. With people and with Gods." He looked at the five of them. "Which means we have our work cut out for us for the next few years. Keeping her alive from our own Gods while we wage a war of survival against the Undead Gods." He pointed to Collins. "You carry her to her quarters. "You two take him" the finger targeted Roland "to medical. When he is able to walk, we will meet in her quarters as we make a few plans." Cratt pinned them each with a sharp look. "You are all still under sentence. She dies by accident, God or design and doesn't return, your sentences are commuted to the lower levels. "Curiss you're with me."

Iarris's tail twitched but she didn't drop his gaze. Collins bent to the body, lifting gently but grunting at the unexpected weight and peeling charred skin under his hand.

Nero's eyes went to the floor, fine tremors along his spine, shaking his body just enough to cause Curiss to look him over once more. He nudged the General slightly, flicking an ear towards the Wolfen

"She's not at the dreaming stage, lad. No more killing dreams, just the normal night terrors we all have." Cratt said, almost gently to Nero.

Nero looked up in disbelief, his ears flat and his lips peeling back. "Lies! She always dreams."

"Those will come later in her life as she gets more Powers, this lass...is about as lost as one of my own kittens not out of school. But enough of that." He turned back to Roland, swaying on one leg. "Take Roar and meet when you're done. I'll be taking Collins and Red on up."

"Roar?" Roland was less than amused at the nickname given to spaced out motorheads.

"Want them to know who you really are? It will save a lot of fuss and food for us all if I do." Curiss gave Roland a wide human smile, with lots of teeth.

Roland flashed fang and said nothing more.

"Thinking our job just got a dwarf star easier," Collins said, trying to breathe shallowly, burnt flesh freshly unfrozen didn't smell worth a damn.

"Depends. If she can't fight and still has her temper, we are shuttle raped." Nero said despondently, slipping Roland's right arm around his shoulders, Nero's upper and lower left arms around Roland's chest and hip. Iarris took the other side, more for Nero's comfort than actually helping with the weight as Nero could bench press two Roland's and not shed a patch of fur.

"Then you'll be able to teach her all your dirty little tricks she was always making you eat mat with in the ring." Collins said cheerfully with his head pulled back as far as possible from the ruined new body. New skin forming under the charred pieces as they walked towards the elevator door. Pink ropey scars that would fade in a month's time.

Nero ears perked up at that. "Hmm...That would be starlight."

"Let's hear it for the new Redeyes," Iarris said with an open mouth grin, showing lots of teeth.

Chapter 18

Lauranya woke slowly. Her eyes crusty along the edges as she tried to open and close her eyelids. She took a deep breath waiting for the pain. The shoulder and leg ached. She ran a tongue over her teeth wondering why they felt so fuzzy. She sat up slowly, careful of the saline drip in her arm. There wasn't even a hint of a bruise from the needle insertion, which Lauranya was prone to. Her arms felt weak, tired.

Frowning, she pulled off the sheet covering her legs. The bandage had been removed and her leg was marred with ropey scarred flesh, red against her normally pale skin. There was no catheter, just a loose diapering. Dry. She had probably been changed recently.

"Arie." Lauranya's voice was weak, dry and scratchy.

"Arie!" Scarring her as much as her physical weakness.

She tugged the IV out, hissing as the needle pulled from under her skin, tossing it to the side once free. She rolled to her stomach. It took a few tries to get to her knees. With no furniture close, it took a moment more to stagger to her feet. The scar tissue pulled tightly as she rose to her feet, only slightly painful. Lauranya stumbled forward, more falling, with her feet mostly under her than actual walking.

She made it to the wall with the only door, when she heard Arie's running footsteps, pattering on the stone floor with her vibrant shouting "Mommy! I'm coming!"

Lauranya slid back to the floor, using the wall as a brace. Her eyes prickled with unshed tears of anxiety.

"Calm. Calm." She sing-sang under her voice, taking deepening breaths. Arie rounded the corner, through the open door and bouncing off the door frame, trying not to stumble on coltish legs.

Lauranya blinked at the child before her. Arie was still a child yet Lauranya could swear her child had a growth spurt as she slept.

"Mommy!" Arie rushed into Lauranya's arms, stopping at the last possible second, to gently wrap Lauranya in her arms.

"Baby!" Lauranya sobbed, stroking the child's hair and planting a kiss on her crown.

"Jacks said you can come downstairs but you'll have to do a lot of sitting before navelgating the stairs." Arie looked up into her mother's gaunt face.

"Navigating." Lauranya corrected gently, with a huff of a laugh. "And I imagine so. Wounds take time." She licked dry lips. "How long was I asleep?"

Arie tilted her head for a moment. "Jacks says about 18 days, give or take."

Lauranya sucked in a heavy breath. Arie's arms kept her from falling over. All the supplies she had not been able to retrieve. She tasted metallic saliva as her stomach clenched.

"Mommy! Mommy! Don't cry. Listen to me." Arie grabbed Lauranya's chin to face her. "Jacks showed me how to get the undead to bring supplies up and arrange everythin'." Arie's face was intense.

"Come see! We have baby chickens and ducks. They are soo cute!" Arie tugged on her mother's hand, bouncing in excitement.

"Arie, please," Lauranya said, barely raising her head, slumped against the wall.

"Arie is correct, my dear." Jacks whispered in her ear, his form misted into being, kneeling beside her.

Lauranya raised her head to look at Arie then to Jacks. "Everything?" Her voice broke midway.

"Everything Camdia and I thought you might need." Jacks said reassuringly. Arie nodded enthusiastically, her hair flouncing with every nod.

"I. I need to see."

"There is hope."

"There is always hope, Jacks; sometimes it's not a viable hope though."

Jacks laughed. "If there was any doubt your family was not always free that right there would show the difference."

Lauranya narrowed her eyes at the ghost, the tightening of her jawline said more than the words she offered. "At least I know the difference." She snapped.

Jacks held up pale hands with palms up, placating. "I am sorry. I didn't mean to upset you."

Lauranya climbed her way to her feet, using the wall as a support. "Let us go and see what we have, oh favoritest child."

The walk down the stairs was the third longest in her life, even if she was walking down. The walk up will be torture, she thought with slow, careful steps, watching where every foot was placed. She rested her left hand lightly on Arie's shoulder, clutching the wood banister with a white-knuckled grip to keep from falling face first as they continued down. Lauranya smiled as she watched Arie's face concentrate on being slow and careful for Mommy, instead of running like she wanted.

The final step to the main floor left Lauranya shaking and covered in sweat. She leaned heavily on the banister for a moment, letting her shaking legs recover.

"Mommy! Come see the baby chicks! They are so cute and fluffy. And the growing space is perfect now!" Arie said excitedly tugging on her mother's limp hand.

"Just a moment child." Lauranya gave a weak chuckle. "Not everyone bounces as fast as you do."

"Ok Mommy let me get you some water. You look a little pale." Arie bounced off to the kitchen before Lauranya could respond.

Lauranya looked around the main room from her seated position, as Arie dashed away. Her jaw dropped. Every planter was perfectly placed. The trees backed against the wall. Their extra branches that had barred them from the back wall, trimmed away, so that the trees now stood against the walls, but full to the front and sides. Everything had been arranged in precise logical placement for maximum light gathering efficiency. To the right where the incubator was, a child's pen of fine mesh has been placed as well as a rather interesting set of plastic containers stacked in a lattice-work fashion, box, space, box then a box over the space held up by the edges of the boxes underneath, doubling the actual holding space.

"Nesting boxes for the chickens and ducks when they are a bit older." Jacks' voice whispered in her ear.

"Ahh. That makes perfect sense. I had not thought of that." Lauranya admitted wryly.

"Camdia was instrumental. She was short on space in many areas, learning how to make do, she was very good at."

"The plants. Arie's eating. So much I missed. How?" Lauranya murmured. "Arie couldn't have done this all even with you and Camdia's guidance."

"No. We were there for her and for you."

"Jacks…how. How am I to train her? I can barely speak with you if she weren't here." Lauranya didn't quite sob, but her eyes prickled with hot tears.

"She'll need to animate and command at least once or twice a season. Use what you were gifted with or watch the gift and your status wither away." Jacks said gently. "Or that was one of the things that my dear space hearted wife would say to our older children when they complained about a particular harsh regime of training."

"Does she have to use." Lauranya stopped herself. "Of course she does." A heavy sigh and a bitter smile.

"Don't worry love, she will be far more circumspect with you training her than if she were found and taken under a God's tutelage."

"I do not want her to become warped with death." Lauranya's eyes misted a little, her voice held fear. She shook her head, to dismiss the image of her sister's face superimposed over her daughter's face. Lauranya's matted hair fell across her face and chest as tears slid down.

"The occasional death happens. There are refugees here who have adapted to the land and water with fins or four feet."

Lauranya's head snapped up. "They can actually breathe water? Shift their forms?" Her hand clenched on the banister once more. "The whiskered cat, which attacked me."

"No. That one was indigenous." Jacks hesitated for a moment. "There was a viral infection under his claws and in his bite. We have nothing that will keep the virus from multiplying more than it already has."

Lauranya's heart flipped over in her chest. "How long?"

"You aren't going to die. In fact the opposite. The virus seems to be doing a better job of cleaning out any potential cancer cells or infections than anything I have ever seen." Lauranya could hear the bitter envy in his ghostly voice. Jacks was dead and could not get his hands on a tissue sample to study or experiment on.

Lauranya gave him a dry chuckle. "If you ask Olorun for a good place to be for your next life, you can come here and study all you want."

"Cruel woman to tease me like that." The affection in his voice made her smile fondly at his ghostly visage. His god of worship was Orunmila, powerful but hard to petition.

She tottered forward to the nearest planter, bracing herself, as she tried to walk to the newly hatched chickens. She ran fingers through churned dirt. It looked as if all non-edible or useful plants had been pulled and small shoots of something else were coming up. Lauranya was going to miss some of the flowers.

"The large tubs have some grains but mostly legumes, roots and vining plants that work well with what is already in the containers." Jacks whispered at her unasked thought. "Camdia and I helped Arie with plant selection. You, and the sweet stingers will still have enough flowers for happiness."

"Not just efficiency." Lauranya finished, with a breathy chuckle. "Thank you Jacks. For everything."

"For you love, it was my pleasure." Jacks brushed ghostly lips upon her cheek before vanishing.

Arie came from the kitchen with exaggerated slow steps to not spill a glass tumbler of ice and water. They met up at a planter not too far from the sound of lively peeping.

"The metal cups are in the sink still," Arie said mournfully. She was still at the age where things seemed to jump from her hands to the ground. So her preference and Lauranya's was for plastic and metal utensils. Less to clean up.

Lauranya took the proffered drink with a sigh of happiness. "Thank you, dear." She said with a happy sigh to a small smiling child. The cool water soothing to her dry throat.

Arie gave a wide grin then tiptoed slowly to the pen. "Camdia said not to run and jump around the chickens if we wanted them to lay unscrambled eggs," Arie whispered loudly, stepping one leg over the pen edge slowly and carefully as to not step on a thumb-sized bundle of fluff.

Lauranya smiled. Camdia had always been good with small things and young things. She would be missed. Lauranya held the crystal up to the light admiring the cut and whirling designs an unnamed artisan had formed on the beautiful and functional piece of art. The overhead lights, filtered through the cut crystal tumbler with small droplets of rainbows on the surrounding stone and flesh.

"Arie, do you think we have everything?" Lauranya asked, sinking down against the back planter in front of the chicken pen as her child cooed at the chicks that flocked around her.

Arie stopped for a moment, watching a bright red chirping fluff ball excitedly waving its wings at her, before answering. "Jacks was very worried when we had to give you the very strong pain meds. But once you started to heal and the zombies brought more stuff up, he seemed to think we would be ok."

Lauranya nodded thoughtfully. There was shelter, food and an overabundance of water. As long as the computers and servers held, there would be knowledge and entertainment. "I think we will be as well. My dear. I think we will do better here than expected."